THE PAST REMAINS PRESENT

Nadi Hemden

God: Thank You for always being You, in spite of me always being me.

My Mother: I hit the jackpot when God allowed me to be your daughter.

My Godson: A ray of sunshine since I first held you in my arms. May God bless you and keep you safe – all the days of your life.

Dr. D.: You chose to be stuck with me and I've only benefitted from having you as my friend and soror. Hopefully, you feel the same way.

Dr. M.: W. C. H. B. S. G. T.

V. J. J.: My real-life version of L. A. F. S. You may have forgotten me but I haven't forgotten you.

CONTENTS

PROLOGUE

"*I ain't a killer but...*"

As I drive my car and listen to the baseline thump, I nod my head. Hard. The volume may be at a deafening level but the noise is only helping to clear my mind. I listen to the rapper gloat about the joy of exacting revenge on a hated rival. His words have become the soundtrack to my life. They're helping to fuel a decision that will have far-reaching ramifications. The song was released almost 20 years ago. No matter. Seems like he's talking directly to me. That damn devil sitting on my shoulder. Encouraging me to do it.

I sigh heavily and think about the twists and turns that my life has taken. How'd I get to this miserable place? Some may call it the point of no return. I call it the point of freedom. My mind needs to finally be at peace.

For all of us, the romance started with so much promise. It unraveled in different ways and for different reasons. There were plenty of opportunities for everyone to walk away – unscathed. Instead, each time one of us opted to stay, another seed was planted. One that would bloom into a life-altering consequence. All hell has broken loose in all of our heads. An unbearable pain has seeped into everyone's heart and become rooted in cement.

Each of us is left with one pressing question: How far am I willing to go, to keep you in my life?

1: WANTING THAT OLD THANG BACK

The unwelcome sound of the alarm clock blared in my spacious bedroom. "Great morning New Jersey! We're Wild Ways 107.9FM. We bring the hits to the Garden State..."

The DJ had way too much enthusiasm, for it to be so damn early. The sun was just starting to break through the night's overwhelming darkness. I needed to silence the noise, even if she was getting ready to give the juicy lowdown on the state that I've called home for the last 15 years.

Quickly, I lifted my head off the satin pillowcase. A crushing wave of uneasiness and nausea overwhelmed me. Immediately, I rested my head back on the pillow. I stared at the tray ceiling, which spun like the inside of a washing machine.

Whoa. I hadn't experienced a bout of vertigo in several years. That last time, it was a major struggle to get out of bed and make it to the bathroom. Those were three days of pure misery. I tried to remember whether I did anything special to get my head back in a clear space. Since I blanked on a panacea, I realized that only time and doing as little as possible made me feel better. Mentally, I prepared myself for a day off work.

I reached for my cell phone. It was understandable that my supervisor's number rang and rang. She was rarely in the office this early. I pressed the number to transfer me to the U.S. Court's sick leave voicemail.

I entered my employee ID and heard my given name, Veronica Elizabeth Glyce. Instinctively, my body tensed. This stupid voicemail and my supervisor were the only ones who called me Veronica. I'd be much happier, if they called me Ronnie, like everyone else.

Although I work as a Federal Probation Officer, my job is antiquated in technology. From home, I could only access my email, so I sent input on today's meetings to my co-workers. All else would have to wait.

Gently, I placed the laptop on the other side of my king-sized bed. Looked at the undisturbed down comforter and smooth pillowcase. A clear indication that no one slept with me last night. More accurately, I've slept alone for a year. The regret of us being over still disturbed me.

A thought flashed through my mind. Today was Tabitha's birthday. My most recent ex. Once upon a time, I would have surprised her with an exotic trip or a nice piece of jewelry. That was no longer the case. There was no reason to even call. Now, the sounds of loneliness echoed in my heart and throughout my sparsely furnished home, whenever I stepped through the front door.

We were together for five years. I ended the relationship and had instant regrets. She quickly found a new love. I resorted to criminal, embarrassing and immature attempts to woo her back.

Unfortunately, I haven't moved forward. Even now, I thought of her, several times each day. Still kept her clothes hanging neatly in my walk-in closet. Hadn't moved her toiletries from her side of the double bathroom vanity.

For the past year, I've been stuck in a monstrous rut. Foolishly holding onto hope that she'd return. Spent too much time longing for a woman who had long forgotten me.

With a new determination, I decided that it was finally time to discard her items from my house, even if my memories of her were carved in stone. Needed to permanently banish thoughts of rekindling our love. Now, it was time to focus my energy on finding a new flame.

2: ONTO THE NEXT

I came across several dating sites. One looked more promising than the others. I started a new email address and would get a burner phone. This was my first foray into internet dating. Wanted to be cautious. I had read too many horror stories about the dangers of immediately giving out personal information.

On the site, I input the necessary information about my preference for feminine women and some general details about myself. There would be no false advertising on my part. Told cyberspace about my likes, dislikes and non-negotiables.

I reread my narrative and was impressed. Life would be much easier, if I could date myself. Then again, maybe not. I had unresolved issues. Thinking about my job and desire for some privacy, I decided against posting a picture.

Taking my time, I read through a lot of profiles, with a fine-tooth comb. Sent messages to several women. Immediately, I felt a mixture of nervousness and anxiety. Made a vow to only check the site once per day.

Okay, I lied to myself. Checked the site a few hours later. Surprisingly, I had twelve messages. All of the women wanted a picture and said they couldn't wait to hear back from me. I stalled on posting the pic but responded to all of them.

The day passed uneventfully. Thankfully, this bout of vertigo wasn't as bad as the last. I got plenty of rest and checked the dating site – again. There were so many messages, I lost count. Even in cyberspace, it was nice to be wanted. Still trying not to seem desperate, I read the messages but wouldn't respond until tomorrow.

I noticed that one woman with the alias of Addictive1 included her telephone number. She preferred to talk. Said that she understood if it was too soon. I liked the way she left the decision up to me. There was something cherubic about her smile. Yes, it sounds crazy. I just got the feeling that she was sincere.

She described herself as a devoted mother, wheelchair-bound educator and new to the same-sex lifestyle, even though she's 45 years old. Hmmm. I bet she had some interesting stories to tell. She made it clear that she wasn't about playing games and valued stimulating conversation. Like me, she wanted to first establish a friendship. I was intrigued.

3: AND THE NEXT

Even with blackout curtains, the sun made its undeniable presence known and woke me early the following day. Slowly, I lifted my head from the pillow. The room didn't spin. Vertigo seemed to be gone. I still vowed to go slow.

After taking a shower, I threw on sweatpants and an old sweatshirt from my alma mater, The University of Alabama. In the full-length mirror, I smiled at my reflection. I had entered my fourth decade of life but still had the energy and slim physique of my 25-year-old self. Today was a bad hair day. I brushed back my hair. Threw on a well-worn hat from the Chicago Bears, my favorite hometown team.

During the walk to the cell phone store, I was among the throngs of people who were enjoying the sunshine and beautiful weather on a lovely Saturday morning.

A guy jogged towards me. He yelled for the world to hear, "It's you! I can't believe it's you! The woman of my dreams! You are a long-legged beauty. Can I get your number?"

People laughed. Half of his teeth were missing and the top of his head barely reached my chin. He was dead serious, though. Confidence is a motherfucker.

There was no need to be rude. I smiled. Paused to acknowledge him and politely said, "Thanks but I'm good."

On the next block, a woman slowly looked me up

and down. She smiled suggestively and winked her eye. I returned the smile but kept walking. Thought about doubling back to chat. In that short time, another woman came out of the store. I watched them walk hand in hand down the street. Oh well.

Somehow, women were better at knowing that I preferred their company, whether I dressed in sweats and sneakers or on the rare occasion when I got all dolled up and wore heels. Most guys didn't have a clue.

I reached the store. Less than fifteen minutes later, I had a no-name smartphone. My first call was to Addictive1. No answer, so I left a voicemail. Her voice sounded nice. I detected an accent that I couldn't place.

Since I was out and about, I walked to my favorite diner, intent on making up for yesterday's missed calories. The waitress appeared. We exchanged pleasantries before I placed my order, "I'll have French toast, double side of bacon and hot chocolate with whipped cream. Oh and may I please have some plastic utensils and a bottle of water?"

She smacked her thigh. "I knew it. You always ask for plastic utensils."

Shyly, I smiled. She was right. While I waited for the food, I went to the restroom and washed my hands. Most folks mislabeled me as a germaphobe. Some of my issues were not that deep. I preferred to tell people that I was a neat freak and had "slight OCD." In my mind, that made me less neurotic.

The waitress returned with my food. Like a kid, I poured entirely too much syrup on the French toast. I smoothed out the large pat of butter, rubbed my hands together and indulged. "Mmm. This is really good," I said to no one in particular.

I had only taken one bite of food. The bells attached to the diner's front doors chimed. Instinctively, I looked up. The food almost fell out of my mouth. Damn! A gorgeous woman entered. She glanced around the diner. Her alluring green eyes did a double...no, that was a triple take when she saw me. We gave each other a quick nod, as the only people of color in the diner.

An intense feeling of heat swept through my body. Felt like I was suddenly drenched in sweat. Took a napkin and patted my forehead. It was bone dry. What the hell was wrong with me?

She looked at her watch. A frown spread across her lovely face. She seemed disappointed. For some reason, her looking upset made me feel the same way.

I guessed that she was from Trinidad, even though she was a dead ringer for a stunning Bollywood starlet. It looked like the possible West Indian had plenty of East Indian coursing through her bloodlines. Like me, she was tall. I had thumbtacks for breasts. Her generous cleavage rose and fell in a pattern similar to the pounding of my heart.

The jeans were a size too small. She carried enough weight to accurately be called full-figured. Lustfully, my eyes slowly traveled the full length of her form. Instead of shrinking from my gaze, she turned to the side. Maybe to give me a better view. Like a trained animal, I dutifully obliged. I swear she smirked. Knew that I was already under her spell. Surely, I wasn't her first victim. Hoped that I'd get the chance to be the last.

Mind you, I hadn't looked at this woman for more than a few seconds. In that time, I noticed her naturally long hair fell to the middle of her back. She wasn't wearing a wedding ring. Her fingernails were freshly manicured.

She carried a genuine Louis Vuitton handbag. A key fob for a Mercedes dangled from her hand.

It was rude to stare. I didn't care. My eyes wanted to soak up every ounce of her. There was nothing about this woman that shouted or even whispered lesbian. From experience, I knew better than to think the cover alone would tell me all about the book.

She fixed her eyes on her target. With a gracefulness that made a group of senior citizens pause from sipping their coffee and whisper to each other, she glided in my direction. She seemed assured and sophisticated. Even her walk shouted, "Look at me!"

By the time the mystery lady reached my table, she was scowling and asked, "Are you Nicola?"

Quickly, I took another bite of food. The lilt of her voice tickled my ears. Now that I had an up-close look, I was even more pleased. Somehow, the anger on her face only enhanced her overwhelming beauty. She had vivid green eyes, whose exoticism could only be likened to the color of an undiscovered mineral. They contrasted nicely with her jet-black hair. For make-up, she only wore lip gloss and a touch of mascara, which accentuated her impossibly but naturally long eyelashes. It was hard to name the fragrance. Its citrusy scent mixed nicely with her pheromones. I couldn't look directly at her for too long without needing to catch my breath.

To bide my time, I slowly chewed my food. Quickly, I fanned myself. When that didn't provide enough relief, I reached for another napkin and patted my forehead. I probably looked like a fool.

The truth was that her being so close made me hotter under my imaginary collar. I had always heard people talk about love at first sight. Thought it was bullshit.

Since I laid eyes on her, I now knew it was possible.

I didn't want her to leave. Had to know whether she was more than just a lovely face. For me, mental stimulation was ultra-important. My lips were numb from nervousness. So much for being coquettish. I hurriedly offered, "Let me buy you breakfast, so I can hear why you look so pissed about Nicola not being here."

Okay, so it wasn't my smoothest pick-up line. Well, honestly, I didn't have any smooth pick-up lines. I could be painfully shy.

She gave me the courtesy of cracking a smile. To my surprise and delight, she didn't turn on her heels and leave. Instead, she glanced at her phone. I doubted she saw the message, missed call or whatever else she was looking for. She put down her purse, scooted into the other side of the booth and announced, "Hey. I'm Jenine."

Her smile was so radiant, it was like the aurora borealis illuminating a dark sky. I was transfixed.

"Beauty has a name. Jenine." I was smiling so much, I probably looked like a hybrid of The Joker and an idiot. "Nice to meet you. My mom named me Veronica but I prefer Ronnie."

Even though I had just started eating, the waitress told me, "Let me take your plate, sugar. I'll place her order and have them to make you some fresh food. That way my beauty queens can eat together."

The waitress was partially right. Jenine had natural glamour girl beauty. The kind that belonged on the cover of magazines.

At the same time, we said, "Tell me something about yourself."

What a coincidence. We already thought alike.

She took the lead. "Rapid fire. I'm 35. Born in Trinidad

though you can probably tell that my East Indian roots run deep. My birthday is January 1st. I'm an only child. Even though my mom stays hittin' me up for money and works my nerves, we're close. Could care less about my father. No kids but eventually, I want to have one. Your turn."

I was so focused on watching her full lips and the beautiful frame they created for her perfectly white teeth that I lost my concentration.

To myself, I thought, "She's not the first stunningly beautiful woman you've ever met. Get yourself together."

"Uh, hello, do I need to call Scotty to beam you back to earth?" She waved a hand. Unnecessarily tried to get my attention. "This is supposed to be rapid fire. Damn. Are you sleeping? Am I that boring?"

If only she knew. I hadn't fallen asleep. Instead, there was a fire burning in me. It was taking the express route. Working its way from my toes to the top of my head. There was no way I would tell her that I already thought the sun rose and set on her.

I put up my finger. Needed a few seconds. This gave me time to take a sip of water and regroup.

"Okay rapid fire. No kids, 40, born and raised in Chicago, only child, incredibly close to my mom. My sperm donor or you know, biological father, skipped town when I was a baby. Unlike you, I'm not pushing out a child but adore the hell out of them."

I reached into my backpack. Pulled out my license to show her that I was born on January 3rd.

A continuous melody of rings and beeps came from her cell phone. Momentarily took her attention away from me.

Stating the obvious, she said, "Too many calls and text

messages." Phone on vibrate, her focus returned to me. "We have a lot in common and were only born two days apart."

"Yup. Where's the Trini accent? You sound like a Yankee." I was teasing that she sounded more like someone from America than the island of her birth.

She dramatically rolled her eyes. "That's a long story. My mother and I fled to Toronto, when I was like 10 years old. If necessary, I can code-switch and chat like the Trini girl that I am."

The waitress returned with our food. While she thought about other things to share, I was stuck on something she just said. "Fled? Who was after you?"

"Wasn't sure you were paying attention. My dad was abusive to my mother. Relatives in Toronto gave my mother the money to leave. There's a strong Caribbean contingent up there..."

With a little too much enthusiasm, I interrupted, "Oh, I know. Driving up to Caribana was a must-do for many years." The smile on my face let her know how much I enjoyed the annual festival that celebrated Caribbean culture via costumes, parades, parties, food, music and much more.

With the wink of an eye, she said, "Maybe you'll share some Caribana confessions."

I nodded my head, as if in agreement. Silently, I thought, "That ain't gonna happen. Stories of my Caribana exploits shall remain under lock and key."

She paused to pour more syrup on her French toast and continued, "Like I was saying, my family gave my mother the money for our move and we were on our way. I love to travel but haven't been back to Trinidad."

There were so many topics to discuss and things to

learn. I felt like we could talk forever and not get bored.

She twirled her fork in the air and added, "I did my undergraduate and graduate work at Syracuse University. It's been almost 10 years, since I moved to Jersey."

Like we were old friends, she reached across the table. Helped herself to some of my bacon. Anyone who knew me would have waited for my meltdown. Even my closest friends knew better than to cross that line. They wouldn't dare take food off my plate. It was part of my "slight OCD" and whatever other issues existed in my head.

She hadn't washed her hands, yet she continued to take more bacon off my plate. For some reason, I didn't mind. I even pushed my plate towards her. Briefly, our hands touched. An electric current roared through my body. I glanced. Her tantalizing smile told me this could be the start of something special.

"So how'd you go from Syracuse, which is, where, upstate New York to here?"

If someone wanted city life, suburbia, beaches or rural living, it could be found in New Jersey. From just about anywhere in the state, you could travel to the big cities of New York and Philadelphia, in less than an hour. There were numerous beaches along the Atlantic Ocean, gambling in Atlantic City and the Meadowlands and thousands of acres of farmland throughout the state. All that being said, most people still didn't decide to move here without a good reason.

"Jersey has grown on me. If it wasn't so expensive and cold, it'd be perfect. At first, I was only going to stay for a few years. I work mainly as an LCSW but I'm also licensed as a marriage and family therapist (LMFT). Thought about getting my doctorate. Got offered a partnership opportunity in a business that treats mental health and substance abuse. Any thoughts of moving to Miami or Southern Cal are officially on ice. I've settled in nicely."

With so many letters behind her name, I guessed that she was beyond intelligent. Her work in mental health and substance abuse made me cautious. How long would it take her to figure out my secrets? Still, I was relieved to know that she wasn't going anywhere, anytime soon.

"You have an interesting background. I wanted to be an attorney but didn't want any debt or more schooling. I did get two master's degrees and applied for a job, as a Federal Probation Officer. Jersey and somewhere in Iowa were the only two places with an opening. They could've quadrupled my salary and I still wasn't going out there, so Jersey won by default."

I smiled. We had a lot in common. "Jersey may be a national punchline but it's cool. More than meets the eye."

"So true. Your job sounds serious."

"Yeah. It's a combo of law enforcement meets social services. After people complete their federal prison sentences, I monitor them, make referrals to different programs and if necessary, arrest them and let a judge decide whether they go back to jail. I've been doing it for 15 years."

I shared more information about my travels. "Traveling is a passion..."

With wide and questioning eyes, she exclaimed, "I thought I was big time with 30 something passport stamps. You've been to almost 100 countries? Seriously!?"

Most people had that reaction. With pride, I replied, "Yeah and 49 of the 50 states. My best friend is an international flight attendant. She hooks me up, sometimes."

"You'll be my inspiration. I have some serious catching up to do."

Her phone continued to vibrate. She responded to a text message and shared, "I only came here to meet Nicola. We made so many plans to get together. Each time, she'd have a last minute excuse. Today, she didn't cancel, so I thought we were good. I haven't heard back from her, though. She never sent me a pic, so I thought you may have been her...think I got ghosted. Blessing in disguise. Otherwise, I wouldn't have met you."

Almost as if reading my mind, she said exactly what I'd been thinking. I watched her eat. Another coincidence. We were both left-handed.

The waitress returned and asked, "You ladies want anything else?"

It hadn't gone unnoticed that she ate almost all of my bacon. I jokingly asked, "No more bacon? Your grubby fingers been in my plate all morning."

She stopped mid-chew, showed me her hands and noted, "You have jokes, I see. Got a manicure earlier today. My fingers are far from grubby. I was so into our chat that I didn't notice." Blushing, she added, "My bad. I'll make it up to you."

Bacon was just the beginning of what I wanted to give her. I refrained from kissing her fingertips. The urge to touch her was strong. There was so much to like. We were barely an hour into knowing each other. She had a brain to match her beauty. We talked about serious and not so serious subjects. Agreed on some. Disagreed on others. Respected each other regardless of our viewpoint. Already, she had me wrapped around her finger.

"Do you want anything else? Take advantage. I'm paying."

Her smile was angelic. Involuntarily, it brought a smile to my face. The ice surrounding my heart melted a little more.

"For now, I'm good." She glanced at her phone. "Sorority meeting in a few hours. I need to go home and change into more appropriate clothing."

Okay, so I finally found one major difference between us. She's a member of Beta Chi Alpha. I'm a member of Delta Zeta Mu. We both pledged in college and remain active in our graduate chapters. Some would say that our beloved sororities are rivals. That may be true. I viewed it as a friendly rivalry. For me, it was all about public service.

Excerpts of our memorable conversation reverberated in my mind. She looked at me and smiled, when I softly placed my hand on her lower back and guided her out of the diner. At her SUV, I didn't want to seem too forceful. I thought of how to ask if we could see each other again.

She disrupted my thoughts and asked, "What time are we having dinner tonight?"

Internally, my stomach was doing somersaults from excitement. Outwardly, I exuded an aloofness. Nonchalantly, I said, "You're too late. I have plans, Broadway and dinner, with a special lady tonight."

There was a slight frown on her face. I didn't want to see her disappointed. Quickly, I clarified, "Miss B and I met from my public service work at her senior citizen building. Do I get a rain check?"

When her frown disappeared the rhythm of my heart was no longer out of whack. I was clearly operating on her frequency.

"Rain check is no problem. Breakfast tomorrow morning. Same place. Twenty-four hours from now."

"Fine with me, Ms. Bossy."

I didn't mind her take-charge attitude. It was one of many reasons for my uncontrollable smile. A feminine woman with an aggressive side turned me on. I felt butterflies in the pit of my stomach. A strong desire was awakening in my most intimate area.

"Unlock your phone."

"Here. It's not locked." I watched, while she added her info to my list of contacts.

In turn, she unlocked her phone. I waited for her to hand it to me, so I could do the same. Instead, she held it tightly and asked, "What's your full name and number?"

That was weird. No big deal, right? Maybe her phone contained codes that could launch nuclear warfare. I went with the flow and gave her my info.

She got in her SUV, rolled down the window and said, "Bye Ronnie. This was fun. I'm already looking forward to tomorrow."

I watched her drive away, until I could no longer see the SUV. Since I first saw her, I was beyond smitten. Walking back home, I stared at her phone number, as though it would unlock the answer to my most perplexing problem. I resisted the strong urge to call. Meeting her made me feel like I hit the jackpot. She had to be too good to be true, right?

I knew the long list of issues that I brought to a relationship. What about her baggage? So many questions that only time would reveal. Of this, I was sure. Veronica "Ronnie" Elizabeth Glyce looked forward to getting to know Jenine Marie Rhett.

At the time, I had no idea that meeting her had

jumpstarted a roller coaster of events that would expose so many secrets and lies, while jeopardizing people's freedom and lives. I would repeatedly question my sanity, in trying to determine what steps I was willing to take, all in the name of love.

4: JENINE'S PERSPECTIVE – PART 1

Dear Diary:

I have some stuff to tell you...

The sunroof was wide open. All of the windows were rolled down. The wind blew my hair in all directions. I didn't even care. The radio blasted Mary J. Blige's empowerment anthem, "Just Fine." That song was a perfect example of how I felt.

I was in a great mood. Finally, I was going to have breakfast with Nicola, a woman that I "met" on the internet. It has taken me entirely too long to get back into the dating scene. Still trying to extract Kayla, my wife, out of my heart, finances and bedroom. You know that it hasn't been easy.

I spent too long living with her, in the condo that we bought. She put herself in some horrible situations, which snowballed into her having financial difficulties. Even though we're legally separated, I still care for...no I still deeply love her, so I'm stuck paying bills in two households. Trust me, nothing about our situation is easy.

Now, it seems like she's lost motivation. With all of the obstacles, she feels like she's trying to swim out of quicksand. I know that my happiness with her has limits, even if my love for her seems limitless.

A few months ago, I moved into my home. Only my name on the mortgage. Kayla tries to rekindle things. Says and does all the right stuff for a few weeks.

Those become my moments of weakness. Despite our legal separation, I have physical needs that the highest-powered battery-operated devices don't fully satisfy. So, we still dip our toes in each other's pool, if you know what I mean. Reality strikes when she loses another job or begs me to pay another overdue bill.

Are we truly destined to do this repeated dance of trial separations followed by uneasy reconciliations? I continue to settle for less. Constantly tell myself that I deserve better. A love that knows no restraints. One that's unbounded.

As I continued to my date with Nicola, Kayla called for the fifth time. I finally answered, "What could you possibly want? Unless it's a dire emergency, why are you ringing my phone off the hook?"

"Hey Wifey. Why are you being mean? I'm home. Been waiting for you. What time you coming through? It's the holiday weekend. No classes today, right?"

Weeks ago, I told her a lie that I was back in school and had to have time to study. Needed an excuse, so she'd stop coming by my house so much.

I assessed the situation. She wasn't cursing. Definitely being too nice. More than likely she wanted something. Maybe a new pair of sneakers. Outfit for an interview.

"No clue why you're waiting for me. I'm not coming through. Whatever you want, I won't be able to get it for you. Meeting someone for breakfast. I plan to be busy all day. Maybe all night."

This was bound to start an argument. She had to accept that I was moving on.

"Bitch! Fuck you mean breakfast and you gon' be busy all day and night?" Her language and volume were at obscene levels.

Hurriedly, I turned down the volume. Clearly, she was trying to shatter my eardrum. An inability to have a civil discussion was another of our many problems. Instantly, I had a headache. Today, I refused to fully stoop to her level. I wouldn't let her fuck up my vibe.

"Look bitch. Don't you dare call me a bitch. Stop acting like this is breaking news. I'm trying to get past you. Told you that how many times?"

She needed to know – again – that I was going to find someone new. Wanted her to do the same.

That bitch had the nerve to laugh at me. "Yeah right. How long you been sayin' that? You're not going nowhere. Been you and me for how many years? We just gotta keep working through some things. I might have a new job. Maybe I can start paying everything on the condo myself, until you come back home..."

Just like countless other times, she said the same thing. We've had this conversation too many times. I was silent, which only made her angrier.

"I know you hear me. You'll be back or...I, I won't let no...else...have you. Don't make...hurt you..."

Usually, I didn't come to this part of Jersey. Maybe I was going through a dead zone. "What did you say? This connection is horrible."

Over an ever-weakening signal, I may have heard her say something about not letting anyone else have me. Something else about she didn't want to have to hurt me. Made me think about one of her exes. They used to regularly put hands on each other. Whatever.

In all the times we've done this break-up and make-up dance, she hadn't tried to hurt me. Well, at least not physically. She could be hardcore. I was the exception, though. When it came to me, her center was softer than a marshmallow. I was sure she'd always be more bark than bite. Right?

I parked my SUV. Reached for the comb. My hair looked like a bird's nest. Wanted to make a good first impression. Touched up my mascara and lip gloss. Combed every hair back into its proper place. Now, I was ready for my first meeting with the ultra-mysterious Nicola. The woman who refused to send me a pic and canceled all our other planned meetings.

The bells chimed, when I opened the door. I scanned the faces. No one looked... What the...!? Why is she here? How did she know?

For an instant, I was close to going into cardiac arrest. At first glance, one of the patrons looked like Kayla. They could've been sisters. I did a triple take, just to make sure my wife wasn't here to ruin my date.

While I got a better look, there were more subtle and obvious differences. That woman had the deepest dimples I've ever seen and longer hair. She was a sun-kissed, darker, caramel color and rail thin. Even before seemingly perpetual unemployment had her sitting home and packing on pounds, Kayla was never that thin. Okay. Undoubtedly, she wasn't Kayla.

We were the only obvious persons of color in the diner, so I gave a slight nod. Rudely, she didn't even respond. All she did was stare at me. Made me feel slightly uncomfortable but not in a bad way. Hard to explain.

Suddenly, I felt self-conscious about only wearing jeans and a form fitting top, even though they were by high-end designers. Damn. I should have worn something that would leave an unforgettable impression.

Wait. Why did I care what this stranger thought?

My focus turned back to my original mission. I

finished looking around the diner, just to make sure no one else might be Nicola. Nope. Only a bunch of old women and even older men. I blew out a puff of air. Waste of time. Another canceled meeting. I was pissed.

Before I headed back home, just wanted to make sure of something. I affixed my best I-am-going-to cuss-you out-face. With an abundance of attitude, I marched up to her and asked, "Are you Nicola?"

She wouldn't look at me. Hid her pretty face under a baseball hat. Flashed a shy smile that showed her blindingly white teeth and those deliciously deep dimples. Kept wiping her forehead like she was sweating. Poor thing was nervous.

After what felt like an eternity, she finally said, "Let me buy you breakfast, so I can hear why you look so pissed about Nicola not being here."

It took all my strength not to bust out laughing. That pick-up line was so damn corny, it was actually endearing. Made me smile on the inside.

I checked my phone. Nothing from Nicola. Missed calls from Kayla. Now, she wants to argue via text. I deserved a break, so I slid into the booth and announced, "Hey. I'm Jenine."

In less than an hour, this woman, Ronnie, blew me away. Challenged me. Made me think way outside the box. Gave me a hint of what I had been missing being stuck on stupid. Stuck on Kayla.

I wanted to spend more time with her. Was she fool's gold or the real thing? Cubic zirconia or a flawless diamond? Full of shit or not?

We exchanged numbers. She was slow rolling about asking me out. I took the initiative. Made plans for us to meet the next morning. I drove away from the diner.

Looked in the rearview mirror. With a tenderness oozing from her pores, she watched me until I could no longer see her.

My cell phone rang. Maybe it was Ronnie. The thought of continuing our conversation sent waves of excitement through me. Already, I looked forward to our mental quickie.

Glanced at the caller ID. Instantly, my headache returned. Kayla. Rolled my eyes. Sent her to voicemail. Started counting down the hours until my first official date with Ronnie.

On the drive back to my house, I chose not to focus on the most pressing questions: How long would it take to extract Kayla completely out of my life? What if she didn't go willingly? Why is a woman like Ronnie single? Why hadn't someone snatched her up?

Instead of trying to figure out those answers, I flirted with the tantalizing possibility that Ronnie may be the woman of my dreams.

5: KAYLA'S CONTRIBUTION – PART 1

No matter how hard I tried, the past couldn't be wiped clean. I've watched my life spiral out of control. Mostly because of my stupidity. Legally separated from my beautiful wife, Jenine, the woman that I love more than life. I'm grossly underemployed. To make matters worse, I barely have any family support.

All wasn't doom and gloom, at least not for today. I had surprise plans. I was going to cook breakfast for her. Copped some free tickets to the amusement park. We would ride the latest mind-numbingly fast roller coaster. A romantic dinner overlooking the Hudson River would follow. Maybe tonight, we could make love. It had been at least two weeks since she let me touch her. That was entirely too long. I needed a release. The pressure inside me was at a boiling point. My pipes were ready to explode.

I looked forward to spending all day with her. Even though I had to call several times before she answered, I couldn't contain my excitement, "What time you coming through? It's the holiday weekend. No classes today, right?"

She was distant. Unlike her usual jubilant self. "No clue why you're waiting for me. I'm not coming through. Whatever you want, I won't be able to get it for you. Meeting someone for breakfast. I plan to be busy all day. Maybe all night."

Streaks of crimson flashed across my now angry eyes. At times, I couldn't control myself. She brought out the best in me. And the worst. Unfortunately, this was one of those times. "Bitch! Fuck you mean breakfast and you gon' be busy all day and night?"

She didn't like when I called her out her name, so her comeback was expected. Her fly girl attitude was a mere snippet of what attracted me to her in the first place. I imagined her pristinely manicured hands motioning back and forth, in an exaggerated manner, like she was the conductor of a world-class symphony.

She proceeded to check me, "Look bitch. Don't you dare call me a bitch. Stop acting like this is breaking news. I'm trying to get past you. Told you that how many times?"

There was silence on the other end. I knew she didn't hang up the phone. This time, I was determined to have the last word. "I know you hear me bitch. You'll be back or I won't let no one else have you. Keep playing with my heart. Don't make me hurt you."

She acted like she couldn't hear me. Supposed to be going through a dead zone. Where the hell was she going that she'd be in a dead zone?

A scary realization crept into my mind. The hair on the back of my neck stood on end. Of all the loves I've ever known, she's the only one who has this effect on me.

Reality was a sharp slap in the face. I struggled to breathe. There was a tightening in my chest. This couldn't be possible. The bond between us was too deep. We had weathered too many storms. For the first time, I seriously considered the possibility that our legal separation may become permanent.

Dejectedly, I stared out the floor-to-ceiling windows that overlooked our condo's swimming pool. Even though we weren't going to have breakfast together, I still cooked the French toast – her favorite – in her honor. For as long as I could remember, she was like an unreachable itch in the middle of my back. There wasn't a pole long enough to reach it.

I thought back to happier times, like when we first met. A friend raved and raved about how fine one of the co-owners was at the place where she received therapy. I had to see for myself. Made it my business to accidentally bump into her. I asked her out. Quickly learned that we had so much in common. She was accustomed to people falling over themselves for her. I played it cool, which made her want me more.

We started in a domestic partnership. Got married when it became legal. I call her my five-star general. She had jaw-dropping good looks, would fuck me senseless, cook a delectable award-winning meal, argue someone into submission on most topics and made me feel like no one else mattered more than me.

We talked of never getting divorced. Always being able to work out any issue. Lavished each other with gifts. Made plans to have a baby. Even stored my eggs at a fertility clinic, while we built our careers. Forget moving up like the old TV show, "The Jeffersons." We were the ideal picture of upward mobility.

Yup. Happiness surrounded us like a protective bubble. My dumb ass still wanted more. When she found out about my other woman, she exploded in anger. I had never seen her that mad. She destroyed my wardrobe with bleach. Kicked me out. Blocked my number. Let loose a jar of spiders in my car. Damn near caused me to crash when they started crawling all over me.

Knowing that I upended our utopia, I gave new meaning to begging for a second chance. Like the agonizingly slow drip of water from a frozen pipe, she allowed me to come back home. We found a way back to the old us.

Unfortunately, I didn't lose my penchant for ruining a great thing. When she kicked me out, I developed a fondness for sports gambling. Initially, I did very well. Saw myself as the only one in history who had a surefire way to beat the system.

I should've known when to cash out and walk away. Instead, I got cocky. Had a string of bad beats. One sure thing after another somehow lost. My once fat bankroll quickly turned into an ever increasing deficit. I used my credit cards to make deposits online. When they were maxed out, I opened new ones. I was determined to win back the money.

Instead of coming clean and trying to get help, I "borrowed" money from the accounts of a few clients. Before I had time to replace the money, several of my "questionable" transactions were audited. Without having time to cover my tracks, I was escorted from the sprawling headquarters that overlooked the convergence of multiple waterways. Security advised that my personal items would be sent via mail. In the blink of an eye, I went from handling multimillion dollar accounts and flying first class to begging my wife for lunch money.

The only saving grace was that my misdeeds were discovered shortly after I placed a sizable bet on a 10-team parlay. That wager won life changing money. I'm talking think about retiring early type of money. Momentarily thought of fleeing to a country without an extradition treaty. Nah. Jenine wouldn't have gone for that. Instead of riding off into the sunset, I used the winnings to make full restitution to all the clients. That was the only thing that saved me from doing serious jail time.

But... There wasn't enough left to pay off much of my credit card debt. I wasn't sure which was in worse condition: my credit score or my professional reputation. I had zero chance of ever finding respectable work in the financial industry.

The gambling fiasco gave my wife another reason to hit the roof in anger. "Kayla!!! How could you be so stupid? You're lucky they didn't arrest you. How are you going to take care of yourself? Help pay the bills?"

All I wanted to do was cry. Bury myself in her arms. Let her make everything right. Again. Instead, I tried to defend myself, "There was too much pressure on me. I was trying to do everything right to get you back in my life..."

She was unmoved by the tears threatening to overflow from my eyes and replied, "There's a lot of competition but that may be the dumbest thing you've ever said... I think we need time away from each other...sell the condo...find our happiness – separately..."

I got on one knee. This wasn't one of our blissful times, like when she agreed to marry me or one of our make-out sessions. Now, I was begging, "You can't ever leave me... I feel like my emotional rope is unraveling. The darkness around me is deep. Debilitating. Impenetrable. Please..."

Although she could be wickedly mean when called upon, she looked past my repeated shortcomings and stayed with me, even though I lost menial job after menial job. I hated that I could barely earn a quarter of my former hefty six-figure salary. Even had to downgrade from my beloved convertible BMW M8 for a fuckin' raggedy Honda Civic. She more than made up for my failings, even though it was a struggle. That's why I was so taken aback when I learned the reason she didn't come home one night.

"Your dinner is getting cold. What time are you going to be home?" Since I wasn't bringing home a paycheck, at least I made sure the house was clean and she didn't need to cook.

"I'm already home."

"Stop playing. I kissed you goodbye this morning and I've been here all day..."

Derisively she said, "That's part of the issue. You being home all day. Not working. I bought a next spot. We have a lot to sort through. I'll be in touch..."

As those old memories faded to black, I thought of the ones from today's conversation. I was wrong for calling her a bitch. I had become the undisputed queen of the fuck up.

Initially, I called her back to apologize for my behavior. My foul language. Everything else wrong that I've done. The more she ignored my calls, though, the angrier I became at the thought of who she may have been meeting. There was something in her voice that told me it was someone trying to replace me. I usually knew when she was lying. Almost sounded like she was rubbing it in my face. I thought about what they may have been doing. Pictured her flirtatiously batting those beautiful green eyes. I saw the unknowing victim being sucked into her orbit.

The wave of jealousy made me send a barrage of angry text messages. With each passing second that my texts went unanswered, I became more resolved to do anything to salvage our marriage.

6: THOUGHTS OF YOU

Miss B and I had an enjoyable night. She chatted non-stop about The Lion King and dinner. Although I was physically present, my mind was occupied with thoughts of Jenine. When I left the house this morning, I had no idea that I'd wind up on a date. Literally, I was counting down the 12 hours until I saw her again. I thought about sending a text but decided against it. The gift bearing Jenine should be unwrapped on Christmas Day and not Christmas Eve. I forced myself to wait.

Once I dropped off Miss B and got back home, I showered and climbed into bed. I glanced at the clock. There were still 8½ hours until breakfast. I was wired. All night I had so much nervous energy that it took me several hours to go to sleep.

By the time I finally woke, I jumped out of bed and yelled, "No! How'd I forget to set the alarm?"

I had ten minutes to meet her. I looked for my cell phone. Of course, I couldn't find it. If I hurried, I could make it to the diner on time. Thankfully, I took a shower before I went to bed. Today would be another ball cap day. Hopefully, it wouldn't be held against me.

There wasn't enough time to walk. In the garage, I hopped in my convertible Audi and saw my cell phone on the passenger's seat. Just my luck, the battery was dead. I arrived to the diner, a few minutes late. Anxiously, I looked around the parking lot. Hoped that she hadn't left. Breathed a huge sigh of relief when I saw her SUV. Took a little time to calm my nerves.

She sat in the same booth as yesterday. There was a frown on her face, as she talked on the phone. She looked up. Saw me. Her luminescent smile reappeared.

Before I got to the table, she ended the call. We hugged and I inhaled the same intoxicating scent from yesterday. While I got high off her, she was breaking me down.

"Are you going to wear a baseball cap the next time we see each other, too? It's like you're hiding."

"Oh. So we'll be seeing more of each other? That's mighty presumptuous."

I tried to add a little levity to the conversation. "I overslept and was rushed. Didn't want you to think that I stood you up. This was the best that I could do." Briefly, I removed my baseball cap. My hair fell past my shoulders. "Satisfied?"

Assuredly, she said, "I'm satisfied for now. To answer your other question, yes, we'll be seeing more of each other."

She smiled confidently. Folded her hands on the table. Like a guru ready to impart wisdom on a student, she boosted my sometimes low self-esteem. "You're very pretty, even though you're not a girly girl. Show your beauty, Ronnie. Folks pay big bucks to have what God gave you. That sexy smile and dimples deep enough to swim in. Your skin is flawless and you don't even wear make-up."

I was speechless. My heart did backflips. Again, I found myself reaching for a napkin to pat my forehead. The same feelings of heat from yesterday were back in full force. Whenever I was around her, it felt like I had a fever.

"Wow. Look at you checking me out."

She flashed a megawatt smile. Stared into my eyes. "Oh yes. I'm checking you out and I'm drawn to what I see."

A knot of desire settled in my stomach. If she was already blowing me this proficiently on a mental level, I could only imagine what she'd do to me physically. I looked at her slowly lick those beautiful lips and planned my escape. I was a mess around her.

"Order anything for me. Be right back." I needed a moment to regroup. I was in such a rush to get to the security of the restroom that I almost fell out of the booth. Glancing back, I saw her stifle a laugh.

Once safely away from her hypnotic eyes, I distracted myself by washing my hands. Took several deep breaths. Felt my heart beating uncontrollably fast. Looking in the mirror, I repeatedly told myself, "Get it together."

When I returned to the booth, I gave her a quick rundown of the evening with Miss B. Ironically, she'd never seen The Lion King. If things continued on this course, maybe I'd treat her to a matinee show. We could spend the rest of the day enjoying NYC.

Damn. I was already making plans to see her again. Do. Not. Get. Ahead. Of. Yourself. I needed to slow down. My first priority was getting through this date, without making myself look like more of a fool.

Back at the table, the auction price for her attention was rapidly increasing. Similar to our first meeting, her phone let loose a symphony of ring tones and beeps. They'd have to wait. She silenced her phone and said, "When I first saw you, I wasn't sure if you were Nicola. You reminded me of someone that I know. Made me do a triple take."

Jokingly, I remarked, "If we look like each other, she

must be amazingly pretty."

That comment only elicited an eye roll from her. I added, "I saw you do the triple take." Naturally, I asked, "Is it good or bad that I remind you of her?"

"Depends on the day."

That evasive answer should have signaled neon warning signs of danger, caution and do not enter to flash all around my head. I didn't even notice. I was more interested in continuing our riveting talk from yesterday. No matter the topic, she added something substantive. I could tell that she was well-read, which only added to her attractiveness.

The waitress returned with our food. Only then did the conversation slow. She reached across the table. This time, she ate most of my sausage. Just like yesterday, she didn't ask. She hadn't washed her hands. I still didn't mind.

Breakfast ended all too soon. I wasn't ready to leave. She offered, "If you don't have anything planned later today, come with me to one of our fundraisers."

Jokingly (but not entirely), I made a face. Probably said something sarcastic about being allergic to hanging with women from BXA.

She smirked and exclaimed, "You've been doing fine so far. I'll text you the info. See you in a couple of hours."

I ran a few errands and headed to meet Jenine. At the park, those arrestingly beautiful green eyes brightened, when I stepped into her view. She wrapped me in a hug that was so comforting, I didn't ever want her to let me go. I inhaled deeply. Her scent sent me on an ascent. In my ear, she whispered, "I'm glad you're here."

I forced myself not to dissolve into a puddle from her touch. She held onto my hand. Introduced me to several of her sorority sisters or sorors, as most people say.

Once the event started, we settled into a rhythm. We quickly finished the 3-mile walk. It was nice to learn that there was a prize for the first person to cross the finish line. Seemed like I beat her by a step or two. The gift card went to me. That gave me some bragging rights. I stuck out my tongue. Waved the card at her, in a teasing manner.

The more I saw Jenine, the more I realized that I wanted to see even more of her. I swore that she could read my mind because she said, "You seem mighty proud of that little gift card. Use it to buy some wine for dinner. My house. Tonight. I'll cook for you."

My tongue felt like it was stuck in mud. I hesitated to give her an answer. She stared at me. Felt like beads of sweat were forming under my arms. The ever present butterflies in my stomach wouldn't let me say no. The longer I looked in her eyes, I plunged deeper into the abyss. I couldn't deny myself the pleasure of spending more time with her, so I responded, "I'm cool with that."

After the park, I went to buy wine, even though I had no clue what was on the menu. The salesman was patient. He helped me select two bottles that cost more than the gift certificate. No matter. She was worth it.

At home, I took a long shower. Looked at my bathroom's double vanity. Pictured her beauty products next to mine. Many questions ran across my mind: Did she have a favorite body wash or perfume? Use a loofah or washcloth? Prefer a shower or luxuriate in the bathtub? Want lights on or off during sex? There was so much more to learn about her.

Thinking back to her words, I put more than the usual effort into selecting my clothes and styling my hair.

During the scenic ride to her house, I had an hour to reflect on our talks. There hadn't been any overt mention of sex. There was obvious chemistry between us. In a flirtatious way, she remarked on the larger than average size of my hands. Since we just met yesterday, I told myself that she was off limits.

7: FIRST OF MANY

I saw Jenine's SUV in the driveway. My Audi would look good parked next to her Mercedes. Material signs of our success. Quickly slowed my roll. Found a spot on the street. Tried to settle the uncomfortable rumbling of anxiety and nervousness in my stomach. I'm not overly religious but still said a quick prayer. Took a deep breath and rang the bell.

She answered the door. Just like at the diner, her beauty took my breath away. Her eyes sparkled like polished gemstones.

While I tried to regain my composure, she looked me up and down. With a devilish grin, she nodded approvingly. "You look very, very nice. I like your hair and that outfit. You're thin but I can tell that you have an athletic body. Those pants show a nice contour of your thighs and butt." She put her hand on my arm and turned me to the side for a better view.

Had I been an ostrich, I would have buried my head in the sand. My cheeks reddened from embarrassment. "You keep feeling me up and I'm going to charge you."

Her hand worked its way down my backside. Settled on my butt. "Name the price. You're worth it."

I decided to quit this sexual innuendo, even though my embers of desire were quickly becoming enflamed. Reminded myself that it was too soon to head down that road.

I gave her the bottles of wine. She smiled. Sounded

like a sommelier, as she confidently stated, "These will pair nicely with dinner. Let me take them to the kitchen, so they can breathe and then I'll show you around."

While I waited, a deliciously fragrant scent of freshly baked cake filled my nostrils. During the tour, I was drawn to the different paintings, statues and other artifacts. She prominently displayed a piece of culture from almost every country that she visited. I had far more passport stamps. Unlike her, my treasures were stuffed in bins and collecting dust in my garage.

We sat by the in-ground pool. "You're here by yourself? Why do you need four bedrooms, 3.5 bathrooms and everything else? Why such a big house?"

"Rough childhood. My mother's degrees that she earned in Trinidad didn't mean squat in Canada, so she had to retake most of her core courses. It was rough. We lived in cramped quarters. Want my future child to have space to run."

After going back indoors, I washed my hands in the half bathroom. I continued to admire her impressive decorative touch. My relationship with one of my exes, Monica, taught me many things, including the ability to have a more discerning eye between low and high-quality products.

Quickly, I came to have more appreciation for Jenine's sense of style. I checked out the expensive pedestal sink, matching mirror and accessories. The soap smelled so good that I washed my hands three times. The hand towel was ultra-thick. Felt like I was drying my hands on a plush rug. I put my hands on the wall. Even the damn paint was luxurious. Kind of felt like suede.

Before I could get settled in the living room, she motioned me to the dining room table and proudly stated, "Dinner is served. Wait. I forgot to pour your glass of wine…"

"No worries. I don't drink alcohol."

"Really? Why?"

With practiced nonchalance, I shrugged my shoulders and jokingly said, "Just trying to be healthier."

I gave the same non-answer whenever someone asked me that question. The full truth of my journey to being a teetotaler was something I rarely shared. Now wasn't the time for that type of confession.

Her probing green eyes hinted that she saw through my deception. Sarcastically she said, "Hmmm. Maybe you can help me be healthier, too."

Nervously, I laughed. I wanted to lighten the mood. More importantly, I needed to change the topic.

"Are you ever going to feed me? I'm starving…"

"Yes. Let's try this again. Dinner is served…"

The roasted broccoli was fresh. Cooked to perfection. And the fettuccine - it was al dente, with the creamy and silky sauce sliding all over those magnificently cooked noodles. I had never described Alfredo sauce in such glowing terms. The aromatic garlic bread was a lovely accompaniment and had just the right amount of crunch. I closed my eyes in bliss, as I ate the lustrous food that was seasoned to perfection.

Tired of waiting, she held her breath and asked, "Well? How does it taste?"

"How'd you know this is one of my favorite dishes? I can tell the sauce and pasta were made from scratch…"

She nodded in confirmation, as I continued, "…this food is delicious. My taste buds are experiencing sensory overload…"

Shyly, she smiled and gave a subtle reminder. "Save

room for cake, too. That'll taste even better than dinner."

From the first time we met, I realized that being so close to her was unnerving. Made me feel like I had a perpetual fever even though I wasn't sick. Looking at her made me feel like I was operating outside myself. Now I knew that she was a fantastic cook. Very quickly, she was accumulating more positive checkmarks.

Despite her continued insistence that it wasn't necessary, she begrudgingly accepted my offer to wash the dishes. After helping her clean up, we settled in the living room. Just like in the diner, her phone repeatedly rang. When she silenced it, the house phone rang and was ignored.

"Feels like I should be asking for your autograph. You're very popular," I casually remarked, while I got comfortable in the recliner.

"Yeah. Sometimes, it's annoying. Especially when it's unwanted attention."

She handed me a plate. I stared joyously at the huge piece of red velvet cake.

While she topped up her wine glass, I took my first bite of the cake.

"Damn. This is so moist. It's melting in my mouth. I'm trying not to lick the crumbs off the plate. Think I could get a next piece?"

She looked satisfied with my compliments. The smile spread fully across her beautiful face.

Maybe it was the sugar rush that made my brain go topsy-turvy. I looked at her. Couldn't help myself. "This tastes so damn good...I may just have to marry you."

For once, she didn't have a sarcastic comeback. She bashfully lowered her eyes and simply said, "Hmmm. Maybe."

Quickly, we were immersed in watching a competitive game between her beloved New York Giants and the Philadelphia Eagles, one of their hated rivals. I listened to her admonish their quarterback for throwing an untimely interception and question defensive alignments.

In an exasperated tone, she asked, "Why are they running a draw play?"

It came as a surprise when she correctly predicted what would happen on the next play. I looked at her in amazement. Ashamed at my foolishness for being shocked that such a feminine woman knew so damn much about sports. Typically, I was the most knowledgeable woman in the room about sports. Clearly, I had met my match.

The game went into overtime. We made a bet that if the Eagles won, I would plan the next date but she'd pay for it or vice versa. Both teams squandered opportunities to win. Just when we thought the game would end in a tie, the Eagles pulled out the victory on a last-second field goal.

I raised my arms and took a victory lap around the living room. She threw a pillow at me. Feeling euphoric, I remarked, "Let me find out you're a sore loser."

"There's no losing with you. I'll gladly pay for whatever you plan."

Daylight quickly faded. I wasn't ready to leave but didn't want to overstay my welcome. "It's getting late. I have to be up at five o'clock in the morning. Lots of people to visit."

"That's way too early. I still have notes to review. Let me walk you to the door."

She took hold of my hand. Intertwined her fingers

with mine. There seemed to be a natural fit. It was said so faintly that I strained to hear her say, "I enjoy spending time with you. Can't wait to see you again."

Simultaneously, we leaned in for a hug. As we separated, our lips were inches apart. I tried to turn my head away from her. She cupped my cheeks in her hands. Looked me tenderly in the eyes and softly said, "You can stay. If you want."

I put my hands over hers. Took a deep breath to gather my thoughts. Seconds of uncertainty were suspended in the air. My body sent undeniable signals that it longed for more of her touch.

"Close your eyes."

Like a star student, she obediently honored my request. I gently kissed her forehead. Lingered and thought some more. Nah. It was way too soon. Anything else would lead to places that I pledged to avoid. I left so quickly, there was probably a cloud of smoke behind me, as I rushed to my car.

A few blocks from her house, my mind toyed with the idea of going back. Succumbing to my carnal desires. A pair of headlights barreling towards me jarred me back to reality. I was almost broadsided by a black Honda Civic with dark tinted windows. Our cars came to screeching stops a few inches from each other. Took several moments to calm my frantically beating heart that felt like it was lodged in my throat. After the near miss, I settled my shaky hands, so I could lower my window.

The other driver was totally at fault. She blew through the red light, as if it was invisible. Instead of apologizing, she audaciously shouted, "Get the fuck out my way, you stupid bitch!"

She sped away. The sound and smell of burning rubber

hovered in the air. It was only a glance but I didn't need more time to know what I saw. The woman who almost ended my life kind of looked like me.

Now stuck at a red light and unable to turn around, I was incensed that I couldn't properly deal with her. In the rearview mirror, I saw her taillights become fainter until they finally disappeared near Jenine's house.

A nagging feeling in my gut told me that we'd meet again. At the time, I had no idea that our connection went way beyond us sort of resembling each other. The strings of that driver's heart and mine were tied to the same woman.

Timing was so important in life. Had I been able to make a U-turn and double back, I would have seen that black Civic peel into Jenine's driveway.

I would have witnessed the angry woman bang on her door.

I would have seen Jenine open the door. Maybe I would have heard her say, "Knew you couldn't resist..."

I would have seen her eyes widen in surprise and heard her hesitant question, "Uh...Kayla, what are you doing here?"

I would have heard Kayla ask, "Couldn't resist what? Why ain't you answering the phone? What the fuck you been doing that got you lookin' so damn happy?"

I would have seen Kayla clench and unclench her hands. Only Jenine would have known that was a telltale sign that she was beyond angry.

I would have seen the terror in Jenine's eyes because Kayla came to confront her face to face.

I would have seen her sparkling green eyes dart up and down the street. Maybe she was looking for me. Maybe she thought that I decided to accept the offer of spending the night.

I would have heard their argument that was loud enough to wake everyone on the block.

I would have seen her usher Kayla into the house, just to keep the peace. Only Jenine would have heard Kayla's threat, "I swear...you're so fuckin' sneaky. Keep doin' stupid shit and you're gonna make me kill you."

Even if I saw everything that transpired, maybe it wouldn't have mattered anyway. I was crushing hard on Jenine. Already making lifelong plans.

I would have made every excuse for her behavior.

Better yet, I would have found every reason to try and make her mine and only mine. Unbeknownst to me, Kayla was intent on doing the same thing.

8: POTENTIALITY

Once I got home and showered, I couldn't go to sleep. Had a wicked case of Jenine on the brain. Falling victim to my newfound weakness, I called. She answered before the first ring ended. "What took so long? You've been on my mind since you left."

"Really? I hope they were good thoughts...just wanted to thank you for dinner and wish you a good night. I left quickly. Should've stayed. Some crazy chick driving a black Honda Civic almost killed me by your house."

Excitedly, she asked, "What?! Did you see her?"

"Yup and I'm still tripping. We kind of look like each other."

Hesitatingly, she asked, "Did y'all talk or anything? You find out her name?"

"She cussed me out. Everything happened so fast. I almost died."

She exhaled. "Phew. That was close."

I thought the relief in her voice was because I wasn't mortally wounded. Instead, she said, "I'm glad y'all didn't need to exchange any info."

"Why does that matter? You haven't even asked if I'm okay."

"I'm sorry babe. Just trying to process everything. Thinking of how I almost lost you. Are you all right?"

"That sounds much better. Yeah. I'm good."

She quickly switched gears and stroked my ego. "By the way, all my thoughts of you are positive. You're...

you're special. I mean that in the most complimentary way..."

There was silence. I thought she hung up. She carefully asked, "So, you only called to say thanks and wish me a good night? Is that all I get?"

"Well..."

It was supposed to be a 15-second phone call. We wound up talking for hours. Neither of us wanted to be the first to hang up the phone. I fell asleep listening to her snore.

*****

The next day at work passed without any incidents. I was able to meet with everyone on my caseload. Jenine texted to wish me a good day. Maybe that helped bring about the day's positive results.

I pulled into my garage. Jenine's picture showed on my cell phone. I smiled. Tried to sound casual, "Talk to me." The butterflies in my stomach were doing aerobics. A simple conversation made my heart arrhythmic.

"Hi, Ronnie. I thought about you, a lot, today. Did you think about me?"

"Hey J. Maybe once or twice."

She called me on my little white lie. "I, sooo, don't believe you."

There was no way I would share that thoughts of her flooded my mind. I even dreamt of her last night.

We didn't have another marathon conversation but we touched on new topics. I learned why she was single. What she wanted from a partner. What she was willing to give towards making a relationship work.

"How'd you even start dealing with women?"

Unlike me, Jenine didn't realize that she was attracted to women until she was close to finishing her undergraduate degree.

"Short version. Senior at Syracuse. Fiancé cheated. I bounced. Married soror mended my broken heart. That first time ignited a flame that I didn't even know existed. Hadn't ever considered being with a woman. My mother thought it was an early mid-life crisis. My conscience got the best of me about dealing with a married woman, so I ended it. Seeing her at events was hard but she was hella mature about everything. No drama." Like she was remembering a painful experience, she softly added, "Too bad every relationship can't end so peacefully."

I had excruciating recollections of being immature when a relationship went downhill. No need for me to chase her away with those sordid details, so I kept the focus on her. "Do you still talk with her?"

"No. After her, I had a few flings but only one serious relationship, my soon-to-be-ex-wife."

Sometimes my hearing was defective. Just to make sure I wasn't imagining things, I asked, "Your who? Don't you think that's something you should've told me when we first met?"

As I suspected. She was too good to be true. "I think I should go…"

"No, no, no. Don't hang up. It sounds worse than it is."

"You have 10 seconds to convince me otherwise."

Like someone watching time count down on a stopwatch, lest the bomb explode, she spoke quickly. "I've been so focused on the house and expanding the business. You see that I was trying to meet someone else when we met. There's a lot to it. We're legally separated. Still own a condo together."

She only took 7.5 seconds to explain. Quietly, I thought about this shocking revelation. In truth, I knew of a few couples in similar situations. Legally tied to each other but living separate lives. Usually for financial reasons. Sometimes for the kids. It wasn't totally unheard of. Just maybe not something that I'd do.

Sensing that I wasn't quite satisfied, she continued, "I caught her, Kayla, cheating. She begged for forgiveness. Stupid me, right? I was in love. We made it work a little longer. I learned that she had never stopped cheating. I already had one foot out the door. She lost a high-income job and was in a bad way financially. Once again, I came to her rescue. Stayed to help, even though we were more like roommates. A few months ago, I bought the house. Needed a fresh start."

This time she took the full 10 seconds. While I was lost in my thoughts and trying to digest this new information, she added, "I constantly encourage her to get her shit together, so she can fully support herself."

"You can't just give her the condo? Why not take the loss, so you can move on? You can't pay her off? Wouldn't that be easier?"

She offered plenty of answers, "I'd lose too much money by giving her the condo. I'm in a bind. Can't make her move or sell without her consent. She won't sign any papers. I know she won't get approved for a loan unless someone co-signs. Her credit is trashed. I'll figure something out."

I asked the obvious. "Is she using the condo to get back with you?"

"Kayla knows that I'm looking to date someone else. I encourage her to find a next boo, too."

After some additional back and forth, she suggested,

"Let's talk about something else, please. There are much more interesting topics. I wouldn't want to hear sleazy details, if you had an ex who couldn't let go. Then again..."

She flipped the script and wanted to peek behind my curtain. I coughed lightly and thought, "Oh, no."

She had no idea. I had my own experiences. I'd be very careful about what I told her, though.

Willingly, I shared, "You know, I've been attracted to girls then and women now, since I was a little girl. Had my first girlfriend when I was a senior in high school. We fizzled because I left to play volleyball at The University of Alabama..."

What I thought to myself and dared not verbalize were the specifics of me physically assaulting an ex, Monica. Nor would I talk about my heartbreak and subsequent breakdown over my most recent ex, Tabitha. I knew that I was keeping secrets. What else might Jenine not be sharing with me?

It had only been three days since I put my profile on the dating site. Not even three full days since I met Jenine. Despite this new information about her being legally separated, for the first time in a year, I felt different about the possibility of finding love. My hope, no, my prayer was that if I indeed found love again, that I wouldn't lose my mind over it or somehow lose even more.

With some hesitation, we prepared to bid each other adieu. "There's a work conference in DC for me this weekend. Can we do the date for the bet next weekend?"

While I went over my schedule, it sounded like her doorbell rang. "I can make it work for Saturday."

"Okay. Have a good night. One of my sorors is dropping off something for an event. Let me go get the door."

I looked at the time. Ten o'clock. In trying to make an event run smoothly, I've had sorors stop by much later. Most folks were clueless about the work that got done behind the scenes to make the show look flawless. Quickly, I pushed any thought that it may have been someone – other than her soror – out of my head.

Before I turned off the bedroom light, the burner phone rang. Only one person had that number. I hesitated. Jenine and I have had mind-bending conversations. There's an undeniable connection. Should I even bother?

After the 5th ring, I answered. As expected, Addictive1 was on the other line. Turns out her actual name was Gisele. Since it wasn't too late, I decided to give her a few minutes. I mainly wanted to determine whether I would enjoy her conversation, as much as I enjoyed her message from the dating site.

Quickly, I learned that she was born in Cameroon. "Your accent is beautiful and your voice is so calming and melodious. I've done a lot of traveling but not to Cameroon."

"Thank you. It's like most places in the world. You can find beauty and ugly, rich and poor, happy and unhappy not far from each other."

We touched on some things from her profile. "My two daughters are students at Stanford Law School."

I gave a low whistle of acknowledgement. Stanford had a stellar reputation for academic excellence, in addition to the high cost of tuition.

"I've worked at Columbia University for almost 20 years. If I remember correctly, you don't have any kids."

"Right. No little ones for me."

I wanted to clear up something. "You've been married. Have two grown daughters. Now you're into women? I'm majorly confused..."

She chuckled. "Sounds like the background for a gripping Lifetime movie, right? Knew my husband from back home. He passed three years ago. Since I was a young girl, I've had an attraction to women. That wasn't an acceptable lifestyle in my country. Even when I came to America, I denied my true feelings, got married and concentrated on living the so called American dream."

Softly, I said, "Interesting."

"God bless his soul. Had he lived, I would have stayed married and never explored my feelings. I'll take this opportunity to live my true life. I've been on a few dates but haven't found a solid connection. Honestly, a lot of people are turned off because I'm in a wheelchair."

"I'm not even sure what's appropriate to ask or say. If I offend, feel free to check me. Why are you in a wheelchair?"

"It's okay. I've told this story countless times. Two years ago, I started having issues with my left foot. I would lose my balance...fall...felt like I was being pricked with thousands of sharp needles. I've seen so many doctors..."

A phone rang in the background. "Ronnie. If it's okay, I'll be in touch tomorrow. My daughters are calling."

"No problem. It's cool."

I hung up the phone. Yawned. Stretched across the king-sized bed. She seemed cool. Maybe, just maybe, we'd become sistah friends.

Inevitably, I thought of Jenine. Weighed the pros and cons on my mental scale. The biggest pros were her assertiveness and intelligence. She didn't seem to have an issue in going after what she wanted. She could talk about so many topics. Add in her physical attractiveness and there was no doubt that she brought a lot of positivity to the table.

The biggest con was her marital status. Truthfully, being legally separated made a huge difference. At least I knew they were headed towards divorce and not just perpetrating. Pros were outweighing that one con.

9: SECOND THOUGHTS

The next day was a blur of meetings and computer work. I made myself leave the office for lunch, even though I didn't get anything to eat. Just wanted to be outdoors. Feel the sun on my caramel colored skin. During my power walk, Jenine and Gisele wanted my company for dinner tonight. Made me smile. Nice to know they were thinking of me.

It was an easy decision to accept Jenine's offer. I had already spent the whole day thinking about her. Now, I could spend a couple of hours basking in her radiant glow. My heart soared to new heights. That euphoria didn't last long. Less than 20 minutes later, my heart was on a rapid descent. She had an emergency at work. Needed a rain check.

Back to the second option. Gisele and I could continue last night's conversation. I recommended that we meet in the Ironbound section of Newark. The area was well known for its Portuguese, Brazilian and Spanish restaurants, which served all types of paella, seafood and endless portions of meat.

Inside the restaurant, I made sure the table had enough space for her wheelchair. I was reading an article on the web and heard her distinct voice. I looked up and we locked eyes.

"Hi. So nice to meet you, Ronnie."

I jumped off my chair and hugged her. She had beautiful skin that was the color of a clear midnight sky. Her hair was twisted in locks that fell to the middle of her back. Even in a wheelchair, she carried herself like royalty, with her head held high and erect posture. Immediately, I felt nothing but positive vibes emanating from her aura.

She was such a worldly woman, who seriously downplayed her job and education. In actuality, she was Dr. Gisele Akaba. The recipient of a Ph.D. At Columbia, she worked as a tenured professor.

I felt as though I was in the company of a griot. With rapt attention, I listened to her spin tales about her homeland. Raising her daughters. Her students at Columbia. Her travels and ultimately, her hopes and desires for the future – romantic and otherwise.

I tended to give credit when due and said, "There's been so much you didn't share, Dr. Akaba. From your education to being a polyglot and having traveled around the world, I'm beyond impressed."

Modestly, she replied, "Oh. There's still so much more that I want to achieve, namely getting back to my old self."

I excused myself to wash my hands. Before we ate, she requested, "Do you mind if I say grace?"

"Of course not. You seem like an angel. God has enough issues with me. I need all the help that I can get," I truthfully replied.

We bowed our heads. I listened, while she thanked God for the food, allowing us to meet and for this to be the beginning of a burgeoning friendship. In harmony, we said, "Amen."

My heart ached for her, as she told me about failed treatments. A glimmer of hope was on the horizon. Recently, she was accepted into a clinical trial that may allow her to not be so reliant on a wheelchair.

"Enough doom and gloom...let me live vicariously through you. Tell me some of your dating adventures. Have you met any interesting women from the site?"

"Only you. But..." I told the story of how I met Jenine. "It's still early. I'll see how it goes." Didn't share that I was close to being obsessed with her.

"Wow. She sounds amazing. Congratulations. We can still chat though, right?"

"For sure. You seem cool. I can be there when you get back to your old self and find the woman of your dreams."

10: SOMEONE WHO LOVES ME

During dinner with Gisele, I mistakenly left my phone in the car. Jenine called twice and sent text messages. It was already late. I dared not call. We tended not to have short conversations.

My mom and a couple of other folks called, as well. I called my mom, a retired public school principal. She still resided in Chicago. Like she was expecting my call, she answered on the first ring. "Hey baby. How's work? When is the last time you talked with Denise?"

The first question was easy. I answered without a second thought, "Work's cool."

My answer to the second question would prove more complicated. I had to tread carefully. Anything I said could cause the conversation to continue going smoothly or go completely off the rails.

Denise was mom's estranged twin sister. Affectionately, she was known as "Aunt D." Like most teenagers, I tried to flex and do what I wanted to do. My mom was intent on showing me that she was the boss. We constantly butted heads. In the end, hers was an overwhelming victory. My teenage stupidity was no match for her. Didn't stop me from trying, though.

Aunt D was the referee and mediator between us. She didn't have any children. Treated me like a daughter. We talk at least once a week, so I simply said, "Aunt D is fine."

I intentionally kept my response short. My mom's animus towards Aunt D was very real. Sadly, it may have been justified. They hadn't spoken in two years, since their mother and my "Nana" died. Aunt D was seven minutes older than my mom and was named executrix of Nana's estate. My mom wholeheartedly believed that the assets weren't distributed, according to Nana's wishes.

Nana owned three pieces of real estate. She also owned a small bus company that had a contract with Chicago Public Schools. I remembered her telling me that she was worth about $2 million. One would never know it. She wasn't flashy. She was a proud child of immigrants from Mali, who somehow found their way to Chicago, in search of a better life. Despite countless obstacles, she and my long-deceased grandfather forged a comfortable life for their two daughters. They were pillars of Chicago's 27th Ward.

According to the will that Aunt D presented, Nana was "only" worth $1 million. Based on that will, Aunt D inherited the real estate and 500k. My mom received a check for 400k. My check totaled 100k. To this day, my mom hadn't cashed her check. I couldn't deposit my check fast enough. It was used it to fully pay the mortgage on my house.

They've been back and forth to court. Several months ago, the judge froze a large portion of Nana's estate. The slow wheel of the judicial system continues to turn. I listened to my mom talk about the research she and the attorney have done, in trying to get the will overturned. She was sticking to her conviction.

I heard soft snores coming through the phone. "Go to sleep. Thank you for getting me home safely." This caused her to perk up a little bit.

"It's late. Where were you?"

No need to go into details, so I nonchalantly answered,

"Oh, a buddy and I met for dinner."

I waited for the usual follow-up questions about what I ate, whether she knew the buddy, so on and so forth. When none were forthcoming, I thought she was giving me an out.

She yawned again and said, "I love you, baby. More than you'll ever know. Call me, tomorrow. I want to hear about this buddy."

Softly, I cussed to myself for thinking I could get one past her. I should've known better.

11: BACK DOWN MEMORY LANE

Sitting in my driveway, I thought that my relationship status was something that my mom and I rarely discussed. She had met the two special women with whom I had been serious, Tabitha and Monica. Tabitha and I had the most intense and longest relationship. After our breakup and my breakdown, I learned that my mom only tolerated her for my sake. I had no clue. Even if she had told me about her feelings, it wouldn't have mattered. I loved that woman entirely too much.

Monica was my first love. We were together for eight years. She ended the relationship. The reason was my fault. I had lingering insecurities from how things ended with a prior girlfriend. One that I caught in a compromising position with a guy. Said she was no longer gay but straight.

Something similar happened with another girlfriend. Said she was no longer gay but bisexual. Asked if I'd allow her to have a boyfriend, while she still dated me. I don't knowingly share that way, so definitely not.

Instead of appreciating Monica for being a phenomenal woman, my mind stayed focused on trying to catch her cheating on me. One day, I was at her apartment. Found some articles of clothing that fueled my need for a confrontation.

While waiting for my showdown with Monica, I downed a bottle of vintage wine from her prized collection. My mind ran wild with concocted stories of her sleazy dalliances.

When she walked through the door, I was hurtling to the edge of drunkenness and being completely unreasonable.

She flicked on the light and jumped back in surprise. She didn't expect to see me. A sincere smile spread across her flawless face.

From the other side of the room, she peered lovingly into my bloodshot eyes. The smile morphed into sadness.

"Ronnie. My love. Why were you sitting in the dark?"

Taking time to remove her heels, she sauntered towards me. Pausing at the empty bottle, she inhaled deeply.

"You drank the whole bottle? Again? Do you have any idea how much that wine cost?"

They were rhetorical questions. I could guess the bottle cost thousands of dollars. Probably given as a gift for her work in pulling together another awe-inspiring fashion show.

She bent to give me a kiss. She stopped mid-peck when I shoved a pair of men's shorts and a T-shirt into her chest.

"Whose are these? Something you wanna tell me?"

I threw the clothes on the floor. Stared defiantly. Dared her to lie.

She abruptly walked away and suddenly stopped. Today, she would not wilt.

"See how extra wrong you are? Those belong to one of my brothers. Remember, he spent the night after all of us went to dinner?"

Through an alcohol-induced fog, I started to remember. Damn. Once again, I mistakenly deduced that she was being unfaithful. Instead of 2+2 equaling 4, my answer was eggplant. I wasn't remotely close to being right.

She saw the recognition of her truth in my eyes. Without giving me time to apologize, she yelled, "Ronnie, you're drunk! Again! You said that you'd get help! I can't keep doing this with you! Stop accusing me of shit that I'm not doing! You have keys to my apartment and spend more time here than at your house!"

Usually, she tolerated my insecurities. This day was different. She walked toward me. Pushed every button to further piss me off. Her mouth once spoke words claiming me as her forever love. Now, she told me how much she hated me.

She pointed those perfectly manicured fingernails inches from my face. The lips that were the softest I've ever kissed hurled vile words that I'd never heard her say. In different languages, she insulted me. I felt spittle land on my face, while she unleashed her verbal tirade. She wouldn't have talked to a stray dog the way she berated me.

This was my woman. My confidante. My lover for many years. Stupidly, I stared at her in complete surprise. She had reached the end of her rope.

To add more insult to my crumbling self-esteem, she not only threatened to cheat but told me that I was easily replaceable. "I swear, it's impossible to deal with you. Matter of fact. Fuck this and fuck you. It won't take long for me to find someone else..."

As if for dramatic effect, she abruptly stopped ranting and stared directly at me.

"Alcohol turns you into a monster..."

The full weight of her words was immediately felt. Intentionally, she picked at one of my old scabs.

"...I'll let Chuck's fine ass take me out. Didn't your old girl leave you for a dude? Makes sense. Probably accuse me so much because you're cheating. I don't even care. I hope you found someone else. I'll send her flowers and a thank you card. At least I won't have to deal with you no more. There's not enough medicine on earth to help your psychotic ass."

I listened to every word. Deserved them all plus more. It didn't matter that she was absolutely right. I could only focus on my anger. Each insult pushed me closer to the breaking point.

While it wasn't the first time that I was dead wrong in my accusations of Monica cheating, it was the first time that I ever hit her or any of my love interests. Like a bull provoked by a matador's cape, I only saw red. I snapped. Must have blacked out. Grabbed her arms to make her stay and listen to me. Undeterred, her insults continued.

I wanted to shut her up. Repeatedly, I punched her in the face. When that wasn't enough, I choked her. It wasn't until several seconds later that her wails of distress brought me to my senses.

All these years later, I didn't have to think hard to recall the look of complete shock on her face when I first raised my hand. That picture plays on a loop, in my mind, whenever I get upset. The sounds of my fist hitting her face were more like a cantaloupe being thrown from the rooftop and landing on concrete. Her screams, so loud and full of pain, while she tried to fight back, still ring in my ears.

Amazingly, no one in her building called the police. She gasped for air. Found a way to flail her arms. Took several wild swings. Connected on more than a few. I didn't bother to defend myself.

Instead, I was in full try-to-make-things-right mode. "Baby, I'm sorry...it's the alcohol...and sometimes I just get so jealous...please...," I apologized. Repeatedly. Profusely. Sincerely. It was all in vain.

She ran to the kitchen. Grabbed a large knife. Waved it dangerously close to my face. Chased me out of her apartment. "You're fuckin' crazy. How could you hit me?! I swear...don't ever call me again! Get out! Nowwww!!!"

That night and the next day, I called and texted her incessantly. She ignored me completely. I had the temerity to go back to her apartment. Knocked on the door. Saw her swollen face. Bruises on her neck. She worked in fashion. Had a meticulousness about her appearance that was unmatched. Part of what made her so damn sexy. It'd be a while before she went back to work.

"Monica, my Muffin, I'm screwed up. I'll talk to somebody. Get some help. Whatever you want..."

Silly me. Using her nickname didn't help. Neither did giving her my most sorrowful look. Apologizing from the depths of my heart didn't sway her. The irreparable damage was done. Some things were truly unforgivable.

Through bloodshot eyes, she stared at me. While I was focused on her distorted face, I didn't notice her hands. Deliberately, she raised both arms. Pointed a handgun inches from my forehead. I was too stunned to move.

She never raised her voice. With a calmness that scared the shit out of me, she slowly said, "Ronnie, if you come back here, your mom will be planning your funeral. Don't make me tell my brothers or anyone else the truth about what happened. You need help. There's no way you can apologize your way out of this. We're finished."

How could I have been so stupid? Why did I have such

an issue controlling my temper, when it came to matters of the heart?

Monica was the consummate good girl. Her two brothers were a different story. They were knee-deep in the drug trade. With a few words to their criminal cohorts, I could have easily disappeared. My mom wouldn't even have a body to bury. I was sure one of them gave her the gun. The fact that no one had beaten down my door told me that she'd already protected me, even though I violated her, in such a horrible way.

I wasn't foolish enough to push my luck. Not even in my wildest dreams did I envision our relationship would end that way. To show that I wasn't a threat, I slowly raised both of my hands and backed away. Before I left for good, I said, "I'm so sorry. Please forgive me."

Unfazed, she kept that gun pointed at me, until we were out of each other's eyesight.

To this day, I hadn't told anyone about that incident. Thoughts of Monica and Tabitha took me on an unexpected trip down memory lane. I shook my head. Tried to clear the cobwebs. Made my way back to the present. I forced myself to trudge into the house. Checked my phone. Texts and calls from everyone except Jenine.

Before I got myself situated for bed, I sent another text wishing her a good night. By the time I closed my eyes for the night, I checked my phone one last time. Still nothing from her.

The next morning, she finally replied. Reminded me that she was headed to Washington, DC, for a work conference, so she'd be busy this weekend. I worked extra hard not to jump to conclusions about why it took her so long to respond.

12: STRENGTHENING THE CONNECTION

While Jenine was out of town, I accepted Gisele's invitation to an art show. We walked around the gallery. Felt like she was my personal curator. She continued to amaze me with her intelligence. The most impressive part was that she didn't try to be a know-it-all. It just seemed like she knew it all. The more time I spent with her, the more I looked forward to calling her a friend. She truly was an amazing woman.

After the art show, I went back home and destroyed dinner. Undeterred and not one to waste food, I dined like it came from a Michelin starred restaurant. Sitting in my favorite chair, I had something to do. Went to the dating site. Saw that I had 22 new messages.

I thought about Jenine. It was still early in us getting to know each other. I had intense feelings for her, which weren't just physical. She challenged me. Made me want to be a better woman. Shit. Who was I fooling? She had a monopoly on my thoughts. Seemed like all I did was think about her. It was an easy decision. I deleted my dating profile. No reason for her to think that I was anything but serious.

Now, I had to plan our date. Came up with several pitiful ideas. Had a lightbulb moment after seeing a commercial. Food had to be included in almost every activity, so time to sit and converse was built into our day. Didn't want the whole day to be helter-skelter, so I decided on something that allowed for maximum relaxation. Couldn't think of a better way to end our day than the last activity that should include lots of laughter and more food, of course.

Once all of the reservations were made and confirmation emails received, I felt content. Folded my hands behind my head. Crossed my feet. Huge smile on my face.

As usual, thoughts of Jenine invaded my head. I called her but it went straight to voicemail. Sent a text. Waited. After several minutes, she still hadn't called or responded. I wondered who or what was taking her attention away from me.

Not quite ready to call it a night and needing a distraction from my fixation on Jenine, I thought about Marisa. I knew a lot of people. Family members. Sorors. Former volleyball teammates. Coworkers. Quantity doesn't equal quality. There was one person, Marisa, who I considered to be my truest friend. She worked as an international flight attendant. More than likely, she was somewhere between New York and another continent. Predictably, the call went straight to voicemail. We usually only talked a couple of times each month, given her work schedule and differences in time zones. I heard the beep and said, "Hey! Checking on you. Hit me back."

Marisa and I met at one of Monica's fashion shows. She moonlighted as a photographer. Back then she had dreams of becoming the female version of Gordon Parks. Didn't take long for priorities to change.

She and Amanda had been together since high school. The only woman she had ever loved. It seemed they were destined for a lifetime of bliss. Sealed it with a commitment ceremony. They bought a house. Started a business. Talked of adopting children. Fairytale beginning. Less than a year later, Amanda overdosed on OxyContin and died. Tragic ending.

To say that Marisa was crushed by Amanda's death was like saying the sun was hot. Some things were obvious. She questioned how she didn't know about Amanda's drug use. Wondered whether it meant that Marisa hadn't loved her enough. Essentially, she found every possible way to blame herself for Amanda's death.

Despite an outpouring of support from family and friends, Marisa became more depressed. She wasn't eating. Became dangerously thin. It was like she was trying to punish herself for not being able to save Amanda. Realizing that she needed help, she signed herself into a mental health facility. To hear her tell the story, each day she had a harder time fighting off the recurring thoughts of suicide. Almost a year later, she was in a better place, although she still struggled with depression.

In part of her coping, Marisa became a flight attendant. She started with domestic routes. Quickly worked her way up to coveted international routes. Now, she lived an almost gypsy lifestyle. Even when not flying for work, she flew here and there for a day or two, just because she wanted to get away. In reality, she spent more time traveling than at her house. Sometimes, I could fly for free and met her for short jaunts.

I had mental health issues and was in no place to judge Marisa. It seemed painfully obvious that she was still running or flying away from the pain of losing Amanda. After the death, she vowed to take her time before having another serious romantic relationship. Almost a decade later, she's been true to her word. She's still single.

13: BIG DATE ↔ BIG APPLE

Jenine and I met at Newark Penn Station for our big date. By the time we got our tickets and reached the platform, there was little time to spare. Just as the ticket taker stepped onto the train, the doors began to close.

I yelled, "Wait!"

He turned and immediately looked past me. When his eyes landed on Jenine, he smiled broadly. Licked his lips. Looked like he was at a buffet and preparing to dig into the choicest cut of meat. He pushed a button and opened the doors. Allowed all of us stragglers onto the train.

At the next stop, the ticket taker made his way to us. He motioned his hands from side to side, showing me that he didn't want our tickets. Instead, he was focused on Jenine.

"Why was a lady as lovely as you running for the train?"

I rolled my eyes. His pick-up lines were worse than mine.

She played the part of a damsel in distress. Batted her eyes, in a teasing manner and said, "We had an issue..."

He seemed all too eager to be her knight in shining armor. He knelt beside her. Put his hand on the armrest. "Oh, beautiful..." He leaned in closer to her and whispered something outside my earshot.

She flashed a bright smile. "Thank you. Next time, I'll remember..."

He looked pleased with himself. I knew what was

coming next. "So, ummm, think I could give you my number? Maybe I can take you to lunch?"

She smiled at him. "That's sweet but...I'm already involved." He followed her finger, as she pointed to me.

"Huh?" He looked confused. "Really? Ohhh..." Darted his eyes back and forth between her and me. Slowly, he came to the realization that his company wasn't wanted. He rose. Shook his head. Walked away and muttered, "But y'all are so pretty..."

We arrived in NYC. Our first stop was getting breakfast at a deli. While waiting for our food, she bombarded me with questions about the day's activities.

"Where will we need to go? How long will our day last? Are we going to be able to finish everything? Am I dressed properly?"

She was incessant. "You'll find out everything soon enough." She pouted and looked more irresistible. I resisted the urge to kiss her beautiful lips and said, "I'll be back."

When I returned from the restroom, she held my hands and astutely noted, "You wash your hands a lot."

"Yeah, it's part of my 'slight OCD.'"

Jokingly she asked, "Sure it's only OCD?"

I busied myself by looking at the menu. Anything to change the topic. No reason to give her, the mental health professional, a glimpse into my well documented mental health and other issues.

After breakfast, we walked arm in arm around the corner. On time, the first clue arrived in my inbox for the scavenger hunt. It seemed simple enough. We needed to find something white that rhymed with cocoon and was bendable. If they were all going to be this easy, we'd finish in five minutes.

She fixed her mind on finding a balloon. I simply reached into my backpack and pulled out a white plastic spoon. She busted out laughing.

Before she could ask any questions or make a smart-ass comment, I warned her, "Keep it to yourself. I blame everything on 'slight OCD.' If I ever kill someone, that's going to be my defense."

The unprofessional LCSW and LMFT in her responded, "Slight seems like an understatement. Medication may help."

Again, I ignored her comments. Especially the insinuation that I may need pharmaceutical help. Two times – in less than half an hour – she unknowingly touched on one of my most sensitive subjects.

Quickly, we moved to the next clue. From there, they got progressively harder. Although she was never an athlete, she had a competitive side. Saw her frustration when I was no help on the penultimate clue. I made up for it, though, because I quickly found the last clue.

We gave each other a high-five to celebrate. In one smooth motion, she had her other hand around my waist. Pulled me closer. It was a good thing she held me tight. I was weak in the knees. Being so close to her shook me to the core.

Out of the blue, she said, "Close your eyes."

I followed her directions. Her lips were tantalizingly close to my ear. "Ronnie, I'm having a great time. Being around you is so chill. A welcome change of pace."

How she remained cool and unfazed amazed me. Guess I didn't have the same paralyzing effect on her. The smell of her femininity invaded my nostrils. She was like a drug. I hadn't even taken a full hit. Already, I was becoming a full-blown addict.

We held hands and walked the streets of Manhattan – the world's most famous island. On almost every corner, just about anything could be found. Counterfeit. Legal. Illegal. Drugs. Clothing. Electronics. Jewelry. The energy was electric.

At the pizzeria, we sat side by side. Had front row seats to see the activity on the street. I told her, "People watching is one of my favorite things to do. I remember this one time..."

While I got ready to share a funny story, she tapped furiously on her phone. I could have told her that fifty million dollars dropped into my lap and we could run away together. She was in another world. Eyebrows furrowed so close together, it looked like she had a unibrow. She didn't look happy.

Naturally, I asked, "You good?"

"Yup."

She showed me that she turned off the phone, as I watched the screen fade to black. Gave me a reassuring smile. Sent my heart soaring to the heavens.

"I'm sorry. All about us today. Okay?"

"I'd like that."

I followed her to the door. Draped my arm around her shoulder. She wrapped an arm around my waist. We walked slowly.

Trying to get our connection back, I said, "Penny for your thoughts."

"You seem too good to be true," she quickly replied.

Had I been eating or drinking something, I would have spit it out in shock. Thankfully, she wasn't looking in my direction and couldn't see my face. I'm sure my bulging eyes would have given away my innermost feelings. Monica and Tabitha were the first two thoughts that came to mind. They would seriously disagree. There was no way I would tell her the regretful details of stalking Tabitha. Nor would I talk about my domestic violence with Monica.

Guess it's sort of like meeting someone new. Sometimes you asked about how many people they ever slept with. Whatever number they gave you, the true answer was probably more. With certain questions or situations, you'd likely never know the truth. Most times, that was for the betterment of your relationship. And sanity.

"Well, I think you're too good to be true, too."

She laughed so loud and for so long that a group of strangers stopped. They started laughing with her, too. "Stick around long enough. You'll see that I'm a major fuck up. For real. You'll need to be patient with me. I like you. Think about you more than I'll ever admit, which is the main reason I'm telling you this."

My mom always said forewarned is forearmed. I was so enthralled with her. Warnings be damned. At that time, I was confident that we'd withstand whatever came our way.

I jokingly asked, "Are you wanted for a heinous crime? How much reward money if I turn you in?"

"Nah. The one person who's probably looking for me doesn't want me arrested."

I waited for her to continue. She went silent. Seemed like there was more she wanted to tell me. More she should have told me.

For once, I was able to look directly at her. Took the time to bare part of my soul. "We all have issues. Leave the past in the past. Let's just see where this leads for us."

*****

Jenine's eyes sparkled when we arrived at the spa. "Oh wow. This is fancy. Extra plush robes, wine, chocolate covered strawberries..."

She looked at me and hesitatingly said, "Don't take this the wrong way but..."

Immediately, I felt defensive and interrupted, "Be nice..."

She flashed that winning smile. Held my hand. Put me at ease before she continued, "...this spa seems very pretentious and grandiose...so unlike you. How'd you know about this place?"

The truth was that Monica turned me onto this spa years ago but I only offered, "Someone I used to know..."

With an inscrutable expression, she remarked, "Basically, one of your ex-girlfriends brought you here."

Was she a psychic? Like a kid caught taking a bite from a cookie just swiped from the jar, I nodded.

Mercifully, she said, "It's cool."

Didn't seem like she was the jealous type. Guess I was the only one with that cross to bear. Quickly, she moved to something more important. "Time to get pampered."

We were treated like royalty. The sea salt scrub had my skin feeling like a newborn baby. The technician worked overtime sloughing all of the dead skin off my heels before I was ready for my pedicure.

She flipped through a magazine. The sorry state of my feet didn't go unnoticed. "There's no reason for your feet to look that way. It's like you don't even care. I'll say it again. You're a naturally pretty woman. Take better care of yourself."

Ignoring her comments, I was more focused on

something else. I had a chance to take a gander at her feet, while we got our pedicures. I had a wicked attraction to women with pretty feet. It kind of felt like Eddie Murphy in the movie, "Boomerang," when he pulled back the bedsheet to look at Halle Berry's feet. Discreetly, I pumped my fist in excitement. Jenine passed the test. Her feet were in pristine condition. I licked my lips, in anticipation of sucking her toes.

She noticed me ogling her feet. "Why are you looking at me like that?"

I tried not to expose my hole card, so I played stupid. "What do you mean?"

"Yeah, right. Have you already forgotten? Told you that I'm very observant." She warned. "You're damn near drooling. Let me find out that you're a foot freak."

I may have been busted but couldn't resist, "Tsk. Tsk. Tsk, Ms. LCSW and LMFT. The correct term is fetish." Felt like I finally one-upped her.

After the spa, Jenine seemed to be energized. I was ready for a nap. The masseuse hit pressure points I didn't know existed. I was so relaxed that I stifled several yawns, while I tried to figure out the best route to our final stop.

At the comedy club, I was ready to laugh and try to find some satisfaction with what I thought would be substandard food. Imagine my shock when everything tasted like it came straight from my Nana's kitchen. The fried chicken, roasted potatoes and sautéed spinach were delicious. They even had homemade cornbread that was drizzled with cinnamon honey butter.

My food was scrumptious. Still, something was wrong. Usually, her fingers would have invaded my plate. "This food is rockin'. You want some?" I pushed my plate towards her.

She scrunched up her nose, like someone farted. "All of the food is touching the spinach."

"The food is…? What are you talking about?"

Like it was the most obvious thing in the world, she shared, "When I was younger, spinach gave me the worst diarrhea. Once I got old enough to decide what I would and would not eat, spinach didn't make the cut."

The look on her face was one of pure disgust. For a final proclamation, she damn near yelled, "I detest spinach."

I went back to eating my food. Looked at her in amazement. During our conversations, she talked of needing to get back in shape. All of those thoughts were clearly long forgotten. She devoured an extra-large portion of oxtails and dirty rice. Forks and napkins be damned, she looked like a vacuum and sucked the oxtails clean off the bones.

Thoughts of her lusciously full lips exploring my most intimate areas flitted across my head. Maybe forgetting that she was in public, she licked, re-licked her fingers and dug way in the back of her mouth. She had lost all home training.

We narrowly avoided a near riot inside the comedy club when the headliner and someone in the audience almost came to blows. Although overwhelmingly pleased with the food but majorly disappointed with the comedy, we stood in midtown Manhattan and vibed off each other.

"Everything that I planned is done, sleepyhead. We heading back to Jersey? Did you have a good time?"

She yawned for several seconds. "If not for those oxtails giving me the 'itis, I'd take you uptown to a private strip club. The owner and I are cool."

Could I get even luckier? "Oh yeah? I'm not the only one who likes strip clubs, huh? Too bad those oxtails made you tired."

"You've been so enjoyable today, maybe I would've shown my appreciation and given you a lap dance on stage."

An uncontrollable smile spread across my face. "That gives me something to look forward to. Let's head back to Jersey."

Like it was our ritual practiced over several decades, instead of a few days, we reached for each other's hand. Walked to the train station. She leaned her head on my shoulder and quickly went to sleep. I kissed her forehead. Whispered to myself, "I could get used to this," as I happily closed my eyes.

*****

Back in Newark, we stood under a streetlight. It felt more like I was under the spotlight. Again, her piercing eyes stared at me intently.

"The night's still early. Come back to my house. We could watch a movie or..." She let the possibility of something else hang in the air.

I had a flashback of her sucking oxtails off the bone. Felt a throbbing sensation between my legs. When she stepped towards me, I moved back. Willed myself to be strong even though my desire for her was immeasurable.

"Absolutely not. It'd be too hard to keep my hands off you."

"Trust, it's not just your hands that I want all over me. Know that I'm not used to rejection. Do not make this a habit."

She wasn't making this easy. Eventually, I'd give her whatever she wanted. Just not tonight.

I spoke from my heart. "If I go with you, we'll be fuckin' like dogs in heat. Won't even make it to your front door..."

"And?"

My crassness only seemed to embolden her. She pulled me closer. Held me tighter. The throbbing between my thighs matched the intensity of a still unsigned yet still hungry drummer unleashing years of frustration.

Her hands traveled across my body like they were following a well-worn road map. No need for GPS or turn-by-turn directions. She already knew how to set my nerve endings aflame. Each touch made my body feel like fire was shooting out of my pores.

Even after a full day in NYC, she smelled like she just stepped out of the shower. I allowed myself some indulgence. Kissed her neck. She held me tighter and softly moaned, "Ronnie. Ronnieee."

Gently, I put a finger under her chin. Okay. I wanted just a little more indulgence. I lightly traced the outline of her lips with my tongue. Kissed her bottom lip and then her top lip. Just as I thought, they were pillow soft. Slowly. Passionately. She returned my kisses. Her lips fed mine. My tongue fed hers. Each touch further cemented our bond.

Seconds passed into minutes. This felt so right. So good. "Damn. That was in...tense." I held her cheeks in my hands. My breathing was ragged.

She didn't realize the depth of my feelings. I didn't want a one-night stand. I'd bend over backwards for her. No way would I admit that I had already envisioned the engagement ring that I'd buy her. I wanted us to share more than this lifetime.

Still... The last thing I intended to do was expose my heartfelt thoughts. If I did, maybe I'd scare her away. Make her think that I had stalker tendencies or mental health issues. I was guilty of both plus more. She just didn't need to know those truths.

After some thought, I finally said, "I want to go about this the right way."

She was unfazed. Unbothered. Unnerved. She asked the same question. "And?"

Feeling the need to regain some semblance of control, I had my question. "Is that the only word you know?"

Now, it was her turn to look away. She seemed hesitant. Unsure. I gave her another soul stirring kiss for encouragement. "Tell me, pleassse."

"You're a fantastic kisser. My body is tingling," she confessed. "It's only been two weeks but I've been wondering... Can we start the possibility of forever? Right now?"

That was unexpected. My heart pitter-pattered with excitement. I could have teased her. Made her wait. Nah. There was no need. Zero shame on my part.

"Jenine, I've been yours since I first laid eyes on you. We're just making it official today."

14: JENINE'S PERSPECTIVE – PART 2

Dear Diary:

My life is like a soap opera. Ronnie is my current romantic interest and future love (I pray). The first night that I cooked for her, she came dangerously close to meeting Kayla, my soon-to-be-ex-wife (I pray) but present (sometimes) love. After Ronnie left my house, Kayla was racing to confront me. She was pissed that I was ignoring her calls. She almost broadsided Ronnie. I would've been horrified had that happened. Equally, I would have been mortified had they actually met. That was entirely too close for comfort.

After the near accident, Kayla arrived – unannounced – at my house. Word for word, I can still recap our conversation. I opened the door and said, "Knew you couldn't resist..." Mistakenly, I thought Ronnie had come back.

"Couldn't resist what? Why ain't you answering the phone? What the fuck you been doing that got you lookin' so damn happy?"

Damn. I had to yank her in the house. Our yelling was already starting to wake up everybody within a two-mile radius. She had the uncanny ability to take ignorance to unimaginably high levels. She was angry that I wouldn't let her spend the night. Shit. I just sexed her senseless a couple of weeks ago. Saw her clenching and unclenching her hands. Knew that she was ready to blow a gasket.

I needed to get her to respect the boundary lines, even

if I'm constantly changing them. She can't just show up unannounced. So glad that she no longer has a key. I have to do a better job of not sending her mixed signals. We must get our legal ties severed. Marriage. Condo. She remains in a bad way financially. I'm stuck footing the bill for the condo, so my damn credit doesn't get ruined. I want to sell. She doesn't because she has nowhere else to go. She could use her part of the sale to get an apartment. Live off that money for a while. The main reason she won't agree to the sale is because that would dash more of her hope that we'll get back together. Something has to give.

*****

Told Ronnie about my marriage. I heard the uncertainty in her voice. No doubt that she wasn't happy. I cleaned it up, as best as I could. Seemed like she bought my reasoning, even if it wasn't entirely true. That was one of those times when telling the whole truth wasn't an option. It was the first major lie that I told her. There'll be more, at least until I can sort out my Kayla situation.

I gave Ronnie fair warning about some of my issues. Admittedly, I'm curious about her issues. I'll figure them out sooner or later. Most people are rarely exactly who they say they are, myself included. I'm pretty sure she's not dealing with anyone else. She talked about having imperfections. I'm not one to judge, especially considering the secrets that I'm hiding.

For now, we're learning more about each other. I like almost everything that I see. Things with her have been magical. It's only been two weeks. Seems like we've known each other for a lifetime. I want to spend more time with her. No way will I let go of someone so good, while I try to get rid of someone who's no longer good for me.

Ronnie and I haven't been intimate. Tried to entice her back to my house, after our NYC date. She actually rejected me. First time for everything. Probably for the best. Standing under that streetlight, I wasn't my usual confident self. Butterflies in my stomach. Quickening pulse. Nervous. Unsteady breathing. Sweaty palms. Never had I felt such intense waves of emotions.

She kissed me so slowly. Felt like she was savoring every millimeter of my lips. If she works my other pair of lips that way, I'm in even more bona fide trouble. I was so caught in my euphoric feelings that I had to make it official. "Can we start the possibility of forever? Right now?"

I was overjoyed with her response, "Jenine, I've been yours since I first laid eyes on you. We're just making it official today."

As pleased as I am with Ronnie and all of our possibilities, I'm equally cautious about Kayla. There's no way that she'll go quietly. She seems intent on making things right. Still thinks there's a chance for us. Is there?

I have to work overtime. Need to untangle this web of feelings and emotions between Kayla and me, so I can fully concentrate on Ronnie. A lover's triangle usually leads to trouble. Secrets can only stay buried for so long. Eventually, those dastardly details ooze to the surface. Just have to hope...no pray...that I'm ready to deal with the consequences and that no one gets hurt.

15: KAYLA'S CONTRIBUTION – PART 2

T hings had been going better between my beautiful wife and me. Occasionally, we spent nights together, whether it was at our condo or her house. I was between jobs, so extra money was scarce. Still, I found ways to spoil her with free tickets to museums, jazz concerts and wine tastings.

The exception to our renewed good times occurred one night when she wouldn't answer my calls. I craved her attention like a fish needed water. A sinking feeling in the pit of my stomach told me that she was up to something I wouldn't like. I took it upon myself to investigate.

As I sped to her house, I flew through a red light. Came within one millimeter of slamming into a convertible Audi. When the other driver rolled down the window, I barely glanced in her direction. A blind rage distorted my vision. I was so focused on getting to my wife. Before speeding away, I yelled, "Get the fuck out my way, you stupid bitch!"

At her house, she smiled like the cat that ate the canary, when she opened the door and breathlessly said, "Knew you couldn't resist…"

I willed myself not to get distracted by her incredible beauty. At an ear-splitting volume, I fired the first shot. "Couldn't resist what? Why ain't you answering the phone? What the fuck you been doing that got you lookin' so damn happy?"

While I waited for her response, I clenched and

unclenched my hands. Anger pulsated through my veins. I talked a lot of shit. Made a lot of threats but I've never hit her. That's a line we haven't crossed.

Thinking back, though, I came close. Menacingly, I raised my hand at her. She stopped me cold and warned, "If you ever do...make sure you kill me because I won't rest until I destroy you."

Then and now, she didn't understand. I just wanted her to love me – like the old days. I watched her and imagined her thinking of a way out of this quagmire. I tracked her striking green eyes, as they nervously scanned the street. Who was she looking for? I leaned in close. The only thing I smelled was the mind-numbing scent of her femininity.

Finally, she spoke, "Stop being so loud. You'll wake up the block. Why are you here?"

She grabbed my arm. Yanked me into the house. My eyes scanned the open floor plan. The living room was spotless. I saw papers on the dining room table. Cautiously, she eyed me, as I walked towards the kitchen.

Before I made ridiculous accusations, I discreetly noted that her fingernails looked like she had just gotten a manicure. I opened the dishwasher. Saw dried dishes. Pressed some buttons. Made sure that it worked just fine.

Satisfied that I could proceed, I turned and calmly noted, "You haven't hand-washed dishes in all the years we've been together. What's this?" I motioned to the wet dishes and cutlery that were neatly stacked in the drainer. I saw two of everything: plates, cups, forks and spoons.

Casually, she said, "Remember...you're the reason we're legally separated...I don't owe you a damn thing."

"Separated? Only thing separated about us is that we don't live together. All else is the same. It wasn't that long ago that you were begging me to go deeper...faster..."

She smiled at the flashback. Quickly regrouped. "I get the point. That was another mistake on my part... Tonight, I'm feeling charitable. I'll entertain your silly insinuations and give you an explanation."

She walked to the red velvet cake – my favorite – and cut a healthy portion. Wrapped it in foil. Handed it to me.

"I had dinner with a soror. We're co-chairs for a fundraiser and need everything to be perfect. We brainstormed. I cooked. She cleaned. Simple as that."

With a shrug of her shoulders, I was expected to accept that was the end of the story. When you've been with someone for so long, you just knew things. She often played me for a fool. I acted as though I had unshakable proof and threatened, "You're a sneaky liar. I'm not stupid. You think you're smarter than everyone else. Keep doin' dumb shit and you're gonna make me kill you."

"I'm not scared of you, so stop your nonsense. I don't know which act is more tired: the constant threats or you constantly needing my help. Me always needing to bail you out must be the dumb shit you're talking about."

Before I could question her answers, she ushered me out the front door. I left her house relieved but not totally convinced. An absence of something wasn't irrefutable proof it didn't happen.

On the way back home, I cautiously passed through the traffic light, where I almost crashed into the other driver. That near-miss had to be an obvious sign that I had been given yet another opportunity. I reaffirmed my pledge to make things right with my beautiful wife.

For the next few weeks, I applied for several positions. I tried to be positive about my prospects of earning a livable wage. In one day, I received five rejection letters.

That was one of the lowest points.

She must have known that I was in the grips of despair. I rang the doorbell. Without a word, she welcomed me back into her loving arms. Led me to her bed. Caressed my body in ways that made me call out her name in ecstasy. Each touch worked to stitch my tattered confidence and hope back together. She promised to always have my back. As long as I had her, everything would be okay. What would I do if she ever left me?

16: START OF SOMETHING GOOD?

There's a downside to quickly jumping into a relationship. You don't have time to learn little and in all fairness, big things about people. Their quirks. Their true likes. Their true dislikes. When they're telling the truth or lying.

I'm a neat freak. My mom's a neat freak. That's probably how the "gene" was passed onto me.

Jenine was the complete opposite. That much was clear from the first time she cooked dinner for me. Her house was nowhere near dirty. It was evident that she made little effort to tidy up. Clothes were strewn on the floor. Her bed wasn't made. In various rooms, there were balled-up pieces of paper by the garbage cans. It almost looked like she tried to throw the papers into the garbage but missed and never bothered to pick them up.

The first night Jenine came to my house, she had plenty to say about what she perceived to be my lack of style, "Ronnie, how long have you lived here? This house is like a bachelor pad on steroids. Only things missing are the video game console and pizza boxes stacked in the corner. Everything looks so bland and uninspiring. You barely have furniture...only one picture on the wall...the paint colors are blah." She paused, looked upward and acknowledged, "The skylights are dope. Lots of natural light and sexy when it rains."

Admittedly, I was far from an interior decorator. Her observations were on point, even if they were a little harsh. "What do you mean? I have a couch, a multipurpose table and my favorite chair. What else do I need?"

Things got worse, as I gave her the grand tour. Like a prospective home buyer, she took note of everything. Once I had shown her all of the rooms, she shook her head from side to side and remarked, "Your house is bigger than mine. You have more empty rooms than furnished ones." She continued to shake her head in amazement. "This place is so clean, I'd eat off the floor and not think twice about it."

Just when I thought she was done, she reserved the best for last and asked, "Slight OCD, huh? Seriously. Have you ever been diagnosed?"

Maybe I was mistaken. There seemed to be a look of pity in her eyes. "Nah. I've never been diagnosed with OCD."

If an answer could be truthfully deceptive, that was what I gave her. I put my hand over hers. Leaned across the table. Kissed those beautiful lips. Wanted a distraction. I knew that her question only referred to my neatness and organization. The full truth was that I had been diagnosed. She just didn't need to know about that forgettable chapter in my life.

On the same night, I showed her my version of romance. She coolly remarked, "Okay. So you get thumbs up for the candles and flowers. Nice touches. The ambiance is nice. But...are we having a candlelight dinner and eating pizza?"

"At least it's not frozen. My cooking tends to look like roadkill...this was my grand idea. Pretend we're at a classy restaurant in Italy."

I held up a slice of pizza. She followed suit. We toasted

by touching the slices and said, "To new beginnings."

After dinner, she went to the living room. I had already set up some warm water, so she could soak her feet. I ducked into one of the bathrooms. Grabbed some warm oil and nail polish. Joined her on the couch.

"Confession. That dinner was sort of romantic. The pizza was delicious. We'll make a deal. I cook. You clean. Fair?"

"No argument from me."

I got the hint, as she moved her feet from the basin to the towel on my lap. I patted them dry. Started at the base. Used my thumbs. Alternated between applying light and medium pressure along the full length of her foot. One thumb went clockwise. The other in the opposite direction. Made small circles. Larger circles. Smiled to myself, as I studied her responses to my handiwork.

At the spa, she made fun of my foot fetish. Now, I watched her head fall back onto the cushion. She inched closer to me. Saw those enthralling green eyes close in a half-mast, under the dexterity of my hands working out the tension in her feet - one nerve ending at a time.

I smiled even more, while she gripped the couch. Quickly, she was learning that her feet were an erogenous area. Listened to her persistently call out my name, "Ronnieee…"

I tickled the bottom of her foot with my tongue. Paused from sucking one of her toes. I couldn't resist myself. "No more smart-ass comments about my fetish, I see."

She licked her lips. Slowly shook her head and stuttered, "I…I'm s-s-orry. This feels sooo damn good."

After turning Jenine onto the erotic feelings in her

feet, I gave her a pedicure. While she waited for the polish to dry, she leaned back against me. Her cell phone rang. She looked at the caller ID. Ever so slightly, I felt her body stiffen.

"More personal bullshit? You want some privacy?"

She declined the call. Ignored my questions. Not even three seconds later, her phone rang again.

I wasn't owed an excuse. She offered one anyway, "No. This is work bullshit. I'll deal with it tomorrow."

I noticed that she didn't just put the phone on silent. She turned it off.

Night came quickly and we fell asleep on the couch. Bodies wrapped around each other. When sleeping with someone else, I tended to be a light sleeper. I was attuned to every twist and turn of her body. Easing away from her, Mother Nature called. Tried not to wake her. The house was dark. Before I was fully up the stairs, I noticed a glow in the living room. It looked like she turned on her cell phone.

A few minutes later, I returned to the couch. Damn. How'd she go back to sleep that fast? While I got comfortable on the couch, I inadvertently touched her phone. The screen didn't illuminate. Just that quickly, she had turned it back off.

Briefly, I wondered what was so important that she checked the phone at three o'clock in the morning. My tiredness overrode my curiosity. She snuggled closer. I wrapped my arms around her. Placed my hand near her heart. Fell asleep to the beat of its rhythmic pattern.

17: PENT UP EMOTIONS

I stared in disbelief at the calendar. Had it been 415 days? I counted again. Confirmed the pitiful truth. It was beyond time to dust off my cobwebs. I wanted my first time with Jenine to be special. Memorable. The beginning of a lifetime of ways to express my love.

The following night, she came to my house. My body shivered with anticipation. During our bubble bath, she fed me fresh pineapple. My tongue sampled various flavors of melted caramel from her breasts. Afterwards, I tied up her hair. Guided her to my king-sized bed. Took time to treasure her body, while I massaged shea butter onto her long and shapely legs. My eyes traveled the length of her silhouette. Her body glistened under the candlelight. Watched her smile at me. She pulled me closer. Repeatedly, she moaned approvals of and desires for my touch, "Ronnni-eee."

Her body was a blank canvas. I longed to make an indelible mark on it. Our mouths and tongues began what I hoped would be a timeless journey of exploration. One in which each kiss and new discovery would culminate in a deepening of our love and commitment.

I wanted every touch and caress to convey the oceanic depth of my feelings that were too soon for my mouth to express. The emotions were too powerful for me to handle alone. I silently prayed to a God that I often disappointed. Humbly, I asked that He would allow her to take good care of my heart. I was so charged up. It felt like firecrackers were exploding inside my body. I wanted to give her all of me. Continuously, I called out her name, "J...Jeninne..."

This was so good. Seemed so right. If I could crawl inside her for eternal rest, I would have immediately done it. Every kiss solidified what I already knew. There was something about her that touched my soul. Parts that hadn't been discovered. Other pieces that needed to be repaired. Tears came to my eyes. Felt like I was releasing the emotions of my breakup and breakdown with Tabitha. My eternal regret over Monica. The desire of forever and beyond with Jenine.

Her fingernails dug deeper into my back. Motivated me to give her more. In harmony, our moans intensified. Every stroke allowed me to pour a heartfelt supplication into her and accept what I prayed would be her eternal love in return.

The sexual feelings were undeniable. The emotional ones were overwhelming. My body felt like it was convulsing from the incredible pleasure of her touch. My heart seemed to be one beat away from exploding.

Our bodies rode a crescendo of passion and emotion to orgasmic heights. We collapsed onto each other from exhaustion. I longed for an everlasting remembrance of this moment. The first in what would be countless expressions of affection. Allow our offspring to have an official record of the love that brought forth their life.

For minutes, I was speechless. I tried to get my bearings. Listened to her unsteady breathing. She circled my navel with her fingernail. Rested her head near my heart. There was no way she could know that it beat solely for her.

"What are you thinking?"

Talk about a loaded question. I could've told her that I was deeply in love. Or maybe that I lost count of the number of times I thought about her each day. Was it too early to confess that I wanted marriage, a house and family with her? Even when she no longer had firm breasts and all the hairs atop her head and in her most private place were gray, I'd still want her. Whenever God called me home, I'd long to be with her. I wondered how far down this rabbit hole I would go. I already knew that I loved her more than Tabitha and Monica – combined. Oh, how that scared me.

Instead of exposing my soul, I closed my eyes. Fought back more tears and finally answered, "I'm thinking that your lovin' is top notch."

She laughed at my corniness. Apparently, there was rarely a better time for pillow talk than after sex, so she said, "Ask me a question."

I was exhausted but found the strength to ask, "What's the worst thing you ever did in a relationship?"

"I cheated, repeatedly." As if reading my mind, she added, "The best thing I ever did was help someone recognize their mental health diagnosis and get the necessary treatment. What's the next question?"

"Which word best describes you?"

"Hmm. One word..." After some thought, she finally answered, "Misunderstood." As an aside, she added, "Sometimes, I don't even understand why I do some of the stuff that I do." Almost like she was recalling unpleasant memories, she had a faraway look in her eyes.

"What's a non-negotiable in a relationship?"

"That's easy." I could feel her shaking her head from side to side. "Don't hit me. We can argue...make threats... talk as much crap as you want...but don't cross that line."

I shifted my body. Had to get her head away from my heart, which beat with the ferocity of a jackhammer. Any mention of domestic violence brought back unpleasant memories.

Like a sponge, I soaked up the information. Massaged her scalp. Buried my face in her long hair. Couldn't wait to bury my face somewhere else.

"That feels good. Your touch is so relaxing."

A few seconds later, she was out like a light. Guess that was the end of our pillow talk. Our next sexual session would have to wait.

I left her on the bed. Kissed her on the lips. Paused to admire her body. After locking up the house, I took a shower. Smiled when recapping our first time. I already looked forward to the next.

Her phone must have been on silent. I didn't hear it ring. Its flashing light illuminated the darkness of my room. I went to the dresser. She had a missed call from a contact named Rehab. Probably something to do with her job. Weird time to call, though. I put her phone back on the dresser – facedown – just the way I found it.

18: MISSING YOU

Just that quick, it was time for Jenine to leave with her sorors for Jamaica. I helped her plan the trip. Even though we were a couple, she didn't ask me to join them. My usual idea of fun wasn't hanging with the ladies of BXA. Still, I could have rented a car and gone on my own adventures. Maybe Marisa could have met me. It would have been nice to enjoy tropical temperatures and pristine beaches, especially since the weather in Jersey was already getting much colder.

At the airport, we held onto each other. Agreed to chat each day. With the seconds quickly ticking away, I honestly said, "I'm already missing you."

She wiped away a smudge of her lip gloss off my cheek. "I'll be back in no time. Behave yourself."

The day that she left, I was busy at work and missed her call. She sent me a text message that they reached safely. They were going to check out one of my recommendations in Montego Bay.

That first night passed without a call. Although disappointed, I didn't stress. She may have had jet lag or found other places to visit. I could imagine the Jamaican men tripping over themselves to please the ladies of BXA. That shouldn't be a problem. Jenine would respect our relationship, right?

*****

Since Jenine and I started dating, my communication with Gisele had pretty much been relegated to texting. Now, she gave me an update through our video call.

"Remember the talk that I had with my girls? Well, it had its intended result."

"Cool. They're on the right track academically."

She turned the focus on me. "How are things going with your lady friend?"

Casually, I chewed a piece of salmon. I tried to project an air of indifference. The luminescent smile on my face told a different story. "Gisele, she's amazing. I like her and want her to be the one... I could talk for hours about her, though. Enough about J and me. Tell me about the clinical trial."

"Well, you know that it started a week ago. So far there's no magical recovery...but no side effects, either." She pointed to the wheelchair. "I remain cautiously optimistic. Keep telling myself to temper expectations and not be unrealistic."

"If I can help, don't hesitate to let me know. Now...tell me more about your new woman?"

Normally, Gisele was the poster child for calmness. Today, she exuded a different energy. "I learn so much from her. Our conversations are amazing and leave me wanting more."

The thought of someone being smarter than Gisele seemed improbable. This woman had to be a brain surgeon. It sounded promising. Maybe she and I had found the loves of our lives.

My phone beeped. "That's my mom. Let me take her call..."

I quickly answered. She was already talking. "Hi, Ronnie. Just want to check that I can visit you on

December 4th. I'll stay for two weeks."

"Is something wrong? You usually visit in the summer."

"I'm missing my daughter. Want to check on you. Find out the reason you seem so happy these last few weeks."

My mom was perceptive. It was only a matter of time before she learned about Jenine. "Look at you thinking you know me. Hold on." While she waited, I booked her flight. "You're all set. I just emailed the info."

"Thank you. I'm going back to working on this family tree. Talk with you later."

I called my weakness. Left a voicemail. Sent a text. Waited but didn't get a response. The women of BXA must be having a good time. I was still riding the high of seeing my mom. Even Jenine's unexpected silence couldn't spoil my good mood. I couldn't wait for them to meet.

The next morning, Jenine's ringtone of "Unthinkable," by Alicia Keys blared on my phone. Quickly, I pressed accept. Saw her modeling a slingshot bikini that left little to the imagination. She'd only been gone for a couple of days, yet she looked more statuesque than I remembered.

"We're going to lounge by the pool." After doing a pirouette, she teasingly asked, "You like?"

I was stuck staring at the phone. For a woman in her mid-30s, all of her assets were still firm and upright.

Reminding myself that she could see my face, I tried to keep my expression neutral. Carefully, I chose my words, "You look amazing. Guess you're having a great time. I've barely heard from you. I miss you."

Now that I had given her a couple of compliments, she'd be more receptive to what else I had to say. I still tiptoed. "You going to the pool like that? No cover-up?"

Despite the attempt to mollify my response, she saw through me. "Do you have a problem with me wearing this? Are you big mad or little mad? Maybe you're jealous, babe?"

Her tone sounded joyous, which put me at ease that this wouldn't turn into our first argument. I was livid. My response would've been anything but playful. I imagined everyone gawking at her. Desiring her. The least any respectable woman would do was wear a proper cover-up.

As I got ready to speak my mind, a woman entered the room and yelled, "What's takin' so long?"

With wide eyes and an open mouth, Jenine had an astonished expression on her face. "I told you to wait for me downstairs. I'm coming."

The call disconnected. Repeatedly, I called her back. She didn't answer. What an inconvenient time to have an issue with the Wi-Fi.

I massaged my temples. A headache was brewing. I was dead wrong for feeling that she shouldn't wear the slingshot bikini. Gave myself some credit for controlling my temper. She could wear whatever she wanted. Maybe the Wi-Fi getting disconnected was to my benefit. Otherwise, she would have gotten a glimpse at my jealousy.

She was supposed to return tomorrow. The more I thought about everything, the more I realized how much I missed her. I had to get the slingshot bikini out of my mind. Coaxing myself into thinking happy thoughts, I shifted my focus to how much I looked forward to seeing her.

*****

While I was getting ready to pick up Jenine from the airport, my phone rang. "Babe, I'm home."

"What? I was supposed to pick you up. Didn't you get the text?"

"Uh, no. Otherwise, I would've responded."

I looked at my phone. Sure enough, she didn't respond. "Guess that's my mistake. Had I been able to talk to you a little more, this probably wouldn't have happened."

That sounded harsh. Tried to clean it up and said, "I know you were having a good time, though."

I had to hide my disappointment. My insecurity. Instead, it seemed like this was another mix-up on my end.

She talked hurriedly, "The trip was amazing. We went to all the places that you recommended. I've already been checking work emails and have so much stuff to do. I'll be busy tonight but we'll see each other soon, so we can properly catch up."

Just like that, my plans for spending the night with our bodies wrapped around each other went up in smoke. I wasn't thinking about the sex – well maybe a little bit. I wanted to hear about the trip. Now, I wasn't sure when we'd spend quality time together.

19: JENINE'S PERSPECTIVE – PART 3

Dear Diary:

I'm writing to you because if I told this to anyone else, they would justifiably slap me for being so stupid. You, on the other hand, are non-judgmental, so I give you the unfiltered truth.

Where do I start? Okay. Ronnie continues to exceed my expectations by leaps and bounds. However, I remain cautious. I'm still looking for her warts, even though there's so much to like. She's attractive, despite putting minimal effort into her clothes or hair. If she could roll out of bed and go, she would. That drives me crazy. It's a minor complaint. Whenever she reaches for a damn baseball hat, I shake my head in disapproval. Then she usually opts for a ponytail, which is only a slight improvement. Baby steps, I tell myself.

We have such insightful conversations. ESPN may be her favorite TV station but she wears out The New York Times and other legitimate news outlets. She's up to date with current events, which keeps me on my toes. Even when we disagree, I love debating with her.

Whenever we hang out, I'm not the only one reaching for the bill. She can take care of herself. Miss Independent. Admittedly, I like to be needed. It's nice to have a woman who can afford to pay for me without a second thought. Unlike Kayla, she doesn't borrow or beg for money.

At her house, I peeked in her organizer. Looked

through her financial statements. Saw that she had tens of thousands of dollars saved in the bank. She said that she has stocks, too. Only owed a few hundred dollars on the credit card. Told me that her house is fully paid. For 15 years, she's worked for the federal government. The picture of stability. She's not rich but seems to be doing better than okay financially.

The sex. Not sure where to begin. She hasn't offered any reason about why her other relationships ended. I'm sure her ability to fuck them endlessly had NOTHING to do with it. I TOTALLY underestimated her. Didn't think her skinny...no...scratch that. She doesn't like to be called skinny (even though she is). Didn't think her slender ass could handle my no longer as thin as I used to be ass. I couldn't have been more wrong.

I'm flexible. Used to study ballet. Still. She had me feeling like I was a pretzel. One leg wrapped behind my neck. Swinging from the ceiling fan. Felt like I was a damn contortionist auditioning for Cirque de Soleil. I'm open-minded but I was hesitant when she wanted to choke me. Surprise. Surprise. I liked it. Heightened the experience. Made the orgasm more powerful.

I could fill page after page. Write ode after ode to her skills. Phew. I'm shifting in my seat, just thinking about it. Remembering every syllable, tremble and moan that our bodies shared and imparted on each other, as we expressed approval in various octaves. She stirs a deeply rooted desire in my loins. Her energy feeds my spirit. Like mummies of yesteryear, I want remembrances of our intimacy wrapped in the finest linens and passed onto future generations. I've lost count of how many orgasms her masterful tongue and maestro-like fingers have induced.

When her mouth explores my most intimate areas there's a ravenous hunger. I feel like she needs me for sustenance. Warms my soul. Looking into her eyes is hypnotizing. Then her versatile tongue overpowers all of my senses. Works me into hysteria. Sends me on a multi-orgasmic wave.

She is masterful with that dildo. Strokes me into a stupor. Hard time talking. Had me stuttering and shit. One step from drooling. Even harder time walking. Felt like I was a newborn fawn. Toes pointing inward, like I was pigeon-toed. I don't think there's a spot on my body that her tongue hasn't touched. Yup. Whether it's fucking or making love, she has turned me out.

I ask the same question: Is she too good to be true? I'm peeling back her layers and like what I see. I checked her phone to see if I'm missing something. Clean as a whistle. She texts Gisele but I know they're just cool. Nothing there. Marisa's her heart but she's rarely around. Like me, she's a momma's girl. No issues with that. Unlike me, she doesn't have a mom who constantly hits her up for money. There's some drama between her mom and Aunt D. Ronnie feels caught in the middle. Nothing suspicious about the texts with friends, coworkers or anyone else.

Well. There's one thing. No, maybe two. She has OCD and can't cook. Haven't met anyone so obsessed with cleaning things and washing her hands. She says that cleaning is therapeutic. Whatever. She can have it. Not the worst issue to have, though. I hate to clean. Love to cook. That gives us some balance.

So, if I stumbled on the magnificence that represents Ronnie, why'd I go to Jamaica with the continued mess that is Kayla? Well, it was her birthday. Before I met Ronnie, I promised her a trip. Okay. Poor excuse. I even had Ronnie help me plan the trip. Told her a lie that I was going with sorors. I was double dead wrong for that. Obviously, I couldn't tell Ronnie the truth. Well, I could have but chose not to. Damn.

For so long, Kayla's been my drug. Yeah, that's the best way to describe her. I know she's no longer good for me but I'm still in Rehab. Trying to kick this habit. Not sure how many more times I'll relapse. The experts say that relapse is a part of recovery, right? Feels like I'm doing better. Maybe.

Kayla and I spent several days on that island paradise of Jamaica and barely kissed. Didn't give her any loving. Not because she didn't try. Believe me, she did. God showed favor on me. Both of us had a visit from Aunt Flo. That was my convenient way out. Made it easier to keep her away from me.

Thinking about one of our almost arguments in Jamaica. "Wifey. Why don't we spend as much time together? It's been a minute since you let me get some of your sweetness."

"Stop smoking so much weed and your memory wouldn't be shot. Told you that I'm back in school. Sex is the last thing on my mind. Need time to study and stay on top of the business. Unlike you, I don't have all day to twiddle my thumbs."

She eased closer to me. Wanted to cuddle. "That's why I love you so much. You stay doing better for yourself."

"Why doesn't that inspire you to do the same? When we first met, you had so much going for yourself. Now, you..."

"Don't get all judgmental because you're doing well. Remember when I paid almost a hundred grand for the down payment on the condo because you didn't have enough money? Don't forget when I helped you buy out a partner. You know that I hit a few rough patches... So long as I have you in my corner, it'll be okay."

"So now you're throwing it back in my face? I won't forget you helping me buy out a partner, so I could have a bigger stake in the business. Now, don't forget that you told me not to pay you back, even though I tried. I know my good fortune can turn to misfortune in the blink of an eye. The difference is that you created your rough patches. Work your way out of them. What happens if, I mean when, I leave?"

She glared at me. Cracked her knuckles. "That ain't gonna happen." Maybe she reconsidered because she laughed cynically. "If it does, only God could judge me for what I'd do."

I send mixed signals. Kayla continues to hope that we're getting back together. Ronnie may be the one who finally gives me the strength to permanently walk away. Kayla keeps telling me that she won't let me go. She's threatened to kill me, if I leave. For sure she's joking. I have plenty of time to figure something out.

20: KAYLA'S CONTRIBUTION – PART 3

For my birthday, my beautiful wife took me to Jamaica. I imagined opening the balcony doors and making love, as we listened to the water from the Caribbean Sea splash against the rocks. Just my damn luck, it was that time of the month for both of us. I had to settle for less than passionate kisses from her, while I begged to hold her at night. Usually, her energy for sex seemed like it was drug induced. The past few months, she hasn't had that same level of desire. She's normally a pro at multi-tasking, so I'm sure it has more to do with me still struggling than her being in school and trying to grow the business.

Even though our sex life wasn't where I wanted it to be, she was still my rock. At the resort, I arranged a romantic dinner. Wanted to show how much I appreciated her help. I also had an ulterior motive. To me, we were back in a good space. I was scheduled to start a new position when we got back. I wasn't cheating, even though I had plenty of chances. Yeah, I still smoked weed but it would soon be legal in Jersey. I wanted to talk about me moving in with her. We could use the condo as a rental property. Get back to building our wealth – together.

I lovingly watched her saunter back to the table. Saw several men openly gawk at her, even though they were dining with women they'd probably be boning later. She was the picture of elegance. She paid no attention to the women who jealously stared at her.

At our table, she placed the napkin on her lap. She was

the epitome of grace. I watched her spread butter onto a piece of bread and cleared my throat. Got ready to share my master plan. Her phone rang. Normally, she waited a few rings before she answered. I looked to see who was interrupting our sacred time. She positioned the phone, so I couldn't see the caller ID. A huge smile spread across her face. Once upon a time, that type of smile was reserved only for me. She answered before the first ring ended, "Hi, Ronnie."

I wasn't familiar with anyone she knew by that name. The volume was too low for me to hear anything that Ronnie said. She ended the short call by saying, "When I get back, we can talk about some of my company's services that may be able to help the people on your caseload."

Now the exuberant smile made sense. That call was about business. Nothing personal, so I flushed it from my mind. She reached across the table. Fed me a piece of her bread. I accepted. Kissed her fingertips.

She looked around the bustling restaurant and noted, "This place hasn't changed since the last time we were here."

Still holding onto my hands, she asked, "What's so important that you wanted to discuss?"

Like someone trying to close the deal of a lifetime, I rubbed my hands together and started my sales pitch. "I start work the day after we get back. Soon, I'll be able to help pay the bills. Let's make money off the condo. Use it for a rental property. I should move in with you. We can even renew our vows. Reaffirm our love."

Her eyes normally told all of her thoughts. I didn't like the ones I saw developing in the background.

"The job is great news...I think we should sell the

condo. My partners and I want to expand the business, so I could use the extra money. You can take your share and get something less expensive to live in."

The muscles in my jaw tightened. I thought the better of causing a scene. In a whisper, I told her, "Nah. I'm not agreeing to sell. If this is your way of inching closer to the divorce that I'm not giving you, stop wasting your time..." Another thought leapt into my head, as I looked closely at her. "Tell the other people you're dealing with that we're not done and we won't ever be done..."

She reached across the table and gently held my chin. Forced me to look at her. "Stop being foolish."

Satisfied that she had my full attention, she picked up her fork, as we held each other's gaze. "Kayla, I'm not dealing with other people, as you say. That's the truth."

She twirled the food around her fork. Offered it to me. I closed my eyes and accepted. Couldn't help but feel that she wasn't only feeding me pasta. Instead, I felt like she had just given me a load of bullshit.

There wasn't much more talk during dinner. I was lost in thoughts, while she studied me. Tried to figure out what I was thinking.

*****

After a stroll on the beach, we showered and settled into bed. I wanted to cuddle even though embers from the argument still burned.

"...When we first met, you had so much going for yourself. Now, you're like a child that I feel responsible to take care of...it's exhausting..."

"Don't get all judgmental because you're doing well. Remember when I paid almost a hundred grand for the down payment on the condo because you didn't have enough money? Don't forget when I helped you buy out a partner. You know that I hit a few rough patches... So long as I have you in my corner, it'll be okay."

"So now you're throwing it back in my face? I won't forget you helping me buy out a partner, so I could have a bigger stake in the business. Now, don't forget that you told me not to pay you back, even though I tried. I know my good fortune can turn to misfortune in the blink of an eye. The difference is that you created your rough patches. Work your way out of them. What happens if, I mean when, I leave?"

My stare burned a hole through her. I cracked my knuckles. "That ain't gonna happen." I laughed at the ludicrous thought. She looked serious, though, so I emphatically added, "If it does, only God could judge me for what I'd do."

We returned from Jamaica. I hit the ground running like my feet were on fire. Most weeks, I logged more than 70 hours. By the time I got home, all I wanted to do was take a shower and go to sleep. That didn't leave much time for my wife and me to reconnect.

I sent text messages and little trinkets of affection. It barely made a dent. She still hounded me about selling the condo. At least she had stopped asking me to sign the divorce papers. I was okay with being in this holding pattern. It gave me more time to show that I was serious about making amends.

21: MOMMA!!!

Like a child awaiting Christmas, I'd been counting down the days. Finally. I picked up my mom from the airport. "My bay-bee," she yelled for the world to hear.

I wrapped her in the warmest embrace. Twirled her around. "Hi Mom. There's so much that I have planned for us..."

As soon as we got settled in the car, she reclined her seat and Aunt D was the focus of her venting. "That damn Denise...the truth will come to light. Just wait and see." She noticed that I was quiet. "You don't have to say anything. I know how you feel about that lying rascal."

Surreptitiously, I rolled my eyes. Silently willed her to change the subject. She talked so much. Acted like we weren't going to spend the next two weeks together. She was more animated and demonstrative than usual. We stopped at a red light and her phone rang. I looked at the screen. Saw her and an older man that I didn't recognize. They were hugging and smiling giddily for the camera. The background was familiar – Wrigley Field – home of the Chicago Cubs.

She saw that I was staring at her. A mischievous smile spread across her face. She answered the phone. I turned off the radio, so I could be nosey.

"Hi Spencer... I made it safely..."

My ears strained but I still couldn't hear what he said, so I was hyper-focused on her words.

"Now isn't a good time to talk." She glanced at me and

implied that there'd be no dirty talk around me. I silently thank God for small mercies. "I'll call later and you can tell me what you miss…"

She hung up the phone. Time for me to get in her business. "Who's Spencer? You seem like a love-struck teenager."

The smile hadn't left her face. "We bumped into each other at Northwestern University. Been seeing each other for a few months…"

She swiped through pictures of them at a jazz concert in Grant Park. Walking along Michigan Avenue. Enjoying some of Chicago's other famous and not-so-famous spots.

"You look happy. Can't wait to grill his ass. Make sure he's worthy of you." I couldn't help but think that my mom had also found someone special.

"Before we go home, let's stop by the supermarket. Just like usual, I'll go vegetarian, so it'll be easier for you to cook."

This time, my decision to forgo meat and seafood wasn't purely altruistic. I probably wouldn't have time to go to the gym. At least I would eat healthier.

After several hours, we finally finished. My mom gave new meaning to going slow, especially when it came to shopping. Jenine called several times, while I carried what seemed like an endless number of bags into the house.

I left my mom to put away the food. Without even being in the kitchen, I knew the routine. She'd take everything out of the refrigerator and freezer. The meats would get moved to the deep freezer. Then she'd wipe down the refrigerator and freezer with bleach. I inherited my addiction to cleaning from her.

On my phone, Jenine's picture flashed. She had never

called me this many times back-to-back. In a panic, I asked, "What's wrong, J?"

"Where've you been? I've been calling you all day. Your mom's here. You haven't let me know what I'm supposed to cook or when y'all are coming over!"

I held the phone away from my ear because she was yelling. She was in a tizzy over dinner. I smiled and thought her jumpiness was cute. In trying to get her to turn down her volume, I said, "Hello to you, too, beautiful. Dinner will be easy. Mom's a vegetarian, so I'm giving up meat while she's here. Maybe we…"

She didn't even give me time to finish, "Oooh. I'm not starving myself with just veggies. I'll do pescatarian. Those are the people who still eat fish, right? That should help me lose weight… I know what I'll cook."

"Sounds good, J. I can't wait for y'all to meet."

*****

I took off a few days from work and focused on my mom. We spent one touristy day in NYC. Matinee on Broadway. Overpriced lunch. Christmas tree at Rockefeller Center. So many people crowded the streets. We headed back to Jersey before the rush hour folks crowded onto the train.

It was rare for my mom and me to talk about my dating life. On the train ride back, I was shocked when she asked, "Who's your new lady friend?"

How'd she know that I was dating? Did she know that I was already in love, too? I tried to make my voice sound neutral and joked, "Look at you all in my business."

She held my chin in her hand. Forced me to look at her. In an unwavering tone, she told me, "You're my baby, so you'll always be my business."

I could hear the clock ticking, while she waited for my answer. This had to be a short conversation. Maybe she thought of my breakdown with Tabitha, which caused me to take much needed time off work. I had to get myself together. The last thing I wanted was for my job to have any clue about the true reason for the extended leave. Best case scenario: They would have taken my gun. Assigned me to desk duty. Forced me to see a shrink before I was allowed back in the field. Worst case scenario: I lost my job.

I didn't like either option. Had a conversation with my primary care doctor that felt more like I was in a confessional. Rarely had I shared so much detailed information about my feelings. She worked her magic, with the clear understanding that I would immediately seek help. On the official paperwork, I was on medical leave for an injury to my arm. The truth was way deeper.

As a lifelong athlete, I could teach a MasterClass on how to stay in tiptop physical shape. My mental health was a different matter. The ending with Tabitha created seismic ruptures in my heart that I needed help to mend. My mind had traveled to pitch black places and my only foreseeable way out was suicide.

For six months, I drove to Baltimore, a couple of times per week, for psychiatric and counseling services. I was also paired with a sponsor and dove headfirst into AA meetings. My new full-time job became trying to get my head in a better space. I was diagnosed and prescribed medications, in order to treat my "mental illnesses."

I used an alias for everything and made sure to pay in cash. Couldn't afford to have anything attached to my real name. The treatment helped tremendously, especially the recommendation to document my thoughts and emotions in journals. To this day, those writings during my darkest moments are stored safely in my basement. They tell the most complete story about my dealings with Monica, Tabitha and other stuff that has troubled me.

Like an infection, my problem with alcohol is ever-present but not necessarily visible or known to others. I still do ongoing treatment via telehealth.

My mother continued to stare at me. Waited for a response. Instead of lying, I took the easy way out. Gave her a short version of Jenine's story. She listened silently. Intently.

"Well, she loves to travel and volunteer...no kids but wants to adopt or have one via IVF."

She didn't need to know about the still unsettled ending of her marriage. Focus on the positive. A retired principal, my mom was a huge proponent of education, so Jenine having multiple college degrees was a plus. "She's an LCSW and LMFT. Co-owner of a thriving mental health practice. May go back for her doctorate."

I dared not tell her that I was already in love and it had very little to do with the acrobatic sex. "She's intelligent, great cook and a homeowner. We're having dinner with her."

It may have been my imagination. I could have sworn that I saw my mom smirk. Only then did she break her silence, "Humph. I'm looking forward to it."

22: DOES SHE LIKE ME?

The big day arrived. My old lady (my mom) was going to meet my new lady (Jenine). When she opened the door, she looked radiant. The beat of my heart skipped like a broken record. Seemed like I was more in awe of her aura each time we saw each other. She wore more make-up than usual. Her hair was swept atop her head with several strands left hanging by her ears. Sexy didn't even begin to describe her.

I handed her a bottle of wine. Noticed that she was wearing a new perfume. The pleasant aroma was an exotic mix of flowers and spices. She seemed tense. I watched her fidget with a necklace. Listened to her talk faster than usual. I reached to kiss her but she backed away. Shook my head in disappointment. She was already trying too hard to impress my mom.

On purpose, I stood to the side, which gave me a better view of my mom's face. She was usually an excellent judge of character. Tonight, her poker face was on point. I couldn't get a read on her feelings.

While Jenine went to let the wine breathe, my mom and I washed our hands in the half bathroom. I quietly asked, "What do you think?"

It was my mom's turn to play like a politician. She never answered my question. She was too wrapped in admiration of Jenine's half-bathroom. "Ronnie, these hand towels are so thick and plush. Did you smell this soap?" She put both hands up to my nose but didn't wait for my response. "This soap smells delicious. Let me wash my hands again. There's no way I would've picked this sink and frame to pair with the mirror. All of the colors play nicely off each other."

She touched the walls. I knew what was coming next. "Feel the wall. Even the paint feels luxurious."

It was like déjà vu. I had the same reaction when I first came to her house.

*****

Jenine served dinner in the dining room. Again, she cooked an outstanding meal. Even my mom went back for a second helping. She was a damn good cook and could be tougher than a food critic.

I listened to them talk about everything from fashion to the usually forbidden topics of politics...religion...sex. They offered opinions. Counterattacks. Agreed on some things. Respectfully disagreed on others.

After I cleaned the kitchen, they were still deep in conversation. I watched TV in the living room. Her first floor was open concept. I could see them and vice versa. I wondered whether they realized I was still in the house. Felt like I was a spectator watching from the sideline. Neither of them asked my input about anything.

Finally, my mom rose and remarked, "It's getting late." Looking at Jenine, she noted, "You, my dear, definitely don't need beauty sleep. We should get going. Thank you for everything. Dinner was delicious. I'll have the leftovers for lunch tomorrow."

"I have an idea. Y'all should come back tomorrow night. We could order pizza or I'll cook something else. Maybe we could have game night...watch a movie...play cards..."

My mom responded before I could agree. "Thank you, Jenine. We'll be out late tomorrow night. Heading to a jazz club."

I didn't know anything about those plans and got ready to correct her. On the sly, she pinched me. A subtle cue for me to keep my mouth shut.

Before my mom headed to the car, she pulled Jenine to the side. I saw a storm brewing in her eyes.

Her voice was barely above a whisper. "She's my only child. Do not hurt her."

The message was unmistakable. I watched Jenine's eyes register surprise, as they grew to the size of saucers.

In less time than it takes a hummingbird to flap its wings, the smile fell from her face. "I..."

Any response she may have proffered was cut short. My mom raised one hand. A definite signal their one-sided conversation was done.

Now, Jenine and I had the chance for a little alone time. We stepped back inside her house and closed the door.

"Think your mom likes me?"

Truthfully, I wasn't sure. I avoided telling a lie by asking a question, "What's there not to like?"

Kisses on her neck. Her nipples strained against the sheer fabric of her silk shirt. My hands were on autopilot. Unfastened her bra and freed her pendulous breasts. Gently, I massaged her large brown nipples in slow circular motions.

Questions about my mom's approval were forgotten. She moaned lightly and sang her song of approval. "You...touch...sooo...damn..."

My hormones were a raging inferno. She was better at self-control. She guided my hands from her rock-hard nipples. Teased my fingertips with her tongue and said, "Oh no. You know how you make me feel. Your mom's waiting. Don't start something that we can't finish."

Any possibility of a quickie was quickly dashed. Coolly, she shifted gears. "It's almost time for our birthdays. Let's do something special."

Maybe she was angling for a special birthday gift. She put her arms around my neck. Kissed me into a catatonic stupor. Her lips on mine. My hands palming her ass. Her breasts pressed against my body had me ready to withdraw all of my assets and deposit them into her account. I was preparing to give her the world. Except. Not that I had forgotten our birthdays. I just hadn't mentioned my plans.

"Damn. I didn't even tell you. Me and Marisa... Phuket...10 days. Trip...booked before...we met."

Marisa spent so much time away from home, she and Jenine only knew of each other. I made an executive decision. "Why don't you come, too? Y'all can finally meet. It'll be our first passport stamp, as a couple."

There was hesitation. Disbelief. "Really? You conveniently forgot about a trip to the other side of the world? That doesn't sound right."

She pulled away. Maybe she thought that I was lying. Crossed her arms. A sign for me to stay away. Any barrier between us was too much.

"Then, I get a last-minute invite, like I'm some afterthought. Tickets are going to be crazy expensive. I just got back from Jamaica. We lost a counselor. I probably won't be able to take off so much time."

I didn't want any problems between us. Slowly, I exhaled and begged, "Don't be mad at me, J. You're my main focus. You make it seem like I'm trying to be shady.

I've been so wrapped up in you. I just forgot."

I could see the wheels turning in her head. There was a definite intrigue about the possibility of an exotic vacation. Didn't seem like she was as upset. "Phuket sounds nice. Never been to Thailand. I'll see what I can finagle…"

The desire for a sexual release would have to wait. My mom was being very patient. I didn't protest when Jenine reached to open the front door and said, "Get home safely, babe." She planted a lingering kiss on my lips. Sent me on my way. As the front door closed, I heard her phone ringing in the background.

At the car, my mom was ending a conversation with Spencer. "I felt you pinch me back there. Now we have tickets to a jazz club? Tell me what's wrong."

"Well…she's gorgeous. A good cook, well-read and…" She gazed out the window, as if the words she tried to find were written in the sky.

Tired of waiting, I interrupted, "And you're stalling."

Candor was one of my mom's many strong suits. She was rarely at a loss for words. I had the feeling she wanted to tell me something that I didn't want to hear. She was uncharacteristically quiet for the rest of the ride. No pressure. I'd wait to hear her thoughts about the woman with whom I wanted to spend the rest of my life.

23: DIFFERENT CONNECTIONS

To my surprise, my mom had three tickets to a jazz club. Clearly, she didn't want Jenine to go with us. On the spur of the moment, I invited Gisele. We met in the West Village of NYC. Unlike Jenine, my mom gushed and gushed about Gisele, like they were old-time friends.

The two of them went back to the jazz club and to several weeknight church services. One day, they planned to meet for lunch. I wasn't invited. They ignored me just like they did at the jazz club. Just like my mom and Jenine did during dinner.

I let my mom take my car, while I used one from work. Made a visit to Jenine's house. She was supposed to be working from home. Her car was in the driveway. I was surprised when she didn't answer the door. Hoping that I hadn't made the drive for naught, I called her phone but didn't get an answer.

Back at the car, I checked work emails. Waited to see whether she'd return. More than likely, she and one of her friends were out and about. After an hour, her phone was still going straight to voicemail. There was no sign of her.

I walked up her driveway. My back was to the street. I affixed a note to the screen door. I saw the reflection of a black Honda Civic with dark tinted windows slowly roll by her house. When I turned towards the street the car picked up speed. The tint was too dark for me to see the driver.

Something about the car just seemed weird. Could

it have been the woman who almost killed me the first night I visited Jenine's house? Had to be a coincidence. After all, Honda Civic was such a popular car. By now, it was too far up the street for me to get the numbers off the license plate. Quickly, I walked back to my car. Wanted to be ready just in case the Civic returned.

I dialed Jenine's cell, again. No luck. Since my mom had been in town, we hadn't spent much time together. She sent me a few seductive videos but our communication was seriously lacking. The note on the screen door would let her know that she remained on my mind and it wasn't just the sex that I've missed.

24: HARD HEADS MAKE SOFT BEHINDS

My mom finished what felt like the fastest two-week visit in history. I parked my car in the short-term lot. Just wanted to spend a little more time with her. At the airline counter, she and the ticket agent were huddled together and whispering. It looked like they were conspiring to take over the world. When they separated, the ticket agent flashed a megawatt smile and handed her a boarding pass.

Unfortunately, it wasn't like the old days, where I could walk her to the gate. Even with my badge, I'd have a hard time getting past TSA without a ticket. We had plenty of time. Took our time and ate breakfast. She still talked effusively about Gisele. In very little time, my mom made a new friend.

We were almost finished with our food. If I had my way, she'd stay with me forever. Unselfishly, I said, "The TSA line is getting longer. Maybe it's time for you to get going."

I knew that she had things to do back home. Volunteering. Doctoral studies. Family tree. There was no sense of urgency. She casually said, "The ticket agent was nice enough to bump me up to first class. I have plenty of time."

Ah. That explained the mysterious looking conversation. I didn't even want to know how she wrangled that perk.

She stared at me. Although I hadn't done anything

wrong, I shifted uncomfortably and guiltily asked, "What'd I do?"

With a steely voice, she said, "Veronica..."

With one word, I was on edge. Even felt myself sit up a little straighter. She only called me Veronica when she meant business.

Her voice trailed off, as she softly remarked, "...I'll always want to protect you. Even if it's from yourself."

She searched for the right words. Finally, she forcefully said, "I know you love deeply at times. Just be careful with Jenine. I'm getting bad vibes. Can't put my finger on it, though. Don't want you to get hurt, again or something worse..."

Undoubtedly, she was talking about Tabitha, even though there was still so much she didn't know. My eyes danced fleetingly around the airport. I thought about the poem, "We Wear the Mask," by Paul Laurence Dunbar. I wore one with her, regarding some of the antics I pulled in trying to get Tabitha to come back to me. She had no clue about me stalking her. More times than I cared to remember, I followed Tabitha to see where she was going and what she was doing. Tried to get more information about the new woman that she was dating. The woman who took my rightful place in her life.

One morning, I watched them walk into a restaurant. That gave me time to break into her apartment. I saw more proof that I'd been replaced. Clothes that I kept in a dresser drawer had been moved. Other items had been carelessly tossed in a plastic bag. A picture of us in Bali was no longer on her nightstand.

Instead of accepting the obvious end, I focused on trying to break up their relationship. When that didn't work, I'd show up unannounced at her apartment.

Our final talk didn't go well. After Monica, I had years of sobriety while with Tabitha. Now, I was heavily under the influence of alcohol. I dropped to my knees. Begged her to take me back, as I clung to her legs in desperation.

She scornfully looked at me like I was shit on the bottom of her shoe and coldly said, "Stop forcing yourself on me. You smell like a distillery. Get some professional help. I don't want you."

Those words started an avalanche. I could feel whatever was left of my mental stability breaking in giant boulders. Finally, I had to face the reality that there was no going back to us being a couple.

I wanted her to feel some of the hurt that permeated through my body. Raised my hand. Made a fist. A repeat of Monica was what I intended. Before my fist descended on her, there was a knock on the door.

She stepped around me. Snickered. Opened the door. The new woman walked in. I, the discarded woman, walked out. Didn't even bother to take my stuff. She could toss that plastic bag to the curb, just like she did with me.

I may not be an LCSW or LMFT but it felt like I had residual trauma from past relationships and alcohol. Tabitha and Monica gave me nightmares. But... I also knew that my mom only wanted the best for me. While I thought about her warning, I hugged her tightly and said, "I love you. I'll try to be careful."

It wouldn't take long for me to realize the truth of an old adage: Easier said than done.

*****

Leaving the airport, my first call was to Jenine. "Yes.

She's on her way...not sure when she's coming back... What's there not to like about you? I'm not avoiding the question... Damn. You can't take off ten days...you're right...we'll have plenty of time for our own vacations."

I was extremely disappointed. Ten days away from her would be torture. I tried to find the silver lining in my suddenly dark cloud. Only things I found were dust and lint. Since we wouldn't be spending our birthdays together, I had an idea.

Before heading home, I made a side trip to the upscale Short Hills Mall. Looked at jewelry in some of the display cases. Like flashing lights beckoning for my attention, my eyes were drawn to the engagement rings. My mother's warning clanged like cymbals in my head. I did a quick about-face and left the store. An hour later, I had splurged a couple thousand dollars for a pair of Christian Louboutin pumps.

There's an old saying that warns against buying shoes for your significant other. Supposedly, they'd use those same shoes to walk out of your life. I looked at the heels. If Jenine decided to go, she wouldn't be walking fast.

*****

Several days later, she drove me to the airport. I dissolved under the soothing touch of her fingernails stroking the nape of my neck. I grabbed my carry-on from her trunk. Disbelievingly, she shook her head. "I don't see how you do it. That wouldn't be big enough to carry my underwear."

"You're dramatic. Believe me, all it took was the airline losing my suitcase when I went to Egypt. That changed my whole attitude. You, on the other hand, are hopeless."

"Whateverrr." She pouted like a child. "I'll miss you."

I kissed her forehead and honestly said, "I'll miss you more."

Intentionally, she was making it harder for me to leave. Normally, I was the one whose hands were like an octopus and feeling all over her. Today, the roles were reversed. She held onto me for dear life. For longer than a moment, I thought about canceling the trip. Decided that wasn't a viable option. The whole trip was a birthday gift from Marisa. She'd kill me. Already, I found myself counting down the minutes until I returned to her tension relieving caresses.

She put a small box in my hand. "Open on your birthday and not before."

"Okay." I pointed to her SUV. "I left your gift on the passenger seat."

"Look at you being slick." She put her forehead on mine and whispered, "Thank you. Have fun. Behave yourself."

She started to walk away, looked over her shoulder and rushed back to me. I expected another kiss. Instead, she held both of my hands and proclaimed, "I love you, babe."

With catlike quickness, she was back in the driver's seat and pulling away from the curb. She didn't look back. It was only the physical distance that grew, while I watched her SUV disappear. Silently, I mouthed, "I love you so much more."

25: CONFESSIONS IN PHUKET

My first time in Phuket. I busied myself reading about different tourist activities, while I waited for Marisa. Someone bumped into my back so hard that I almost fell. I blurted out, "Watch where you're going."

Damn, I hadn't even been in this tropical utopia for an hour. Already, I was aggravated. I turned with my fists clenched and prepared to whoop someone's ass. Marisa jumped on me and my anger instantly faded. Her arms wrapped around my neck and her legs found their way around my waist.

We did that dance for a little while before she climbed off me. For several seconds, we sized each other up. It had been entirely too long. She'd always been thin. Somehow, it looked like she'd lost even more weight. That usually happened when she was stressed. I'd have plenty of time to find out what had been happening in her life. Her naturally curly Afro was so big that Angela Davis would be impressed. Her childlike smile melted my heart. She looked like the epitome of Bohemian cool.

I couldn't help but stare. Marisa laughed nervously and asked, "What?"

Shaking my head to gather my thoughts, I asked, "You're a good-looking bitch. You've lost weight, though..."

She lowered her head. "There's so much going on... we'll have plenty of time to talk about me...you... Jenine..."

The mention of Jenine's name naturally brought a smile to my face. She looked at me and smiled because she knew me too well. We put our arms around each other's shoulder and walked to get a taxi, as I showed her the brochures and said, "I've been thinking..."

*****

We did the countdown from New Year's Eve into New Year's Day and watched the fireworks illuminate Patong Beach. There was a 12-hour time difference. Jenine's birthday over here but not in Jersey. I called and she yelled, "Happy New Year in Phuket! I wish I was there with you."

I could see that she was in the beauty parlor. She was preparing for a black-tie affair to ring in the New Year. "Happy birthday beautiful. I miss you sooo much. It's hard to hear you but send me pictures when you're ready for the runway..."

Marisa hovered but didn't ask any questions. The next day, we went on our first excursion. We had lots to discuss. She started, "You know the commercials that talk about learning your background?"

"Absolutely. You did it? My mom is big on that genealogy stuff, too."

"Yes. I finally got up the nerve. I'm so tired of not having answers."

Her mother passed when she was a toddler. She never knew her father. She was passed from one auntie to the next and was sexually abused by more than one relative. Child Protective Services became involved. Placement in foster care. Eventually, she was adopted by a family that nurtured and loved her. Surprisingly, criminal charges were brought against the relatives. The legal system did its job of convicting the men and sentencing them to long prison terms, which caused a major rift in the family.

My mind was like a locomotive going downhill. Remembering her to be a sensitive soul, I forced myself to slow down and carefully asked, "You want to talk about the results?"

"Yes! Got the email about three weeks ago. Roughly, I'm equal parts Italian, West African, Cherokee and Scandinavian. The bigger shocker is that I know my father's name."

My eyes widened in disbelief, as she continued, "He died three months before I was born. The website links everything. I have info on maternal and paternal relatives. I even have names of half-siblings, who want to be contacted."

"This is so overwhelming but in a good way, if that makes sense. I'm going to take a sabbatical. Hit Italy first and meet some relatives."

I cautiously asked, "Are you sure that's a good idea?"

"This has to be done. It'll be okay."

Although she was a little older, I felt the need to protect her. There was still an innocence about her. Sensing that she was in a good space, I bombarded her with questions, "When are you...? What did you...? How will you...? Did you ever learn how to fight?"

She laughed and confessed, "You're an idiot... I'm excited but nervous... You of all people know I'm no fighter." She smiled broadly and said, "Remember when..."

We recalled an incident from 10 years ago. The details were so fresh, it seemed like everything happened yesterday.

"I can't forget...rental house...getaway weekend. Supposed to only be two couples: you and Amanda. Monica and me...."

"...No clue why Amanda invited everyone else. I can still see your face when you found out there was only one bathroom..."

"...I was pissed. Monica was already taking our bags back to the car. I wasn't sharing one bathroom with nine other women..."

"...One couple started arguing..."

"...You were trying to be the peacemaker, as usual. That one chick thought you were making moves on her woman..."

"...Thank God she was already drunk...she would've knocked my head off my shoulders..."

"...I swear. It felt like everything moved in slow motion. For as long as I live, I will NEVER forget you curled on the floor and yelling...:"

"...I've never had a fight...please don't hit me!"

We busted into hysterics. That story would always be funny. The less funny part occurred the next weekend when Amanda overdosed.

Invariably, the conversation turned to relationships. Unlike our discussion about her family, she was short and to the point. "Nothing has changed. I have the same friend with benefits in London... I still miss Amanda..." All these years later, the pain on her face looked fresh.

She didn't have the chance to turn inquisitor on me. The guide announced our arrival at one of the national parks. Along the way, we took plenty of pictures, at the waterfall and in the natural pool. We learned about the man-made threats to rainforests around the world. In addition to the detrimental impacts on climate, medicine, animals and other things. Without saying it in these exact words, the guide basically told the group that humans sucked because we were destroying the earth.

*****

I wasn't properly seated for the ride back to the hotel before Marisa dove headfirst into my business, "Okay. Yes or no. Your mom, the job and volunteering are all good?"

"Yup."

"Cool. Now, gimme the stats on Jenine."

At times, we could be like hormonally driven teenagers, when talking about women. Today, I'd do better. After all, Jenine was special. I wouldn't subject her outstanding physical attributes to our immaturity.

"Let me tell you..."

Still not quite ready to delve into that part of the conversation, I first talked about meeting Gisele and our burgeoning friendship.

She quickly interrupted, "Don't even...you work for the federal government but it's not the CIA. Stop being so damn secretive. Gisele sounds great...sure she'll make some woman happy. I want to hear about Jenine. You wasn't lying. That bitch is fine. I see why your eyes light up when her name gets mentioned."

First my mom. Now Marisa noticed the effect that Jenine had on me. I buckled and shared, "Remember that we met in a diner. That's crazy! I looked up and I swear... it was..." I came up with the best description that I could find. "...it was like all of the planets in the solar system revolved around her. The attraction was that strong."

She dramatically rolled her eyes and had a "yeah right" expression on her face. "Do you intentionally try to be so damn corny or does it come naturally?"

Thinking about the randomness of it all, I shook my head. "Marisa. I like her. A lot. She's funny. Intelligent. Femme aggressive. Independent. Sexy as fuck. And she's a bona fide good cook. Even my mom complimented her cooking. You know she's fussy as hell."

"Word? If she met your mom then she's special. Momma Glyce don't play when it comes to you. Where's the wedding invite? I know that I'm the maid of honor. She seems perfect."

My smile faded a little. I confided, "Be clear. I didn't say my mom liked her." She nodded knowingly. "Anyway, the wedding has to wait. It's still early for us. Plus, she's already married…they're legally separated…"

Almost like I had to defend Jenine, I added, "…but she's working on getting it dissolved." Part of me felt like I already said too much. No need to mention my mom's warning.

Marisa and I had an uncanny connection. Our brains tended to operate on the same wavelength. Like Jenine and me, we complemented each other. So, it wasn't unexpected when she asked, "What's the issue on ending the marriage?"

That was the question I wanted to be answered the most. I only repeated what she told me, "They own property and she's hanging that over her head. She won't sign the papers. Trying to take care of everything is on her list of things to do."

The words weren't fully out of my mouth. Already, I realized how foolish I sounded.

Marisa was a sweetheart. The one who'd sincerely apologize, even if she didn't do anything wrong. I've seen her cry because she mistakenly stepped on an anthill.

She was usually one of the most considerate people I had ever met. That's why I was in complete shock when she looked me squarely in my eyes, laughed in my face and said, "That bitch's pussy must be platinum-coated... maybe y'all have circus sex...or she slipped something in your food. Whatever it is...those excuses sound like bullshit and she's playing you for a fool."

I glared at her in disbelief. "That's why I keep stuff to myself. I thought you'd be happy for me. Not jealous..."

Still the somewhat peacemaker, Marisa refused my invitation to an argument. "If you could get your head out of her ass long enough to be sensible, you'll see that many things sound suspect. I'm the friend who tells you the truth whether you wanna hear it or not. You can be mad at me once you get back to Jersey. This trip cost me a grip. We're going to have a good time whether you want to or not..."

Like a petulant child, I crossed my arms. Turned my back to her. I didn't care that the trip cost a lot of money. She didn't need to talk to me like that.

Thinking of my mom and her. Unknowingly aligned in their thoughts. Neither of them seemed to understand. I was so far gone. There was a much bigger question... How much was I willing to sacrifice for Jenine and me to continue growing as one?

*****

The disagreement didn't stop us from having a wonderful vacation. Still, I looked forward to getting back to Jenine. On the return flight, it felt like time stood still. I fingered the diamond hoop earrings that she gave me for a birthday gift. They were just my style. I couldn't wait to thank her in person.

Walking out of the terminal, I saw her in the arrivals area. I nearly tripped over my carry-on. I was in such a rush to envelop her in my love. Everything now felt right in my world. She wore extra lip gloss and those beautiful lips were talking to me in our special language.

During the vacation, I sent plenty of pics and videos. She was more than aware of how much fun we had. Now, I wanted to find out what she had been up to, so I said, "You kind of went missing in action. We only chatted when you were at work. Even when I called at night, I couldn't reach you." Playfully, I asked, "Who kept you so busy?"

"Did you hear about the mass shooting?"

Although I was halfway around the world, I kept up to date with the news. "Yeah, a little. Happened in South Jersey. Ten people killed, right?"

"I did some volunteer work...only got back home yesterday. I didn't want you to worry. I'm mentally drained. Even though you use every available resource, it just doesn't feel like enough."

Now, I felt like a complete ass. On the return flight, I thought about the warnings from my mom and even Marisa. I had resolved myself to talk with her about selling the condo and ending the marriage. Obviously, this wasn't the right time. At least there was a legitimate reason to wait a little while longer.

"I want to hear some good news. Tell me about your trip. From the pics, it looked like y'all turned Phuket upside down."

My mind was elsewhere. With little enthusiasm, I said, "Uh, yeah, it was amazing. We had a great time."

She pulled into my driveway but didn't unfasten her

seatbelt. "You're not staying?"

"I need some time, babe." She held my hand and assuredly said, "I'll make this and everything else up to you. Please be patient with me."

26: LOVE ON A SEESAW

A night after my return, Jenine finally introduced me to food from her East Indian roots. Like a teacher for a remedial class, she patiently gave the culturally appropriate name for each dish that she cooked. I felt like an intellectually challenged student on the short yellow bus. Kicked myself for not paying better attention and not taking notes.

My mouth experienced the full array of flavors – spicy, sweet, sour and hot – individually and simultaneously. Whether it was the chicken tikka, dosas filled with veggies, raita, chickpeas, naan or malai kofta, each dish made me smack my lips and lick my fingers in appreciation.

As a measure of thanks, for the delicious dinner, I looked forward to feasting on her, as my scrumptious dessert. Before our bodies were twisted around each other, I worked on cleaning up the kitchen. Upstairs, she prepared for our romantic evening. Love songs. Candles. Melted chocolate. Relaxing bath.

I scraped the scraps of food in the garbage can. Saw something that stopped me in my tracks. An empty package of spinach. That was odd. Jenine abhorred spinach. I remembered that from our date at the comedy club.

I looked at the empty package. Tried to connect dots. For a week, she stayed in South Jersey, while volunteering as a grief counselor. She had only been home for one night. Said she needed to work on her notes. Why would this be in her garbage can?

Many people who work in law enforcement are stereotyped as overly aggressive. Often, I took the opposite approach, which caused people to underestimate me. Usually, I was polite and soft-spoken. I could have the patience of a high-stakes poker player. There were times when I tended to let things build for too long before addressing them. Tonight would be an exception.

I ran up the stairs and casually asked, "When'd you start eating spinach? Did anything that you cooked tonight have spinach in it?"

Without hesitation, she responded, "No. Babe, you know I don't eat spinach. Maybe you're confusing me with one of your other women."

It was said in jest. I had a plethora of issues. Cheating wasn't one of them.

"I saw this empty package in your garbage."

My positioning was wrong. I should've been facing her. From my vantage point, I wouldn't be able to see her reaction. She stayed with her back to me for a few additional seconds, while she unbuttoned her shirt. Was she stalling?

Finally, she nonchalantly replied, "Oh that...potluck lunch at the office...decompress from the volunteer work. I got stuck making potato spinach casserole."

We hadn't been together long enough for me to know her tells, as far as whether she was lying or not. If pressed, I would have bet that she was violating one of the Ten Commandments and being less than truthful. Over spinach of all things. It didn't make sense.

I chose to give her the benefit of the doubt. After

Monica, I had vowed not to make any accusations, unless I had irrefutable proof. I couldn't afford to be wrong. That would create a different set of issues, so I bided my time.

The next week, we were going to the movies. I was early. Pulled up to her house. Saw a guy delivering three dozen red roses – a symbol of love. He assumed that I was Jenine. No need to correct him. Gave him a tip and read the unsigned note: "Jenine. My baby. I love you more than life. Thank you for being you and putting up with me."

I knew one thing for sure. I didn't send them. Roses put back on the porch, I returned to my car. Drove up the block and waited. I had so many questions. Waiting for her to show up, I had time to come up with my own answers. Ones that I didn't like. Ones that I hoped were wrong.

She pulled up. Read the card. Smiled. Took the roses in the house. I repeatedly told myself, "Stay calm," as I drove back to her house. Rang her doorbell. Hugged her tightly. She walked me to the bathroom and waited, while I washed my hands. The roses were prominently displayed on the counter. Showtime.

"Nice flowers."

"Yeah. Thank you. Why didn't you sign the card?"

"You're thanking the wrong person. Who sent them?"

"Stop playing. You did."

She pulled a rose out of the vase. Smelled it. Smiled. Looked at me. She digested my crossed arms and the lava that was beginning to spew from the top of my head. I was livid. Her smile quickly faded. In its place was a look of utter confusion. "If it wasn't you, then I don't know who sent them."

Going back to the roses, she reread the card. Handed it

to me.

I went through the motion of reading the card. Tossed it on the counter. "Don't. Play. With. Me. People don't just send all of these damn red roses for no reason."

Her volume rose to match mine. "You're trippin' and it's annoying. Jealousy doesn't look good on you." She backed away. Crossed her arms to further mimic me and defiantly said, "Can't tell you what I don't know."

Back and forth we went. I was a juror hell-bent on finding the defendant guilty. She was so adamant, in all of her denials, that the sands started to shift. I began to believe her. Had this been a movie, she would have been the unanimous winner of the Academy Award for Best Actress. Either she was telling the truth or she should go to Hollywood and start a new career in show biz. She was just that damn convincing.

Finally, she had an "ah ha" moment and reached for her cell. Oozing with confidence, she looked at me and said, "You owe me an apology."

The phone on speaker, I heard her mother's heavy Trinidadian accent, as she asked, "Why yuh nah answer when me call? Tank yuh, fah helpin' me. Yuh get da roses?"

"Yeah, I got them."

In deliberate circles, she massaged her temples. "I blocked your number because I so vex wit' you. How do you stop paying your mortgage for more than a year? If it happens again, I swear, do not call me. That was more than fifty thousand..."

I listened to Jenine admonish her mother for being financially irresponsible. While their talk wrapped up, I silently expressed thanks that I was wrong about the roses. To be honest, I was even happier that I kept my cool. Despite my doubts, I didn't say or do something that I'd regret. Maybe I was having a breakthrough moment.

27: BABY ALOHA

As a surprise, Jenine took me to Hawaii. I had done Maui but this would be my first time visiting Oahu. We took the public buses to get a more authentic feel of the island. First stop: Diamond Head State Park. Made our way up the stairs and to the top of the crater. The panoramic view of the island was breathtakingly beautiful. No matter where I looked, there were postcard worthy views of aquamarine water, lush vegetation and mountains that seemed to reach the sky.

With the arrival of more tourists, the tranquility of the place became a distant memory. She suggested, "Maybe we can walk back to the hotel. It's just a couple of miles."

I looked at her, as though she spoke in tongues. She was the one who'd drive around the parking lot, umpteen times, in search of a closer spot. She rarely wanted to walk. Inwardly, I smiled. She was up to something.

She stroked my hand and said, "Babe, you know that I want to have a baby. We talked about in-vitro...using Diego's sperm. Remember? He'll sign away all rights to the baby. Plan B is being a foster parent."

Guess I didn't realize that I was holding my breath. Maybe I had been preparing for bad news. Something told me this would be momentous. Feelings of relief washed over me. I exhaled loudly. "When is he coming back? How soon does everything start?"

Diego's her gay friend. An attorney for a prominent civil rights organization. Several months ago, he went back home to Brazil. His mother's cancer diagnosis didn't give her much more time to live.

Now, one of his brothers was dealing with pending criminal charges. He faced the possibility of decades in prison, so Diego helped with his defense strategy. I hadn't met him in person. Through video chats we bonded over our love for Jenine and soccer.

"It'll be a couple of months." She stopped walking and looked at me. There were questions in her eyes. "If the baby will change anything between us, tell me now."

I kissed her hand. Told her the whole truth and nothing but the truth. "I've been ready for marriage, a house and two point five kids, since the first day I saw you. In this life and the next, I want it to be you and me."

"That's exactly what I wanted to hear." She wrapped her arm around my waist. Leaned her head on my shoulder. "Have you given any more thought...? How do you feel about donating your eggs? I'd carry the baby but you'd have a genetic relationship."

"I remember those conversations..."

When we left Jersey, I thought we were only going on vacation. My three primary objectives were to not get sunburn, find a way to have sex on the beach and relax.

I was quiet. Reflecting not solely on the magnitude of what she just asked. I also thought about the steps that brought us to this exact time and place. Like a long swipe through the photos in my phone, I saw so many smiles. Good times. Blissfully happy memories. Then I came upon the one thing that caused all of our arguments.

Standing outside the hotel, she looked at me. Normally, she was good at reading my mind. This time, she thought my silence meant that I was retreating. She tried to pull away from me. I wrapped my arms around her shoulders. Rested my forehead on hers. No need for telepathy. I spoke from the heart, "We're not going to argue...you've been working on something for a while..."

She put me on pause. Pecked me on the lips. "Trust. I haven't forgotten. There's something for you in the room. I'll be upstairs in a little bit. I need to talk with the manager."

*****

I took the stairs up to the room. My phone rang when I was halfway to our floor. I stopped on the landing and saw Aunt's D number. Normally, I would've answered immediately. Now, I thought about the last conversation with my mom, right before Jenine and I left for Oahu.

"Ronnie, I got her ass."

"Since when do you like ass, mom? You have a confession? Did I get my so-called queer gene from you?" I laughed.

"Goodness you're a cornball. Just hush and listen. The court agrees with me. Nothing's finalized but Denise may face criminal charges. She's going to have to pay us, more money. Praise be to God."

No need to ask if she was serious. Once God got thrown in the mix, it was a wrap.

"Whoa. Back up. You and me?"

"You're not laughing now, huh? Nana left you more money...not sure how much, though. That's part of what needs to be figured out..."

With that conversation clearly in my head, I decided to answer Aunt D's call. May as well get this over with. "Hello. What took you so long to call?"

A pained expression formed on my face. I frowned

deeply. Listened to the woman, who's been my second mom, detonate the foundation of our relationship with fifteen words. "Your mom was right. I lied about everything. The will was forged. I'm so sorry."

She cried. Begged for forgiveness. Told me that I was owed an extra 150k. She didn't want to go to jail. Apologized to me endlessly.

This time, I was the mature one. Offered my own fifteen-word salvo. "You owe my mom an apology, too. I'm not gonna disrespect you. We'll talk later."

Not waiting for her response, I ended the call. Made my way into the hotel room. Hands washed, I saw an envelope, with my name on the front. Tipped my head to the side for a better view. It was Jenine's handwriting.

The conversation with Aunt D was on its way to putting a serious damper on my mood. In opening the envelope, a smile slowly spread across my face. I was looking at paperwork that showed the end of Jenine's marriage was a reality. Now, our possibilities truly seemed limitless. I intended to use some of the extra money from Nana's will to pay for what I dubbed "Operation Baby." There was one other important thing to do.

Dear Diary:

Since losing her high-profile job, Kayla was intent on becoming the queen of living the high life on a shoestring budget. She'd spend hours scouring the internet for free giveaways, entering raffles and trying to procure any type of discount. Most times, she fell woefully short of her desired outcome. Other times, like today's phone call, she surprised me with an incredible find.

"Wifey, put on something sexy. We're going out."

"I'm supposed to be working. Am I paying for it?"

"Nah. I'm paying...well...not exactly. I won two free lunches for the buffet at the five-star place by the waterfront that we used to go to. They included endless martinis, too. I'll come scoop you up in an hour."

"Oh, okay. Their food is sinfully good. Guess I could spare a few minutes to get something to eat..."

At the restaurant, we were seated at "our" table. The one that had the best view of the NYC skyline. I ate like someone coming off a hunger strike. She was determined to set the record for drinking the most martinis in the allotted two-hour time limit. Anyone looking at us wouldn't have had a clue this used to be our regular hangout spot.

With a smile plastered on her face, we sat in her car. She rested her hand on my thigh and stroked it back and forth. "Thank you for coming. I had a good time."

I couldn't disagree and said, "Yeah. I'm glad that I

came. A nice distraction from work."

I held her chin in my hand. Stared into her eyes. Maybe it was the alcohol that softened her personality. There was none of the arrogance. She looked defeated. Downtrodden. Helpless. Nothing like the woman who once swept me off my feet.

While memories of our happier times moved to the front of the line, I sighed deeply. I kissed both of her cheeks. Wordlessly, she started crying. I closed my eyes. Tried to absorb her pain. Make it easier for her. I kissed her on the lips. Almost allowed myself to get carried away in the moment. A thought of Ronnie caused me to come to an abrupt stop.

"Why'd you stop? Wifey, I'm trying. Believe that I'm trying. It's so hard, though. Most jobs don't pay anything."

"I know, Kayla." Subconsciously, I rubbed her hands and offered other alternatives for her to get out of her misery, "You might need to go back to school. Get another degree in a different field... Maybe try some different training... People do it all the time..." It wasn't necessary but I added, "You know I'll help..."

"No idea what I'd do without you. I've been looking at programs. I'll think about it some more..."

Before I shifted her car into first gear, she rested her head against the window. Seconds later, her heavy breathing told me that she was already in a deep sleep.

While I expertly navigated the ride back to my house, my heart and mind were at odds. I found myself caught in the sentimentality of the day with Kayla. We had an enjoyable time. It was like the old days, before she cheated, when we finished each other's sentences and laughed hysterically at stupid things. She didn't beg me for money or sex or ask to move in with me.

I turned onto my street. Saw my other reality standing on the porch. Normally, seeing Ronnie brought a wide smile to my face. Today, terror swept through me. Brought me crashing back to earth. I let loose a loud gasp. Kayla's body shifted from the noise. Silently, I prayed that she wouldn't wake up. There'd be too many questions that I wasn't ready to answer.

My fight or flight signals got crossed. Instead of speeding away, I slowed down. I felt waves of gratitude when I was sure that Kayla was still sleeping.

Almost like she sensed my presence, Ronnie turned towards the street. Only then did I come to my senses. I accelerated so quickly that the back of my head slammed against the headrest. In the rearview mirror, I saw a quizzical expression. I was thankful for the darkly tinted windows that kept us safely hidden from her prying eyes.

I drove to the other side of town and finally turned on my phone. As expected, I had plenty of messages from Ronnie. Sent her a text that I was with a co-worker and wouldn't be back home until later in the evening. It was getting harder to keep my blatant lies and partial untruths straight. How much longer until they would come back to haunt me?

*****

Ronnie and Marisa went to Phuket. My invitation was made at the last minute and felt half-hearted. I couldn't afford to take off that much time from work. A couple of days after Ronnie left, I got an urgent call from Kayla. Met her at our condo and walked into a huge surprise. I asked, "What happened to you?"

"I broke my leg at work. They fired me. Said they saw me on camera joking around and it was my fault! I should sue them."

"You called me for this? Why not your mom, sister or somebody else. You know that I'm busy."

"They're not reliable. You know that. No one else takes care of me like you."

I still had issues reconciling why Kayla cheated on me. "Listen to what you just said. How good I treated you. Yet you still cheated, right? Between you and my mother... y'all act like I have a money tree in my backyard that I shake whenever y'all need something. My name isn't Wells Fargo. At least she thanks me by sending roses. You...you don't do anything right. Can't keep a job...won't leave the condo...allergic to paying a bill...it's just excuse after excuse. All you do is beg for more. Now what do you want? How much is this going to cost me?"

Some folks believed that a lawyer who represents herself has a fool for a client. Would the same apply to me, if I tried to diagnose myself?

My heart and brain were often first-class passengers on a plane flying through storm clouds. No one else would comprehend my inability to let her go. Some things weren't meant to be understood by a spectator. Nothing fit nicely into a box that made any sense, unless you had walked that path.

When we first got together, she earned more than triple my salary. Had intelligence beyond measure and a swagger that should've been patented. Ours wasn't always a one-sided exchange.

Even though I now had the upper hand, I still needed to play this correctly. Her mobility was severely compromised. She needed me, so I pushed all my chips to the middle of the imaginary betting pile and said, "If you don't agree to let me sell the condo and sign the papers to end our marriage, I'm not helping you."

I watched her try to shift her body. Listened to her cry out in agony. Willed myself not to succumb and immediately make her feel better. The pain was cemented on her face. "That's mean as hell. You're kicking me when I'm down. Where am I going to go?"

Silently, I waited. Watched her toss alternate solutions in her head. She's always been arrogant. That was part of my initial attraction to her. Now, it just aggravated me. I knew she wouldn't immediately agree to everything, if anything.

The picture of who-gives-a-shit, I busied myself with filing my fingernails. Sent text messages to Ronnie. Responded to a few emails.

Finally, she spoke, "I love you, so much that it hurts. If it'll make you happy, sell the condo. You know that I need time..." Before I had the chance to ask, she firmly said, "... and don't say nothing else about the other papers."

She willingly signed my hastily scribbled contract. I wanted everything in writing before she changed her mind. We haggled but eventually agreed on a timeframe for her to get her things together. After that, I could sell the condo.

At least one problem seemed like it was on its way to being solved. She put her hands over mine and said, "I've been messing up but things are getting better. Guess what? I stopped smoking. My mission is to get the old us back. Then maybe you'll stop rationing the sex with me. Can I at least get a kiss?"

Part of me wanted to laugh in her face. Momma didn't raise a complete fool, though, so I knew better. Even a one-legged Kayla was dangerous. I pecked her on the cheek. Turned my cheek when she tried to kiss my lips. Gave my best faux smile. No time to dwell on what felt like a partial victory. There was a lot more work to be done.

*****

Our fifth-floor condo was in a walk-up building. Since I agreed to what amounted to babysitting duty, I let her stay at my house for a week. I slept on the pull-out couch with her. Otherwise, I would have been up and down the stairs whenever she needed something. Said hell no each time she asked for my legendary loving. That was a major step. I let her cop a few feels on my tits and ass. That was to avoid glass shattering arguments. Compared to Ronnie, her touches sometimes felt like barbed wire being scraped against my skin.

Spending so much time with Kayla meant that I wasn't free to chat via video with Ronnie. Had to come up with something on the fly when she returned from Phuket. She had a seriousness about her that made me cautious.

Almost like she was trying to set a trap, she said, "You kind of went missing in action. We only chatted when you were at work. Even when I called at night, I couldn't reach you." Playfully, she asked, "Who kept you so busy?"

Unknowingly, she touched on a live wire. I dared not tell her the truth, so I asked, "Did you hear about the mass shooting?"

Even halfway around the world, I knew that she kept updated on the news. As confirmation, she sadly remarked, "Yeah, a little. Happened in South Jersey. Ten people killed, right?"

"I did some volunteer work...only got back home yesterday. I didn't want you to worry. I'm mentally drained. Even though you use every available resource, it just doesn't feel like enough."

From the corner of my eye, I watched. Her eyes were curious but held not a hint of suspicion. I guessed that she bought my lie.

I hoped to reach the point where I could be completely honest with her. How far in the future will that be?

*****

Knowing that I couldn't let my new girlfriend find my wife on my couch, I sent Kayla's ass back home. She was nowhere near fully recovered. Paid for someone to stop by the condo for a few hours each day.

Thought I had everything covered until Ronnie saw the package of spinach. She called me on it. I felt so much shame that I couldn't meet her eyes. No clue whether she believed yet another lie that I told.

Once Ronnie got back from vacation, Kayla's broken leg turned into a blessing in disguise. Ronnie and I got to spend more time together. No worries about Kayla popping up at my house or work. I was able to have my cake, eat it and have mine eaten, too. Ha. Love the play on words.

Often, I reminisce on one escapade. We were out back by my pool. A drizzle of rain fell from the moonless sky. Innocent talk turned into lustfully tearing off clothes. Frantically groping each other. Like a drill sergeant barking orders to a subservient, she ordered me onto the diving board. I looked at her nervously and said, "This is the deep end. You know I can't swim."

"Don't you trust me?"

"Of course, but..."

"I want you face down and ass up on the diving board."

I did as she instructed. Wondered whether my neighbors were watching. If so, I was ready to give them a show.

She tied me up with a dexterity and quickness that only came from experience. I was at her complete mercy.

Even when the clouds surrendered drops of rain, she wouldn't stop. The pleasure was relentless. Unbearable. Yet, I still cried out for more. To this day, she won't tell me what she did or how she did it. Something to do with cucumbers, honey and a remote-control dildo – appropriately named Earthquake – which doubled as an electro stimulating sex toy that sent waves of delight through my whole body. After four, I lost count of my orgasms.

*****

Transported back to the present, I subconsciously rubbed my wrists. The rope burns are long gone but the delightful memories remain fresh.

Damn. I'm distracted. No more sex talk. I need to update you on everything.

I met Ronnie's mom. No doubt, she doesn't like me. She's too much of a lady to act otherwise. Aunt D was instantly wrapped around my finger. Even the future father of my child, Diego, can't get enough of her.

Ronnie met my mother. They cackled like old hens. My mother had nothing but positive things to say about her. "That Ronnie sure has a lot going for herself." "Seems like you finally found a good woman."

"Wow. Ronnie's so articulate and has so much formal education." "Ronnie this..." Ronnie that..."

She's right but I didn't need the constant reminders. If I didn't know any better, I may have thought she wanted to date her. As far as my mother is concerned, Ronnie is Miss Wonderful.

My mother knows enough about the new Kayla to see that Ronnie is a marked improvement. Her comments were uncharacteristic. She didn't usually say much about my love life.

Recently, she made an exception. Called and woke me from a sound sleep. Groggily, I wiped the sleep from my eyes and whispered into the phone, "It's two o'clock in the morning. What's wrong? Who died?"

Slowly and silently, I began to extract my naked body from Kayla's viselike grip. Maybe she didn't hear the phone.

She held me even tighter and sleepily asked, "Where are you going? Who's that?"

So much for my smooth getaway. Quickly, I answered, "My mother..."

I didn't need to offer more of an explanation. Kayla's unnecessarily loud grunt told its own story.

From the first introduction, their dislike of each other was legendary. The mileage between Toronto and New Jersey meant they only saw each other a few times each year. Even that was often too much. I wound up paying for my mother's hotel stays. Anything to keep the distance and peace during those visits.

Wrapping my sex-satiated body in a silk robe, I hurried to the ensuite bathroom. My mother was already spewing her venom.

"Was that useless Kayla? I thought you finally came to

your senses..."

It was too early for this nonsense. I cut her short, "I don't monitor your bedroom activities. Stay outta mine..."

She responded with lightning quickness, "My pickney...don't get cross with me."

"Yes, I'm your child. Sometimes you forget that I'm all the way grown..."

"I didn't call to argue. Listen to me."

Her English was crystal clear. That usually meant she wanted to have a serious conversation.

"I had a dream. You died...and Kayla did it."

She was an ardent believer that dreams were accurate predictors of real-life events.

Momentarily speechless, I was now wide awake. Tried to hide my uneasiness but shakily said, "Oh, you're, you're being ridiculous."

"No. I'm trying to save you. Remember the dream. Be careful. She's dangerous..."

I had a fitful time going back to sleep. My mind fixated on my mother's ominous warning. The unsettled issues weighed on me. I replayed a frequent conversation with Ronnie. Same questions and comments. Just expressed on different days and in different tones of pissed off-ed-ness. "It's cool that you can sell the condo. What's the hold up with ending the marriage? If there's something I need to know...tell me...don't make me assume."

Ronnie didn't know but I had been trying. Kayla may have relented on the condo but she wouldn't listen to any talk of signing the papers to end our marriage. Just the other night, there was a reminder of how I'm in a seemingly no-win situation. "Kayla. This needs to end, officially. I'm ready to move on."

"You're supposed to be the smart one, right? I told you to drop it. Since you keep finding your way back to help me, you obviously ain't trying to let me go. I'm not going nowhere and neither are you."

*****

I took Ronnie to Oahu. Wanted some time alone with my babe. Had some important things to discuss. A long time ago, Kayla and I talked about having a baby. Took the initial steps. Her eggs were still at the fertility clinic. She continues to hold out hope that we'll get back together. That I'll have our baby.

Normally, Ronnie's incredibly patient. Now, she's persistent. More insistent. I mentioned having our baby. Knew that she'd only be hesitant for one reason. I had little choice but to show her some fake divorce papers. Diego will soon be back in the States. Operation Baby is moving forward, just like my damn biological clock. I have less time to waste. Seems like I solve one problem but create two more.

Slowly, I'm formulating a plan. I refuse to lose Ronnie, while I figure out the Kayla debacle. Only need to keep the cosmic forces from colliding. I know that I'm surrounded by gasoline and playing with matches. All it takes is a spark before someone is blown to smithereens.

29: KAYLA'S CONTRIBUTION – PART 4

I carried old problems into a new year that was supposed to be epic. For so long, I had been doing everything right. Getting to work on time. Working extra hours. I had even stopped smoking. Plus, I was saving money and not depending on my beautiful wife so much.

I should have paid attention to the warning from my horoscope that trouble was on the horizon. It wouldn't take long for my world to get turned upside down. Again.

Some of my coworkers and I were on break. We were joking and having fun. For a week, a recent hire had been secretly flirting with me.

On the sly, the new hire followed me to the restroom. I had just washed my hands when she came out of another stall. Her shirt was raised. Her breasts looked so firm, they had to be implants. Her pants were pulled down just enough to show that she was freshly shaven with a thin line that led to her honeypot. She looked at me lick my lips in desire and proceeded to tighten the lasso around her catch. So much for my vow to stay away from my latest temptation.

As if reading my mind, she said, "They're real. Feel." She moved towards me. My lips found the way to her boulder sized nipples. I teased them with my tongue. She threw her head back and groaned in pleasure. Her moans intensified. I started to pull her pants even lower. I justified our tryst because my wife rationed her loving on me. She'd be my short-term pleasure. Getting back with my wife remained my long-term obsession.

Suddenly, she said, "Stop."

I thought someone saw us. Why else would she stop? I knew how to make a woman feel good.

A mischievous smile crossed her face. She flirtatiously said, "Let's save the rest for later."

The little tease scooted past me and ran out of the restroom. Jokingly, I ran after her but didn't see the "slippery when wet" sign. The floor was freshly waxed. I lost my balance. Felt my leg twist in the most unnatural position. The sounds of her laughing echoed in the hallway, as I hollered from insufferable pain.

There was little doubt that I chased her. That much was caught on video. As far as why we were running, well, her story was a lot different than mine. She swore that she was escaping from me – the predator. That bitch really said that I sexually assaulted her. There weren't any cameras in the restroom, so it was my truth against her lies. The job thought her lies were the truth. I was fired before the ambulance arrived to whisk me to the hospital.

At first, my pride wouldn't let me call my wife. Instead, I tried the woman who gave birth to me. Unsurprisingly, she didn't answer. I left a message, "Hey. It's your firstborn. You know I don't ask you for much. I'm in a bad way and need your help."

For days, I tried hard to do for myself. Everything was a struggle. I barely moved from the couch and couldn't even wash. My frustrations boiled over and I called my wife. I pledged to go to my grave without telling her the truth about that episode. That would be one more thing for her to throw in my face. We had enough issues.

It took a little convincing but she came to our condo.

Concern flashed on her face when she saw my cast. She used my pitiful plight to her advantage.

"I called my mother and sister...they're not reliable... No one else takes care of me like you." I asked myself the question that dangled on her tongue: Why did I ever cheat on her?

"Listen to what you just said. How good I treated you. Yet you still cheated, right? Between you and my mother...y'all act like I have a money tree in my backyard that I shake whenever y'all need something. My name isn't Wells Fargo. At least she thanks me by sending roses. You...you don't do anything right. Can't keep a job...won't leave the condo...allergic to paying a bill...it's just excuse after excuse. All you do is beg for more. Now what do you want? How much is this going to cost me?"

The pounding in my ear from her yelling at me was only matched by the pain in my heart, while I reflected on my endless stupidity. Everything she said was true. All of it hit below the belt. Made me feel so useless.

She played her powerful hand and demanded, "If you don't agree to let me sell the condo and sign the papers to end our marriage, I'm not helping you."

Her insensitivity crushed my spirit. I couldn't even shift my body without crying out in agony. She didn't make a move to help me.

"That's evil. You're kicking me when I'm down. Where am I going to go? You know my mother still hasn't called me back?"

She shrugged her shoulders and waited. I thought of options that would shift the odds back in my favor. She was unfazed. Filed her nails. Played on the damn phone.

Maybe it was the pain that clouded my ability to think. I couldn't come up with any tangible alternative. Still, my ego wouldn't let me give her everything that she wanted.

"Wifey...I love you, so much that it hurts. If it'll make you happy, sell the condo. You know that I need time to heal and find another job. Please be patient with me..."

She looked so damn smug. The smile was wiped from her face when I added, "...and don't say nothing else about the other papers."

*****

For a short time, my broken leg was the best thing that happened to me in a long time. I moved in with her. She waited on me like I was royalty and she was my subject. Even though she doled out her loving in drips and drabs, I had the pleasure of waking each morning and looking at her lovely self.

The two of us being under the same roof extinguished all thoughts that she was involved with anyone else. The only people who came to the house were ones that I already knew. There weren't any late night calls where she whispered into the phone. I was hyper-focused on trying to turn my sudden good fortune into a long-term arrangement.

A week later, the rug was pulled from beneath my feet.

"Wifey, why are you taking me back to the condo?"

"Something's come up and it's easier for you to be there and not here."

"Something like what?"

"There's a lot going on and I need space to handle everything. With you here, it's like looking after a baby... I'll cook the potato spinach casserole. At least you can eat off that for a couple of days..."

I eyed her suspiciously but couldn't say or do much

more. She still came to check on me but her attitude was different. She seemed distracted. Maybe even happier.

At least she hired someone to come to the condo for a few hours each day. It was nice to have company. My family acted like I didn't exist, especially after I lost my lucrative job. Since I couldn't help them financially, they had little use for me.

I was waiting for the aide, when I got a call from a childhood buddy that I hadn't heard from in years. "Hey, Kayla. It's me, Shawna."

"Oh shoot... It's been a minute since I last saw you..."

I was all set to get updated on the happenings from our old neighborhood. My pride told me to be discreet in picking and choosing the current details of my life that I'd share with her. I wasn't doing nearly as well since the last time we'd seen each other.

"Don't play with me. You literally bumped into me at the bank today. Almost knocked me over. You feeling yourself because you're skinnier than when we were in college and still sinfully sexy? Even when I called your name, you looked right at me but kept going out the door. Acted like you didn't even know me. That was rude as hell."

"What are you talking about? I have a broken leg and damn sure ain't slim and trim no more. My ass hasn't seen the inside of a gym in far too long."

Subconsciously, I patted my belly because I had put on too much weight.

"Are you serious?"

I took some pics and sent them to her. "There's all the proof you should need."

"Damn. Kayla. Your leg is jacked up. The woman I saw...y'all looked like each other."

"That's bonkers. Don't even know what that's about. Listen, I gotta call you back. The lady's here to help with my leg."

*****

Later that night, my wife came for a short visit and brought me a sack full of snacks. Greedily, I tore open the biggest bag.

"Guess what? I spoke to Shawna today. She called to cuss me out because she thought she saw me and I ignored her. Said the other woman looked like me."

My wife behaved like she saw a ghost. Her eyes widened and she backed towards the door. As though the words were caught in her throat, she asked, "Really? How crazy is that?"

"That's weird. They say everyone has a so-called twin. Guess Shawna saw mine today..."

*****

I continued to heal. Focused my attention on trying to get compensated for unjust termination. I received a very small settlement and was basically told to be happy I got that much. Times were still hard, so I gladly accepted. The extra money gave me a little breathing room.

While I tried to get my life back in order, it seemed like my wife was plotting something. I saw it in her eyes. Heard it in her voice. Felt it in her movements. In one conversation, she still mentioned getting a divorce. I shut that down before she even put the key into the ignition.

In the next conversation, we talked about her having a baby. She was still willing to use my eggs. Made it clear that I had to bring more to the table. Otherwise, she'd do it solo. There was a new seriousness to her. Told me that she was going to Oahu, to get her mind right. She expected a realistic plan for me to get my shit together by the time she got back. Like her biological clock, I feel like the expiration date on our marriage was quickly approaching. Time wasn't on my side.

30: MORE QUESTIONS

Vacation in Hawaii was a pleasant memory. Jenine and I were back in Jersey. Operation Baby was in overdrive. Multiple visits to the fertility clinic. Blood was drawn. Tests were ordered. Results were returned. No issues so far. Diego's supposed to be back in less than a month.

We fanatically adhered to a special diet, which was high in fat, moderate in protein and low in carbs. She took prenatal vitamins, multivitamins and monitored her caloric intake. Supposedly, this regimen would increase fertility. I was dubious but tried to be as supportive as possible.

Beyond Operation Baby, something else, about Jenine, wouldn't leave my mind. I couldn't talk about it with just anyone. Went through the list of my confidantes. It was short. My mom was at the top. Unfortunately, she hadn't changed her opinion of Jenine. If anything, it was more deeply entrenched. There was no way that she could give me an unbiased viewpoint. She had made a few return trips to NJ, so she and Jenine spent more time around each other.

I don't think Jenine realized that my mom was only cordial to her for my sake. As such, I hadn't told my mom about us having a baby. If I wasn't ready to talk with her about the impending pregnancy, there was no way I could talk with her about another equally important decision.

I thought about Aunt D. Months ago, I took Jenine to Chicago. It was important for her to get a better idea of where and how I was raised. She met Aunt D, who adored her from their first talk. The opposite of my mom. Just as I expected.

Admittedly, I was still working through my emotions of her lying about Nana's will. I had this monumental decision to discuss. The expression of trust being lost in buckets and won back in drops held true. She was now firmly outside the trust box. I had no idea, when or if, she would work her way back into my good graces.

After our vacation, Marisa left for Italy. I had apologized for saying she was jealous. She forgave me. We were good.

She'd only been gone for a couple of months. It seemed like so much longer. Initially, she sent weekly updates. Now, it had been almost a month and I hadn't heard back from her. I made one more call. Left one more message. "Marisa. What's going on? I'm sending out the bat signal. Are you okay? I need to hear your voice. Politic about some life-changing stuff with you. Call me, please."

Like me, she hadn't ventured onto social media. Bat signal was our not-so-secret code that something was important. Surely, she would respond. I was at a loss on how to reach her. I hoped her newly found relatives hadn't tossed her into the Adriatic Sea.

I continued on my list. Landed on Gisele. She and Jenine met at several community events. Maybe it had to do with her professional background. During most conversations, Jenine made you feel like her focus was all on you. No one else existed. What you said was of the utmost importance. That was part of how she sucked people into her cypher.

More than once, I listened to Gisele share information about lifelong issues with her father. Hopes for her daughters. Improvements from the clinical trial. Regrets from her past. She told Jenine stuff that she hadn't even shared with me and she was my friend! Each time, they looked like two lifelong comrades reminiscing on decades of shared memories. Jenine was equally moved. For weeks thereafter, she talked about those conversations.

Gisele spoke positively of Jenine. Then again, I hadn't heard her say a negative word about anyone. It wasn't a far-fetched notion that she could find something positive to say about the devil. Maybe I wouldn't get an objective opinion. I couldn't talk with her, either.

This was frustrating. The last person who came to mind was Jenine's mother. We've met twice. The first time, Jenine and I went to Toronto for her mother's birthday. The other time, her mother came to Jersey for a weekend visit. It seemed like we got along well.

I did a quick search and found two phone numbers. Between sips of ginger tea, I called them both but they were disconnected. There was an email address. Immediately, I received the automated reply that it was no longer valid.

This was proving to be more difficult than expected. I didn't want Jenine to know that I was trying to get in contact with her mother. She was nosey and that would lead to endless questions. Driving would take too long. I could fly. Be back on the same day. No. That was doing entirely too much. I just had to get her phone number without Jenine knowing, which meant that I needed to get into her cell phone.

Although there'd been some instances where I questioned the true reason the marriage wasn't dissolved sooner, I hadn't gone through her phone in search of answers. It would've been easy enough. I was pretty sure that I knew her passcode. This time, I justified doing it because I wanted her mother's number. Told myself that I wasn't snooping.

*****

Later that night, we brought bags of groceries into her house. Intentionally, I left the ice cream in the trunk. She put her purse and phone on the kitchen table.

I was putting away the food and said, "Hand me the ice cream before it starts to melt."

She looked through the bags. "It's not here, babe. I'll check the car. Maybe we forgot a bag."

I heard the front door open. Grabbed her phone. Punched in the passcode but it didn't unlock. I took my time and tried again. Bingo! I checked her contacts. Found her mother's information.

Had I not seen the twelve missed calls and sixteen text messages, I would have simply locked the phone and put it back on the table. Instead, I hurried to the front door. Saw her looking in the backseat. I glanced at her phone. My mind went in one thousand nine hundred and thirteen different directions.

Another peek out the window. She found the ice cream and was on her way back to the house. My finger hovered over her phone. Beads of sweat formed on my temple, while I vacillated between my choices.

I said a silent prayer this didn't blow up in my face. Decision made. I pressed the text message icon. Saw that two of the texts were from her mother and one was from a cousin. The other thirteen were from someone whose contact name was rehab. I could read part of the last message: "You've been so good to me. Don't say it's too late for us to reconcile. Please. I really need you. Call me. I'm sooo sorry."

Seeing that name brought back a memory. Until now, I had forgotten about that night when I saw Rehab's name flash on her phone, at like three o'clock in the morning. Even at that hour, the name alone made me think it may have been work-related. Now, I wasn't sure. I stared at the phone. Heard her at the screen door. She was talking with one of the neighbors. Yanked me back to reality. I rushed to the kitchen. Felt like a junkie trying to get clean. My hands wouldn't stop shaking. I pressed the home button, locked the phone and put it back on the table.

My head throbbed. Coaxed myself into taking deep breaths. Constant contriteness over Monica filled my thoughts. Guided my actions.

"Don't lose your cool," I repeatedly whispered to myself. So many other things I thought to myself: Was rehab Kayla or someone else? Why were there so many messages? Were my plans of forever unattainable?

Jenine triumphantly put the bag onto the counter. "Mystery solved. Ice cream was in the trunk." Seeing my stoic expression, she asked, "What's wrong?"

We were planning to have a baby. I wanted forever in this lifetime and beyond with her. I needed answers. "Your phone's been ringing."

"Why didn't you answer it?" She skillfully deflected back to me.

"ID said rehab. Thought it might be something to do with work."

She looked at the phone. What seemed to be relief flooded her face. She looked in my direction. Phone on speaker, she returned the call and explained, "This is work-related. Now they want to call back. Ring my phone off the hook...I've been..."

Someone answered and hurriedly said, "Hello, Ms. Rhett. Please let me explain. You're one of my best resources. I'm sorry it took sooo long to get back to you... staffing issues. If you have time, maybe we can talk about the referrals that you..."

"Seriously, save the apologies...until recently, we've had a great working relationship. I shouldn't have to call you umpteen times and wait several days before I get a response. You've forced me to reach out to someone else..."

Jenine excused herself and went into another room. They'd probably discuss sensitive information that I wasn't supposed to hear. I understood but still listened by the door.

That conversation just reaffirmed that I was tripping. I could confidently move forward with everything. That rehab was not Kayla or any issue that should concern me.

31: FUTURE PLANS

Now that I had no hesitation about taking the next step, I called Jenine's mother a few days later. "Hi, Ms. Rhett. This is Ronnie."

She screamed almost incoherently. Even after living in Toronto for almost three decades, she sometimes spoke with a strong Trinidadian accent. I focused extra hard to understand what she was saying.

"Huh? Who are you talking about? Nobody did anything to your baby."

She still wasn't convinced that everything was okay. "Yuh...me...yuh...sure?"

"Ms. Rhett, everything is cool. I need to talk with you about something important. Don't tell Jenine about this conversation, please."

Now assured that Jenine was all right, the Trinidadian accent was gone. "If you're sure that she didn't do anything and nothing is wrong, I'll keep this between us. What's on your mind, love?"

I was worried. Cleared my throat. Took a deep breath. Spoke from my heart. "Ms. Rhett. I love your daughter. We're continuing to build our relationship. Making big plans. I'm asking for your blessing. I want to ask Jenine to marry me..."

Silence filled the line. Hadn't thought about what I'd do if she didn't give me her blessing. I had no choice but to wait.

Finally, she said, "You're a wonderful woman. I know

that you only want to add to Jenine's happiness. She loves you. Of course, I give you my blessing. Keep being patient with her."

I had been unnecessarily on edge. We spent some time talking about Operation Baby and her excitement at becoming a grandmother. She was already making plans for the baby's extracurricular activities. "I want that baby to learn how to swim and do martial arts. Goodness, I'm so excited."

"I used to be a lifeguard, so I can teach the baby to swim. Why martial arts?"

"Remember. I was an abused woman. No one taught me but I made sure Jenine learned to protect herself from young. She has a brown belt in karate. I want my grandbaby to have some training, too."

"Ronnie, love, I have to get back to work. Our talk will be a secret. Remember. She loves you. Things don't always happen when we want or how we want. Patience is the key word with her."

While Operation Baby continued to unfold, I was getting more excited, at the thought of becoming a mother, raising a baby and marrying Jenine.

32: OPERATION BABY: I DO – NOT

Out of the blue, Jenine told me to take a half-day off work. We met at her house. She gave no hints as to where we were going. To add to the drama, she blindfolded me. That didn't stop me from asking lots of questions. Exasperated, she said, "Enough. You're worse than a little kid."

The SUV stopped. She squealed in excitement. Opened the driver's side door and warned me, "Don't take off the blindfold. Play the game properly."

Ms. Bossy opened my door. An unfamiliar pair of hands helped me out of the car. I heard a baritone voice. The accent. Slower than I wanted, the pieces came together.

In Portuguese, the man said, "Bom dia linda," which I knew meant "good morning beautiful."

She removed the blindfold. Diego and I cautiously eyed each other. The same positive vibes that I got from our countless video chats continued. Operation Baby was one step closer to reality.

In person, he was even more handsome. Like Jenine, he had those same spellbinding green eyes. His boyish smile broke down anyone's defenses. He had an easygoing nature. I thought we were taking him to his condo. Instead, we went directly to the fertility clinic. We'd already been notified that there weren't any issues with our bloodwork. Now it was Diego's turn for testing.

During the day, it was almost impossible to find legal

street parking in Manhattan. The garages were a major rip-off. While they went into the clinic, I cruised the streets in her SUV. Watched people go about their daily activities. An hour later, I picked them up and we dropped off Diego at his condo.

It was still early. I asked, "Anything special you want to do?"

From the corner of my eye, I saw her take off her shirt, unfasten her bra and wiggle out of her pants. I was trying to concentrate on driving. When I got a better look, she wasn't wearing any panties.

She shrieked, "Ahhh!" I looked back to the road, just in time to slam on the brakes. I came within a fraction of an inch of rear-ending a Jaguar. The driver behind me honked furiously.

Considering I almost totaled her SUV, she was taking it well. She laughed and told me, "Pay attention."

Such a double entendre. I told her, "You're the one distracting me."

Although I tried to concentrate on driving, I couldn't resist sneaking glances. I got aroused when I saw her sucking her own nipples.

Feeling emboldened, she leaned toward the driver's seat. Flicked her tongue in and out of my ear. She did not play fair. Involuntarily, I squirmed. "Pleassse stop. You know that...my ears...weakkk spottt."

My head went rapidly back and forth between watching the road and watching her. She guided my hand between her legs. Now, I was distracted by someone else. We had unwelcome company. Through the open sunroof, I saw a truck driver staring at us. His mouth was agape. With tobacco-stained teeth, he smiled and yelled, "Y'all want some company?" Like a rattlesnake, he quickly moved his tongue back and forth. I drove faster. The voyeur would no longer be part of our unplanned exhibition.

"Babe...find somewhere to park. I wanna fuck."

Again, we were thinking the same thing. I cut off a car and found the nearest spot. The SUV was barely in park. She was already climbing in the back and folding down the seats. I couldn't unbuckle the seatbelt fast enough. She yanked me towards her. Like a ripe peach with juice bursting through the flesh, she begged to be devoured. I was all too happy to oblige.

The windows were quickly fogged. Sweat clung to our bodies. We found sixty-nine ways to another orgasm.

*****

I surreptitiously looked at her. She decided to stay naked for the rest of the ride back to Jersey. This woman felt very comfortable in her own skin. Until I wiped down the seats, I wouldn't ride again in her SUV. I pulled into her garage, so unseen by neighbors, she could go directly into the house.

For more than an hour, I had been cleaning every nook and cranny of the SUV. Like someone whose puppy had mistakenly been left outside for too long, she came looking for me. "What's taking you so long? You could've just sprayed everything with Lysol."

It wasn't exactly how I had it planned. I wanted her with every fiber in my being. Long ago, I had learned that she was untraditional, in some regards. I'd been carrying something with me, while I tried to decide on the right time.

This qualified as unconventional. It wasn't a hot air

balloon ride in Kenya, the Blue Grotto on the island of Capri or skydiving in Dubai that I had envisioned. Instead, this was bare bones.

In her garage, while she wore flannel pajamas, had her hair in rollers and a charcoal mask on her face, I knelt on both knees and offered, "Jenine Marie Rhett…from the first day we met, I've looked forward to this day. Will you please spend all of eternity with me? Will you marry me?"

I held the simple titanium engagement band. The look of surprise was evident. I saw tears forming in her eyes. She took the ring. Kissed it. Placed it on her right hand. Got on both knees with me. She rested her forehead against mine and spoke her truth, "Please know that I do love you. This can't happen right now. I need you to trust me…"

I felt myself blinking back tears. Her mouth kept moving, so I guess she continued to talk. I couldn't hear anything else she had to say. The tears that I refused to let fall pooled in my eyes. They drowned out her voice.

In trying to find the bright spot, I thought to myself, "At least she didn't say no."

33: ARE YOU POSITIVE?

Jenine may not have been ready for marriage but Operation Baby continued. There were no issues with Diego's test results. All the other necessary steps were taken, which continued up to the all-important embryo transfer.

On that date, I had an emergency. Called to give her the update. "J, I have a dire situation at work. I'm not going to make the appointment."

"Are you serious? You know the importance of this day. You take time to play golf and whatever else. You should've taken off for this, too. Do what you need to do. I'll find someone else to go with me. Someone who'll be supportive."

She sounded upset at me, instead of being concerned about my pressing situation. I blamed it on pre-pregnancy hormones. I didn't have the time or desire to defend myself. It was easier to just agree with her. "You're right. I know. I'm sorry. Don't cancel. Let me know how everything turns out. I need to go."

At work, I was a bundle of nerves. Later that night, she gave me the run-down. "I'm still mad that you weren't there. Two embryos were transferred to my uterus. I'm supposed to wait at least 10 days...preferably 14...before the pregnancy test. I don't want to take any chances, so no sex, either. That might cause the embryo not to implant in my uterus."

It was hard to pay attention. After she said, "No sex," I

was lost.

"Had you been at the appointment, you would've heard the same info. For the next two weeks, I'm going to pamper myself. You're going to help. That means more foot massages. I must take medication and keep eating healthy. There's a lot of products that have harmful chemicals, so they have to go in the garbage."

Seconds later, she sent a text with a long list. I thought she was being extra about the stuff we should and shouldn't do. More than one reputable website confirmed that she wasn't being a drama queen. I still wasn't feeling the no sex part. If it was for the benefit of the baby, I'd learn to deal with it.

*****

On the 14th day, Jenine came to my house with three separate pregnancy tests. She waited outside the house and tasked me with the responsibility of telling her the results. After the instructed amount of time, I checked and one of the tests already showed two lines, which meant that she was pregnant. Tried to calm my jittery nerves. Maybe it was a false positive. I didn't want to get my hopes up too high. There were still two more tests.

The second test seemed to make things clearer. It had two lines, as well. I reread the instructions. Okay. Two lines equaled pregnant. That was another good sign. Nervousness still gripped me.

Just one more test to go. I read the instructions twice. All right. I was ready. The third test showed a plus sign, which meant that she was pregnant. Only now did I scream, "Yesss!"

Almost like hearing my call from the wild, she walked

through the front door. There was no chance at me playing it cool. I placed my hand on her belly and yelled, "We're going to have a baby!"

Dear Diary:

Baby, baby, baby. I have plenty of news for you. Have to go chronologically. Otherwise, I'll forget stuff and it'll make even less sense.

I dodged a major bullet. Through my work, I helped a woman start a substance abuse treatment facility. If appropriate, I referred clients to her. She and her team do great work and have helped a lot of people. We had a fantastic working relationship until she went missing for a few days.

Honestly, I thought she may have relapsed. There was no response to my numerous calls, texts or emails. Just when I was ready to cut her off, she replied with a flurry of messages and calls.

As usual, Ronnie was so transparent. I saw the look of suspicion in her eyes when she said, "Your phone's been ringing."

I was ready with a snappy comeback. "Why didn't you answer it?"

Thankfully it was that rehab. I intentionally let Ronnie hear our conversation. Saw the relief on her face, when she learned that the calls were work-related. A cat gets nine lives, right? How many have I used?

That issue solved, another presented itself. Diego's back stateside and met Ronnie in person. He's in love with her. No. Not that type of love. Remember, he's gay. He's in love with her essence. Starting to get on my damn nerves. He knows that I'm wrong. Feels like it's his damn duty to constantly remind me. I know that I'm wrong but he doesn't need to be so extra.

"Jenine... When Ronnie leaves, you'll only have yourself to blame."

"Diego, it's not that easy. Kayla won't leave me alone. I've offered alimony. Tried to hook her up with someone. Nothing works. She only wants me. I give her a little, sometimes to keep the peace. At other times because I still have feelings for her. Just need more time to figure something out."

"More time? How long have you been saying that? I think you like the drama. The mess. This isn't a game. I don't think you'll like the final outcome, when Ronnie wises up...or when Kayla..."

"No negative juju. Don't even put that into the atmosphere. You sound like my mother."

There was no way I would tell him or anyone else about her dream. Last thing I wanted was to speak it into existence.

Since I was becoming an expert at keeping secrets, I dared not tell him or anyone else that Ronnie asked me to marry her. I'm laughing even though nothing is funny.

She stared at me with expectant eyes that I – shamefully – could not meet. At that moment, I wished to disappear into the incredible depth of her dimples. I didn't want to bear witness to the inevitable pain that would soon cross her face and inundate her heart.

My heart screamed, "Yes!!!"

Too bad I knew the web that I still needed to untangle with Kayla. For that reason, my mouth said, "Please know that I do love you. This can't happen right now. I need you to trust me..."

That was my attempt to ease what looked like her heart shattering into a million pieces. I wear the ring on my right hand. How much time before I move it to my left? I need to keep Ronnie and Kayla from finding out about each other. Phew! In so many ways, my life is a mess.

*****

I'm truly saving the best news for last. Need to tell the full story, though.

Diego had been back and forth to Brazil. More family drama. Ronnie was super busy with work. She couldn't go with me to several appointments, including the most important one of all – the embryonic transfer. So, for every appointment that Ronnie missed, I called Kayla. No surprise that she was all too willing to accompany me.

Admittedly, it felt like the days when we planned to have a baby. I may have gotten too caught up in recalling those moments and said some things. Agreed to some things. Fed into Kayla's belief that there was more than a glimmer of hope for us...

What is the end result from those visits, bloodwork, tens of thousands of dollars and everything else? Yours truly is PREGNANT!!!

There are times when words aren't enough. That's how I felt from the moment Ronnie and then Kayla told me the results. To know that another life is growing inside me. That almost all I do will impact the baby's life is overwhelming. It's a journey that I embrace. I pray for our health. I pray for the strength to get my life in order...

My wife's call wasn't totally unexpected but I was still somewhat surprised. "Are you at work?"

"Yes, Wifey. Getting off soon, though. Are we meeting at our spot by the lake?"

"This isn't about sex, Kayla. I've given this a lot of thought. Bringing another life into this world. We have so much history. I want you to take me to the embryonic transfer. Pick me up in two hours."

"No problem. I knew you wouldn't give up on us. Now that you're going to use my eggs, we'll be bonded for life through the baby."

I floated out of work. Forget Cloud 9. I was on Cloud 999. All the way to the fertility clinic, I rubbed her belly. Just wanted a little practice before she got pregnant. She smiled at me. We talked about names, how to decorate the nursery and so much more. Just like the old days.

*****

Two weeks later, she stopped by my apartment with a pregnancy test. I watched her face beam with excitement, as the plus sign turned bright pink.

I placed my hand on her belly and beamed, "We're going to have a baby."

From that point forward, all I did was centered on keeping her and our baby safe.

I called Diego but he didn't answer. My calls went

straight to voicemail. I couldn't think of a reason for him to block my number. Even messages sent on social media were ignored.

We've never had a good relationship but I swallowed my pride and called my mother-in-law, too.

"Hello, Mother Rhett. This is Kayla. It's been too long since we talked..."

"Not long enough for me. I thought she dumped you. Don't ring my phone. Goodbye."

Well damn. That was inconsiderate. She hung up the phone on me. I only wanted to talk about planning a baby shower. Thankfully she resided in Toronto and we wouldn't need to see too much of each other. That woman hated my guts. Can't say the feeling wasn't mutual.

Even when I was in corporate America, she didn't think I was good enough for her precious daughter. Said that I was too rough around the edges. I'm sure she thought even less of me now, especially if my wife told her about my financial struggles.

I could be the bigger woman. We needed to get on the same page now that the baby – who would forever tie us to each other – was on the way.

*****

I didn't want anything to unnecessarily stress my wife. That included me, so I wasn't offended when I showed up unannounced at her house and she told me to go home because she needed to rest. Anything for her and our baby, I told myself.

Not quite ready to return to an empty apartment, I made a detour to see the woman who gave birth to me.

Akin to a bloodhound tracking the scent of money, she called me shortly after Jenine sold the condo. My siblings happened to be there, as well. Seemed like everyone had a sob story and needed some money. Like during my more successful days, I helped them.

Yeah, I used to work in finance. Should've known better. If I stayed on the current path, it'd be the same old story of my money and me continuing to head in opposite directions.

In some ways, I was still a little girl. The one who yearned for acceptance. Even if it was from the woman who used to tell me, "I should've aborted you," way more than she ever told me, "I love you."

36: WELCOME

Although I didn't tell Jenine about the extra money from Nana's will, I made good on my vow to pay for Operation Baby. After insurance paid its paltry portion, the remaining balance was 45k. I looked over the medical statements and could only imagine the cost, had there been major issues, instead of minor ones. Without her knowing, I sent a check to the fertility clinic for the full amount.

From the beginning, Jenine had the pregnancy glow. The baby shower was attended by more than 100 women. There were so many gifts that I had to rent a U-Haul truck. Diego and I spent hours putting all of them into the spare rooms. At her house, I painted. Assembled the crib. Decorated the baby's room. Organized everything else. Diapers and clothes wouldn't be needed for many months. All that was left to do was wait for the little one to arrive.

*****

Unexpectedly, my job sent me to Pittsburgh, PA for training. Jenine called and screamed, "Babe. My water broke!"

Stupidly, I suggested, "You just have to hold it."

"When did you start drinking? You know it doesn't work that way. I'm having a baby. Not trying to hold my pee."

Normally, that question would have put me on edge. Today, it didn't even register because I was wrapped in a cocoon of anxiety.

I smacked my forehead and clarified, "That came out wrong. You know what I meant. They can't give you a drug or something?"

"Think babe. It's close to my due date. There's nothing I can do but get ready to push...and you're not even here..."

"I'll be there as soon as I can..."

I wasn't sure whether she tried to make me feel horrible. If so, it wasn't necessary. Immediately, I booked a return ticket. I felt a trifecta. Apprehension. Fear. Unease. All of them swirled in my stomach. Made me feel like I unwisely mixed dark and light liquor. Not a good combination.

*****

Once I arrived in Newark, I made the gas pedal kiss the floorboard and drove like a madwoman. I just had to get to her. At the hospital, I parked with no concern about the car getting ticketed or towed.

I arrived well after visiting hours. I showed my badge. Maybe the guard would do me a solid favor. Let me see Jenine and our baby.

He looked at me curiously and asked, "Weren't you here earlier?"

"Nah. I just got off a plane from Pittsburgh."

As if clearing cobwebs, he shook his head from side to side and offered, "It's been a long day. My mistake."

He escorted me to the maternity ward. I saw a blue blanket covering the bassinet. At 7:46 that night, our son, Klark Alexander Rhett, graced the world with his presence. He weighed eight pounds and six ounces. I held our bundle of joy. Briefly, he opened his eyes. Could have sworn that he looked into mine. At that moment, he was imprinted on my heart. The smile on my face was a country mile wide. He was the blueprint of perfection. I softly rubbed his head. Prayed that God would order his steps for all the days of his life.

Any thoughts of me not being present for the birth were quickly forgotten. All that mattered were the woman lying in the bed and our son, who rested in my arms. He had so much to learn. I relished the chance to be one of his first teachers.

While I recited the ABCs and 123s to Klark, I thought of Diego. Without him, this moment wouldn't have been possible. Unfortunately, he couldn't be present for the birth. He had returned to Brazil. The same brother whose criminal charges he helped to get dismissed had been killed by the police. The official story was unsatisfactory and left more questions than answers. He felt an obligation to investigate. I tried to call him but couldn't get a signal inside the hospital. I wasn't even sure he knew about his son.

37: BIGGER RESPONSIBILITIES

At my house, Klark had a bedroom, which was a mirror image of the one at Jenine's house. Days passed into weeks, which turned into months. Klark continued to be my primary focus. I spent as much time as possible with him and settled nicely into being a mom. My relationship with Jenine was strong, even though we didn't live together. I had come to terms with that aspect of our relationship.

Surprisingly, my mom had turned a page. Well, sort of. Since Klark's birth, she visited much more frequently. Every now and again, I caught her looking sideways at Jenine. Kind of like she was trying to fit together the pieces of a puzzle. The magnetism of Klark was too hard for her to resist. With each visit, she fell more head over heels in love with him. We were equally passionate in helping him exceed pediatric milestones.

During this visit, Klark was asleep. My mom and I caught up on things. Offhandedly, I mentioned, "You haven't said anything about Spencer."

She seethed, "That sorry motherfucker..."

The fact that she cussed told me much of what I needed to know. Turns out that even senior citizens can have a saucy side.

"Spencer," my mom started, "was quite the man about town. One of his lady friends called and cussed me out. Another wanted to fight me. I didn't know about either of them. Can you believe that nonsense?"

My mom had more juicy details. "I confronted him with everything. All he did was lie. Usually, I read people well but not him. I blocked his number. Threatened to get a restraining order, if he called me again."

I tried my best to keep a straight face. I thought about Spencer being a playa well into his 70s. What's the old saying? Something about a woman's tongue and man's eye will only rest when they die.

Out of the blue, she said, "I've been thinking about getting a condo out here. That way, I can spend more time with you and Klark. What do you think?"

I jumped off the chair and wrapped her in a massive hug. "Finally! That's the best news I've heard all day."

"It'd be easier for me to have my own space, especially if you and Jenine ever start living together."

The last comment was said with more than a little sarcasm. She cut her eyes at me. Looked like she was prepared for a battle. I refused to give her the satisfaction of a response.

Aunt D finally presented Nana's actual will, which was authenticated by the courts. My mom received almost $2 million. Unless she was trying to buy a whole housing development, her budget offered a lot of flexibility.

"I'll put you in touch with a realtor. You'll get a nice spot."

Aunt D was still alienated from my mom. She had some criminal issues, as well. The thought of her going to jail seemed like overkill. I said as much to the prosecutor. My mom would take some convincing. She was being stubborn and wanted "maximum punishment." In a side conversation, I asked the prosecutor for time to talk some sense into her. She was operating purely off emotion, which I knew often led to making the wrong decision.

I watched my mom get sentimental, while we talked about Nana and some of her witty sayings. "Ronnie, your Nana was wise beyond her years. Just about everything she envisioned came to pass."

One thing Nana would often say that proved true – time and time again – dealt with deaths or bad things "happening in threes." Soon I would realize that from the grave, Nana was speaking to me.

38: HAPPENS IN THREES

Event #1: Jenine and I tried desperately to get in contact with Diego. It was like he disappeared. One of his sisters eventually responded to her on social media. Dropped the cruelest news that he'd been killed. Initially, we thought the message was an unfunny joke. Not until his sister attached articles and pictures from his funeral could the truth no longer be denied.

I've heard it said there are three versions of a story. Side A, Side B and the truth. According to the official version of events from Side A or law enforcement, Diego was shot and killed by an unknown assailant. They didn't have any suspects. It was an active case. Curiously, no one had been assigned to investigate. Many of the files had mysteriously disappeared. Short and to the point.

More details and a markedly different version came from our many conversations with Side B or Diego's family. He was in Rio de Janeiro and walking to a meeting. A single gunshot sounded. People ran in different directions. Once things settled, Diego was in a pool of his own blood. He'd been shot through the heart. He was dead before his body hit the pavement.

His family portrayed him as a marked man. While he was the lead attorney for his brother's defense trial, he painted law enforcement in a bad light. He exposed issues of corruption that still impacted the country. More than once, he was warned to leave and not return. He became the enemy of some very influential and criminally connected people. Instead of staying away, he was defiant. Determined to expose more corruption. He asked uncomfortable questions. Pissed off even more people. His family fully believed that his dogged determination resulted in his murder.

Truth. Such a difficult word. Meant different things to different people. Most times, the truth rested somewhere between Side A and Side B. Diego's family, Jenine and I had negative confidence that the full truth would ever be known. There seemed to be too much at stake for too many powerful people. In all of our conversations, Diego never gave a hint about the dangers he faced in Brazil.

*****

Event #2: My mom was back in Jersey and offered to watch Klark. Jenine and I took advantage of the free time. Each month, we rotated taking each other on a date. I planned a full day of activities. Breakfast at the diner where we first met. Relaxing walk back to my house. Matinee movie. Onto the park, where we feasted on a cornucopia of fruit, while I gave her a pedicure. Dinner at my favorite hibachi restaurant. We finger-fed each other because she couldn't get the hang of using chopsticks.

She mistakenly thought the date was finished after dinner. Not quite. The real treat was an intimate concert, followed by a meet and greet. I could only get tickets from a resale site. He was her favorite musician. I lived to make her happy, so I paid the inflated price.

I watched, as he gave her a rose. Serenaded her on bended knee. She basked in being the center of his attention. She smiled contentedly throughout the show. The ways she pleased me afterwards made everything worthwhile.

Her measures of thanks started with a striptease. Seductively, she swayed her hips. Twerked. Gyrated. It looked like her ass had a motor attached to it. I was hypnotized. Our lovemaking lasted until the sun began to rise. Maybe it was the exhaustion of her relentlessly exploring my body. It could have been her unending quest to make me surrender to her touch. Whatever the reason, she was uncharacteristically behind schedule and running late for work.

On the way to my car, I stopped short and noticed that her SUV looked like it was leaning. Upon closer inspection, I yelled, "J. You have a flat tire!"

She was just closing the front door and groaned, "Not today...I can't be late for this meeting." She glanced at her watch and declared, "I don't have time to wait for AAA..."

"I got you...this'll be my reciprocation for how well you screwed my brains out this morning. You were... mind blowing..." As usual, she left me wanting more. I asked, "Round 2 tonight?"

She tossed her stuff in the backseat. Got comfortable in the passenger seat. "I wanted to thank you for everything. You're my dream come true, Ronnie."

She saw me looking at her. Fantasizing. She put an immediate stop to my lascivious thoughts. "Round 2 we can do. Right now...I have to get to work. This Audi is supposed to be a sports car. You can't drive any faster? Let's go!"

We got to her job with no time to spare. "Thank you, babe. Remember, I won't be available until lunchtime. I love you." She blew me a kiss. Grabbed her stuff from the backseat. Hurried into the building.

A few minutes after I dropped her off, I was surprised

to hear her phone ringing. By the time I pulled to the side of the road, it was silent. Caller ID showed an unknown number. The phone rang again. Thinking it may have been Jenine, I answered. "J. You forgot..."

"Who the fuck...?! Where the fuck...?! Why the fuck...?! I'ma fuck...!"

After the fourth fuck, I hung up the phone. That woman was loud. Angry. She must have called the wrong number because she didn't call back.

I tossed her phone on the passenger seat. Pushed the button to lower the convertible and let the sun warm my skin. Turning back onto the road, I cranked up the volume and drove towards my job.

Listening to the radio, the segment focused on callers dishing the dirt about the worst thing they ever saw in a significant other's phone and vice versa. It was the usual. Dick pics. Pussy pics. Child porn. Unexpected hotel receipts. Paternity results. Cross dressing. On and on...

One caller shared too much information on the finer points of snooping. Sounded like she was a private eye. Or a woman that someone shouldn't try to cheat on. She brought up so many valid points. Nowadays, if you wanted to know the truth about someone, look through their phone. Take your time. Try to find hidden apps and photos. Dig deep into their text messages. In their emails, look in the drafts folder for messages that hadn't been sent.

The cell phone was like a window to the soul. Social media accounts. Bank statements. Credit card bills. Internet search history. So much information that could give useful insight into any malfeasance.

First, I thought about what Jenine would find if she went through my phone. Quickly concluded that it was clean. For the longest time, I didn't even use a passcode, until she lectured me about what could happen if I lost my phone. Blah. Blah. Blah.

I thought about the time I looked in her phone when I needed her mother's number. I was rushed. Saw the text message that raised some questions. Turned out that I was wrong about that rehab. If I had more time, would I have found something else?

Now, I had a grand opportunity. Part of me wanted her to realize that she left the phone and call me. Weirdly, I felt that would sway me not to look. When she didn't call... I pulled into my job's parking lot. Thought about the concerns of my mother and Marisa. Slowly, I punched in her passcode. The phone immediately opened to the text messages. I followed the path laid before me.

Through narrowing eyes, I looked through what felt like tens of thousands of text messages. I found that Kayla's number was listed under Rehab, with an upper-case R. The work contact for the substance abuse treatment facility was listed under rehab, with a lower-case r. One capitalized letter made a world of difference.

She and Kayla went to several appointments at the fertility clinic. Their marriage hadn't ended. She and Klark spent time at Kayla's apartment. Et-motherfucking-cetera. It felt like someone drop-kicked me in the chest. The air was being snuffed out of my lungs. I had a hard time breathing.

I refocused. Saw what looked to be more damning information. Although she and Kayla sold their condo and split the money, Kayla thanked her for always having her back. For three months, Jenine sent her weekly transfers of $350, which allowed her to pay the arrears and avoid getting evicted. Quick math told me that was twelve weeks. Too much of a coincidence. For the same amount of time, I had transferred $350 to Jenine.

Supposedly, she started a 529 plan for Klark. Thinking that I was helping to secure the financial and educational future of our son, I readily agreed. I hadn't felt the need to ask for proof that she made the deposits. I just sent the money. I was sure of two things: she was giving my money to Kayla and she was stealing from our son.

There was an app inside an app that contained hundreds – no thousands – of pictures. In seeing Kayla, my mouth dropped wide open. I shook my head in disbelief. It couldn't be possible. I remembered her as the woman who almost killed me the first night I left Jenine's house. Clearly, I recalled Jenine being more concerned about whether Kayla and I talked than my well-being. All this time she knew how close we came to meeting and didn't say anything.

The pictures showed them at the movies, day cruises and acting very much like the happy couple. How'd she gather the energy to do all of this? There were even times when Jenine went from my house straight to Kayla or vice versa. I had pictures with her in the same outfit.

Feeling like I saw a ghost, I looked at pics of Jenine and Diego. They were such good friends. What did he know? There weren't a lot of texts between them but I read through some of the last ones:

Diego's Text: You're still playing this game? I told you from the beginning that you were making a big mistake. If Ronnie finds out that may be the end of your relationship.

Jenine's Text: Don't do the I told you so routine. You think I don't know you were right? That I should've listened to you? I'm still figuring out some things.

Diego's Text: You sound stupid. What's there to figure out? You're like a fly stuck on Kayla's shit. Get it together. Even you trying to decide whose eggs to use was a fiasco. Kayla thinks y'all are back on the road to being a happy couple. If either of them knew the truth... You're screwing up BIG TIME.

Jenine's Text: I knowww. Maybe doesn't seem like it but I love her so damn much. I'm still thinking about how to handle some things.

Diego's Text: That's part of the issue. Who do you love so much?

Jenine's Text: You just need to have the last word, huh? I'll let you get that. My client is here. Ain't this some shit? I help people solve their problems. Can't handle my own. We'll catch up later.

Unfortunately, later would never come. One question was answered, though. At least Diego had my back. Too bad the woman that I once asked to marry me was twisting a knife in it.

Still stunned, I made my way to her Facebook page. Saw that it was private. Some of my buddies had mentioned sending her friend requests that went unanswered. Guess if she accepted, that would push her secret into the open. She was cunning. I was inane. No. Some things needed to be simply stated. Long ago, I graduated up to a doctorate in stupidity.

Although I still had more searching to do, it was time for my meeting. I dragged myself out of the car. Willed myself not to cry, while I sat stone-faced through the longest meeting of my life. Thankfully no one asked me any questions. My voice couldn't be trusted not to crack from the misery that I felt. It seemed like the foundation of our relationship had imploded.

*****

On autopilot, I went back to Jenine's house. Waited for AAA. She finally called my phone. I looked at the screen. Smirked. Repeatedly sent her to voicemail. Decided to let her wait and wonder.

I thought about the information that I found on her phone. How should I handle everything? What did this mean for us? Now wasn't the most ideal time for that talk but I couldn't wait forever. I called her back and asked, "Did you want something?"

"What took you so long to answer? Somehow, I left my phone at the house. I see it on the app on my iPad. Wanted to let you know, in case you needed to talk to me."

I wouldn't expose all my cards. "Hold on, Jenine." I muted the call.

The guy from AAA looked perplexed. Wanted my attention. "Miss. This tire can't be fixed. Looks like somebody slashed it. I'll tow you to the shop, so you can get a new one."

I wasn't sure that I heard him correctly. "What'd you say?"

He slowly repeated what he said the first time, as if there was something wrong with my hearing. When it rained, it poured and now, I was being inundated with bad news. "Okay. Fine. I'll meet you at the shop."

Focused back on her, I made the call as quick as possible. "I'm busy now. I'll get your tire fixed and text you the info. You'll have to get your SUV from the shop and pay for it, though. I can't do it. Gotta go."

"Babe, but..."

Before she could fully respond, I hung up the phone

on her. Klark was the only reason I took care of her SUV. Otherwise, I would've left her conniving ass stranded.

My mind had already been overflowing with questions and two more just got added: Who slashed her tire? Why would anyone do such a thing?

Afterwards, I retreated to the comfort of my home. For the extended weekend, I shut out the world. My heart felt like it had been splintered by a thunderbolt. Like I was chanting a war cry to stop the deluge of rain, I repeatedly tried to talk myself out of another breakdown. I yelled. Threw stuff. Cussed. A lot. Cried a river of tears. Punched walls. Slammed doors.

In my weakened state, I remembered a bottle of tequila that Jenine kept in one of my cabinets. I had more than a year of sobriety. Sitting in the shower, I held the tequila – tightly – with both hands. Rocked myself back and forth. Water cascaded down my body from the oversized showerhead. It seemed like nothing would stop me from inching closer and closer to jumping off the ledge and landing in the pit of a complete mental breakdown. Slowly, I opened the bottle and expectantly licked my lips.

*****

Event #3: My mom and Jenine shared an interest in genealogy. In working on the family tree, my mom definitively learned her background when she submitted her DNA to one of those ancestry sites. Prior to meeting me, Jenine had done the same thing. I remembered them talking about being surprised by some of the results.

Now that Diego was gone, my mom bought the same test for Klark. Supposedly it was top of the line. The advertisements said that it would reveal everything from health predisposition reports to trait reports to ancestry reports. She thought it would be beneficial to learn more about his background. More importantly, it might help him identify medical issues, especially considering Diego wouldn't be around.

I considered Diego being born in Brazil and its large diversity of backgrounds. For vacation, I spent three weeks down there. Saw a wide range of people with different skin tones and hair texture. Despite the vast differences in looks, they primarily spoke Portuguese and identified as Brazilian, even though their ancestors came, voluntarily or involuntarily, from many different parts of the world.

I had little curiosity about my ancestral background. My feelings for Klark were different. I wanted him to have as many answers, as possible. With that sentiment in mind, I ordered the same test for myself. Didn't give much consideration in notifying Jenine. I'd surprise her with the results. Thought about my grandparents being born in Mali. Maybe I'd learn that my lineage extended to the great Mansa Musa. That would be quite a story to tell. Especially since some folks regard him as one of the richest men of all-time.

When the kit arrived, Klark watched me swab my cheeks and clapped his hands. All he wanted to do was play. I made a game out of doing our swabs. He thought it was the funniest thing. Hoping that I followed the instructions correctly, I put him in the stroller. We made our way to the post office and mailed everything.

A couple of days after I emerged from my self-imposed exile, from when I found the damning trove of information on Jenine's phone, our ancestry/DNA results arrived in my email. Any hope of me not waging an all-out war was destroyed, when I read that there was no possible way he and I were genetically related. Surely, I was seeing wrong. Each time I read the results, it sparked a thirst for revenge that I thought had long been extinguished.

Immediately, I thought back to the text messages in Jenine's phone. The ones that mentioned going to the fertility clinic and OB/GYN with Kayla. Time and time again, Kayla referred to Klark as their son. Jenine didn't bother to correct her.

Even when Jenine and I were deciding on names, she was insistent on having an "unusual" spelling. I preferred Clark or even Clarc. She was steadfast on Klark. It didn't take long to convince myself that the spelling of his first name with a K was her furtive way to honor Kayla.

Most of her money from the sale of the condo went towards growing the business. She and her partners were already recouping their investment. She didn't need me for a financial lifeline. Still, I took it upon myself to pay for the fertility clinic.

Why would she allow me to be such an integral part of his life, if Kayla had the actual genetic relationship? How long did she think this secret could last? My mind was spinning. I became dizzy off the need for retaliation.

As Nana would say, "Don't try to keep nothing that ain't yours." No one seemed to understand. Despite this Harlequin-like drama, Jenine was interwoven through my entire existence. Without her, I somehow felt incomplete. I just had to find a way to keep her and Klark in my life.

Supposedly, there's a bright spot in every shadow. While my heart was growing darker by the millisecond, the thought taking root in my head caused me to perk up.

Masterminding my plan was the equivalent of gathering all the ingredients and then baking a cake. Undoubtedly, the infallible execution would be the icing on top.

I looked at myself in the mirror. Didn't care that like a stone tossed into a pond, the ripples of what I intended to do may extend endlessly. For the first time, in what felt like forever, I genuinely smiled, as I thought about how I was going to kill Kayla.

39: COMING TOGETHER? FALLING APART?

It felt like the stars were aligning. My partner and I made an unscheduled visit to pick up a probationer on a violation. He was a senior citizen, with a penchant for young boys and guns. When I reached for my handcuffs, he grabbed his chest and fell to the ground.

My partner and I thought he may have been bluffing, so we stood back. He looked eerily still. I got on my knees and shouted, "This dude ain't moving!" I checked for a pulse and felt sick to my stomach. "I think he's dead!"

While my partner called 911, I started CPR. After several minutes, I said, "My arms are tired. Let's switch. Maybe we can still save him."

As I began to stand, a glint of metal caught my eye. I looked a little closer. There was a handgun under the bed. Before making another move, I thought of his case file. He had a criminal history dating back several decades. I was pretty sure the gun wasn't registered to him. My partner still tried to save the old guy's life. He didn't see me take the tank top off the bed and wrap it around the gun.

The paramedics arrived just before the police. I opened the front door and kept walking to the car. Placed the gun inside my backpack for safekeeping. Because the probationer expired, I had to spend extra time giving a statement and completing my paperwork.

At my house, I went straight to the basement and put on several pairs of latex gloves. I spent hours taking apart the gun and cleaning it.

On the way to the gun shop, I discarded the bullets in different locations. I stopped by the store and bought a tin of cookies and continued to the gun shop to buy a box of bullets. Eschewing a paper trail, I paid for everything in cash.

Once back home, I donned new latex gloves, wiped down the cookie tin and loaded the gun. I wrapped it in a new T-shirt and put it inside the cookie tin. On the highest shelf, I placed the cookie tin next to the box that stored my volleyball keepsakes and more importantly, my secret and therapeutic journals. Step 1 was complete.

*****

The next step was getting another burner phone. I knew that Miss B took extended afternoon naps. Under the pretense of checking on her, I called. "Hi, Ms. B. Are you okay? Need groceries or anything?"

"Oh. Hi Ronnie. I'm okay. Jus' sitting here watchin' TV. It's almost time for my nap."

A few minutes later, I heard her heavy breathing. I didn't disconnect the call. Instead, I put the phone to the side and left the house. If anyone had a reason to check, my cell phone records would show that we talked for many minutes. The signal would show that the phone didn't leave my house. I had no worries if anyone asked Miss B for specifics about the call. It would be my word against that of an octogenarian, whose memory wasn't quite what it used to be.

I walked to the station. Took the train to Philadelphia. The cost of the tickets was paid in cash. Taking extra precaution, I wore sunglasses, a hat and a coat, which made me look much heavier. Looking at my reflection in the window, I was sure that even my mom wouldn't recognize me.

Once in the "City of Brotherly Love," I saw a woman standing on the corner. She asked, "Can I get a dollar?"

I switched to a faux West Indian accent. She understood that I wanted to know if she needed to make some extra money. She was streetwise and remarked, "I ain't wit' that freaky stuff."

Although I assured her that it was legal, she still looked askance at me. The offer of a $20 bill made her an easy convert. Her eyes widened and coruscated like 4th of July fireworks.

I stood across the street and waited. In she went to the store. A few minutes later, she emerged with a phone under the very common name of Jane Smith. I paid my debt and watched her run in one direction. I took the battery out of the phone and hurried to catch the train back to NJ. Step 2 was complete.

*****

When I was out and about, I saw a black Civic, with dark tinted windows, for sale. I looked over it thoroughly. Didn't see any readily identifying dents or scratches.

The next day, I went back and talked to the owner in "Portuguese." He had no clue that I was talking gibberish. The language of cash money crossed all barriers. He readily handed over the title and keys without asking to see my ID. The inspection sticker was valid for six more months. I wouldn't register the car but needed license plates.

Later that night, I stole plates off another black Civic. I

used black electrical tape and changed the F and L letters to look like an E. If I got pulled over, my hope was that my badge would cause the cop to give me the benefit of the doubt.

Now, I was better able to focus on my mission and put my "new" car to good use. Kayla worked overnight, which I thought would make her an easier target. I watched when she took a break around four o'clock in the morning and went outside to smoke a cigarette. Through binoculars, I watched her video chat with an older woman. A little after seven o'clock in the morning, she left work. Most days, she went straight home. Some days, she drove by Jenine's house, almost as if she was checking to see if she had company.

When not stalking Kayla, I walked as much of her commute as possible. I tried to locate vantage points, where I could set up a post and kill her. There were a couple of places that gave me a clear shot. Fortunately, for her, it wasn't that simple.

The reality was that most people simply went about their daily business. They paid little attention to the number of cameras that recorded our activities. I couldn't find a spot where it felt that I was truly out of sight from a camera that I could see. Add in the possibility of cameras that I couldn't see. Undoubtedly, I wanted revenge. More importantly, I didn't want to get caught. Remembering to go slow, I told myself to exercise more patience. There were other pieces that still had to be put into place. Step 3 was incomplete.

*****

On the burner phone, I searched for information on

how to buy a silencer. If done legally, I'd have to provide identification, which defeated the purpose of doing something in secret. Even some activity on the dark web was traceable. I was certain that a few guys on my caseload could get one. No way would I give them that kind of leverage over me. Step 4 was incomplete, too.

Reminding myself not to rush, I needed to give this a lot more thought. Right now, my master plan was seriously flawed. At this rate, I was only going to end up in jail. This wouldn't be as easy as I hoped.

40: UNSPOKEN AGREEMENT

Jenine called while I was at work. "Babe. You've been so preoccupied these last few weeks that we haven't seen each other," she complained. "You don't even have time for Klark. We want to spend more time with you."

I would give her exactly what she wanted. This time, it was for my benefit. Had to keep things status quo, so suspicions wouldn't be raised. Admittedly, I had another thought. One that fed my ego. If they were with me, they couldn't be with Kayla, so I said, "I've been busy...but my schedule is lighter now."

Later... She was waiting on the couch when I stepped through the front door. Didn't feel as though the AC was working. Like the stifling humidity on this hot summer night, the tension between us was so thick my shirt clung to my body.

"Why are you here?"

"Where have you been? It's late."

"I had a date. Answer my question."

As one perfectly shaped eyebrow arched to an impossible height, she asked, "A date? With who?"

She wasn't accustomed to me pushing back on her. With a cockiness that I didn't usually display, I shot back, "That's not your business. You lost that right when..."

My loose lips were close to torpedoing my ship. I refocused. Gave her a dose of her own bitter medicine and sarcastically asked, "Why so quiet? Are you jealous, Jenine? Doesn't feel good when the shoe is on the other foot, huh?"

An unfamiliar emotion etched its way onto every space of her still lovely face. It was the first time that I had seen her look genuinely fearful. She resembled a gazelle who stumbled onto a pride of lionesses. Her usual bravado vanished.

Maybe she thought of losing me. Her normally calm and sunny exterior changed. Quickly. She was frantic. Like someone in an unprepared midwestern state whose weather alerts malfunctioned and now a tornado was sweeping into town.

Had our roles reversed? Was I now in control? Dominant? Silently, I stared at her and wondered. Did I desire to be malicious towards her? Was she now submissive? Willing to do anything for me? To keep me?

She looked solemnly in my eyes. Evidently, she decided against asking more questions. Instead, she patted the couch for me to take a seat next to her. I didn't trust myself to sit too close. The temptation to pounce was too great. I sat on the other side of the room. As far away from her as I could get.

"Answer my question! What are you doing here?"

I could feel that our synergy was off. There was a distance and silence between us that was unnerving and uncommon, yet welcome.

Slowly, she rubbed her hands back and forth. Finally, she broke the impasse. "We both know more than the other thinks we know. Neither of us knows the entire truth."

"What?! I'm sooo not in the mood for more of your shit." A look of confusion covered my face. I felt my temperature rising. I was becoming angry. "Did you come here to tell me riddles?"

"No. This only works if we answer with complete honesty."

I was so surprised to hear her talk of honesty that now my eyebrows shot through the roof. "You? Complete honesty? That's funny. I'm pretty sure L-I-E is how you spell honesty."

A sarcastic smile formed on my lips. Before I decided whether to play her game, I asked, "Why now?"

Her response was cryptic, "Someone's going to get hurt. This is spiraling out of control. No more lies."

After everything, how couldn't I question her ability to be honest? The grimace on my face reflected the mosh pit of emotions that I felt in my heart. I needed to keep her and Klark close, for everything to work.

As if she knew that I'd agree, she pulled out the index cards and started to write. Before I had a chance to change my mind, I said, "Let's get this over with."

Jenine's 1st Question: Do you believe that I love you?

Ronnie's Answer: You've lied so much, I'm not sure.

Jenine's 2nd Question: Will you give me time to make it right?

Ronnie's Answer: You can't be serious. Everything can't be made right. You've already had so long, yet you still want more time. I don't know about any of this.

Jenine's 3rd Question: Answer the question. I know it's a lot. Please, if I can make things right, will you at least THINK about forgiving me? I can't imagine my life without you.

Ronnie's Answer: Am I being punked? Is this a joke? You should've thought about that when you did every possible thing to push me away. Forgive you? I don't know. Make things right? I'm not sure. You've done so much dirt. I honestly don't know, if I can do it.

I had way more than three questions. Unsure where to start, I paused and considered the heaviness of what I would ask. What her answers would mean. After much thought, I finally started to write.

Ronnie's 1st Question: Do you know the depths of my love for you?

Jenine's Answer: Yes. The intensity of your love is overpowering. You're not the one who should clean up this mess. I apologize a million times and still owe you a billion more. Please allow me to show you that I'm worthy.

Ronnie's 2nd Question: Why should I trust you, at all, especially now?

Jenine's Answer: Understandably, my word doesn't mean much to you. Please have a little, well a lot, more patience. I constantly tell you that I love you. Let me show you that my actions will back up my words.

Ronnie's 3rd Question: How much time?

Jenine's Answer: A max of two months. PLEASE stand down. Let me try to handle this situation.

Since Jenine handed me the first index card, we hadn't said one word to each other. Yet, we had come to this unspoken agreement. Unknowingly, she was doing me a favor. The two months would give me more time to patch the holes in my plan to kill Kayla. I took all the index cards, put them in the fireplace and set them on fire. There'd be no written evidence of our discussion. Just my word against hers.

We walked to the door. She tried to hold my hand. I wouldn't let her touch me. She turned to kiss me but I backed away. On the way out the door, she said, "I know the clock has started."

Dear Diary:

The greatest news in the world!!! I'm a mom, madre, mãe, mère... Whether you say it in English, Spanish, Portuguese or French, it means the same thing. I'm the mother of Klark Alexander Rhett. He's perfect. I give him everything that I have to give. If that's not enough, I'm willing to take from someone else.

Newsflash: Ronnie has been amazing and sees herself as his personal tutor. If I listen to her say the ABCs and 123s one more time, I'm going to scream. She wants him to learn, so I deal with it. I support him being as intelligent as possible. Him being adorable is a given. After all, I'm his momma. She's already buying him stocks and planning for his long-term future.

Kayla. Oh Kayla. What can I say? She tries. Prefers to waste whatever money she can scrounge up on Baby Jordan sneakers that he knows nothing about, could care less about and outgrows in a few weeks. Considering she used to work in finance, you'd think she'd be better with money.

My bundle of bliss has rapturous green eyes, just like Diego and me. A headful of curly hair. He'll be tall. Already, women fawn over him. It'll get worse, as he gets older, I'm sure. Ronnie swears that he looks like her. Kayla says the same. I keep my mouth shut and don't feed into either of them. They both love him unconditionally. I'm happiest about him being healthy and blowing past those pediatric milestones with ease.

*****

With the changing of the seasons, I received the most devastating and incomprehensible news. My Diego is gone. I'm shocked. Still trying to digest what I refused to accept as true. Unsure how to feel. What to do. Such a complete surprise. He was killed in Brazil. Cops don't have a clue. Probably not trying to get a clue.

Now, he'll never know the bundle of joy who shares his DNA. Klark won't have the benefit of such a great man being his mentor. I've lost my moral compass. The one who had no issue calling me on all my bullshit. Not just with Ronnie and Kayla. A man who supported me. The one who would've walked me down the aisle. He'll be sorely missed...

*****

Proof that time waits for no one, life continues to move forward. I want it to stop, just so I can catch my breath. Ronnie's mom bought a condo in Jersey. She spends more time out here than in Chicago.

I'm sure Ronnie didn't tell her about the failed marriage proposal or any of our other issues. If so, she may have come banging on my door. Her mother is super protective. Now that I have Klark, I have a better understanding of why she's not feeling me. Eventually, I'll need to bury the one-sided and well-deserved hatchet that she has towards me. For now, that'll have to wait. Other things demand my attention.

*****

Usually, I can read Ronnie like a book. She's so damn transparent. Not this time, though. It's like a few pages or a couple of chapters are missing. I'll just say that she's up to something. She knows a lot but not everything. Kind of like me. Whatever has her pissed off, I think she got the info from sneaking in my phone. If so, I'm not mad. Served me right. I should have been more careful. Nah. I just shouldn't have fucked up on a remarkable woman. I'm doing the same thing to her that Kayla did to me.

As a therapist, I've heard damn near every sob story and excuse known to humankind. I look at Ronnie and see the hurt in her eyes. It makes me sick to my stomach. I'm the one who put it there with every lie and partial truth that I've told.

Before she does something that can't be undone, it's beyond time that I got my shit together. I need to address the river of bad blood that runs between Ronnie and Kayla. I'm the reason behind it all.

There's a long way to go but Ronnie and I have an unspoken agreement. Maybe I watch too much Dateline NBC. I'm hesitant to write everything, in case anyone ever finds you. Let's just say that officially, in trying to right my many wrongs, I'm hastening the steps in my journey of what seems like one billion miles...

I thought about the happiest days of my life: graduating from college, marrying my beautiful wife, each time we made love and buying our condo. All of them combined didn't come close to the euphoric feeling when I first held our son, Klark Alexander Rhett, in my arms.

Sitting in the hospital room, I gave thanks to God for allowing him to be healthy. My wife was fast asleep but I gave silent thanks to her for allowing me to help create our angel. I held onto his tiny hands and thought about the outfits that I purchased. He would be the best-dressed baby. With his genes, I was sure that he would be tall and handsome, so maybe modeling was a possibility.

I still talked with Jenine about letting me move into her house. She still hadn't budged. Now that our baby was here, it would make things easier, especially since I wasn't keen on daycare. She was stubborn but I vowed to keep working on her.

*****

It seemed like good news was followed by bad news. My wife brought our son to my apartment. Reaching out to hold him, I said, "Hi handsome. You came to see your other mommy? I got you some new sneakers."

I couldn't help but notice how much he looked like me. While I played with our son, my wife was stone silent. She hadn't even said hello. Just sat on the couch and ran her fingers through her hair, a sure sign that she was stressed or mad.

I started to panic. There was no way she could have known about my lady friend who visited earlier. I was all set to defend myself and explain that I needed her to give me more intimacy. The other woman didn't mean anything.

Maybe she knew more about the reasons for my dwindling bank account than I told her. My family hadn't paid back the money I loaned them. Neither had my lady friend after I paid part of her son's tuition.

Still intent on getting back in the black, I placed a few more wagers and lost – again. Lady luck continued to elude me. Like a song playing on repeat, I was in the same pathetic position of relying on my wife to come to my rescue. I hoped she didn't come to tell me that I'd have to find my own way. When I saw crocodile tears falling from her eyes, I knew it wasn't because of me.

"Wifey, what's wrong?"

She extended her phone towards me. I held our son in one arm. Saw several Facebook posts about Diego being killed. The large turnout for his funeral. Other links hinted at a possible cover-up in the investigation of his killing.

How do I say this delicately? Fuck it. He and I detested each other. We almost came to blows the first time she caught me cheating. I appreciated him for helping to bring forth Klark. However, that was where my fondness for him started and ended. Honestly, I was kind of glad that he wouldn't be around to constantly tell her that she could do better than being with me.

Now. I've done many foolish things but I'm not a fool. I knew the depths of her feelings for him. Since I'm in a constant state of trying to get back on her good side, I bit my tongue and diplomatically said, "I'm sorry. I know you're hurting."

My wife needed time to work through Diego's death, so I didn't see her or our son, as often. Just as well. I had no desire to hear her wail about how much she missed him, their close friendship and things wouldn't ever be the same. Blah. Blah. Blah.

*****

While she mourned, I worked like a dog. Even with her help, I struggled to make ends meet. The overnight shift was taxing on my body. So many boxes, deliveries and packages. I headed straight for the exit, once my break started, so I could get some fresh air. Since the job did random urine screens, I couldn't smoke weed. Instead, I picked up the nasty habit of smoking cigarettes. I inhaled deeply and stared at the sky.

A chill went through my body that caused me to shudder. It felt like I was being watched. Cautiously, I looked around the expansive parking lot. It was the eeriest feeling. Even though I didn't see anyone, I snuffed out the cigarette and went back to the building. Better safe than sorry.

I made it through that shift. Under the guise of dropping off clothes for our son, I went by her house when I finished work. I just wanted to see them before they started their day. Coming down the long block, I thought I saw someone pulling out of her driveway in a convertible Audi.

Once I got to the house, I tried to make sense of what I thought I saw and rang the doorbell. She didn't answer. I peeked in the garage window but didn't see her SUV. Back at the front door, I called on the phone. "Wifey! Great morning. I'm at your house."

"What did I tell you about stopping by unannounced?"

"I needed to talk and drop off clothes for our son. I think somebody else was here, too. They had a sweet convertible Audi."

"Really? An Audi? Did you see who it was?"

"No. Where are you?"

"I got an early start. We can talk later."

Something didn't feel right. She sounded nervous. I stared at the phone. Replayed scenes in my head. Thought about many of our conversations. Suddenly, I had other questions. The issue was that I didn't trust my wife to give me truthful answers.

43: RIGHTING WRONGS

Week #1: Jenine and Klark spent that first night at my house. "Jenine, if you want extra blankets, I already put them in the other bedroom," I yelled.

She followed the sound of my voice. "Stop being so loud. You'll wake the baby." Looking at the blankets, she remarked, "You're serious!? And when did you start calling me Jenine?"

"You're lucky I'm not calling you out your name. I've thought about it. This is how it'll be. I moved your stuff from my bathroom to the other bathroom up here and your clothes are in there." I pointed to the closet. "If you don't like it? Take all your crap and take your ass home."

Even though I struggled to push down my anger, the tone of my voice was rising. I thought about Klark and tried not to talk too loud. "Know this...I don't want you in my bed. No worries about me trying to touch you. Don't even think about touching me. On everything I know and love...this isn't open for discussion."

In the time that we've known each other, I barely cussed at her. Unless we were fucking, there were only a few times when I could remember raising my voice at her. I tended to stew in silence. This was different.

She opened her mouth, as if to respond and promptly closed it. Correctly, she assessed my rigid posture and defiant stare. I dared her to challenge me. She knew better. Instead, she busied herself by unfolding a blanket.

That next morning, she and Klark were out of the

house before I even opened my eyes. On the kitchen counter, she left two keys and a note: "Mi casa es tu casa." So now I finally had keys to her house. Hmmm. It was a nice sign that she may be serious about making amends. She still had a lonnng way to go.

*****

Later that night, we ate dinner at her house. Klark was with my mom. By a force of habit, she stretched to put her legs near my lap, so I could massage her feet. My look of disdain stopped her cold in her tracks. My first instinct was to slap her feet away but I refrained. In case she didn't take me seriously, I quickly moved the chair and reminded her, "I told you don't touch me."

Out of the blue, I demanded, "Let me see the statements for the baby's 529 plan."

She had no time to prepare a smart-ass comeback or hide anything. What she did was equally surprising. She pushed her cell phone across the table and said, "It's the purple app at the top." She went back to eating her food, as if she didn't have a care in the world.

"Here. Unlock your phone." I pushed the phone back to her.

"No more lies. You know the passcode because you looked through my phone, right? Don't try to be cute." She pushed it back to me.

I hated when she was right, especially at my expense. I punched in the same passcode that started us down this rabbit hole.

Painstakingly, I scrutinized each line of Klark's college savings account. Saw that she had indeed started the 529 plan. There were my weekly deposits of $350 for three months. I even saw her bi-weekly deposits of $350. No money had been withdrawn.

I squinted. Kept looking at the statements, like I could magically make them change. Force them to show what I thought I knew to be true. Surely something was amiss with my eyesight. Could I have been wrong about the money?

She got up to take her plate to the farmhouse sink and suddenly sat back down. She recognized the shocked look on my face.

"Why are you suddenly so interested in seeing his account?"

I watched her normally luminescent green eyes narrow and become clouded with suspicion. She came to a realization and exclaimed, "You think I was taking your money?!"

I never realized how many times statements and questions were expressed at the same time. A part of me was incredulous that she had the hubris to ask why I had doubts. "Are? You? Kidding? Me? Don't ask me something so stupid. We're in this situation because of you!"

I pointed my finger inches from her face and gave a partial confession. "I read the text messages. You were giving Kayla $350 each week, right around the time that you asked me for the same amount of money. That was too coincidental. With what you've been doing, what was I supposed to think?"

For emphasis, I slapped the table with the palms of my hands. I gripped the sides of the table so hard that my fingers began to cramp.

Startled by the force that caused the table to shake, she jumped off the chair. I stalked towards her. She didn't entirely back away and asked, "So now you wanna hit me like..."

Her words caused me to stop mid-step. I was beyond angry but that hadn't crossed my mind. "Like what? Like who? Why would you think something like that? Finish what you were going to say."

"It's just that I've never seen you so mad. I didn't know what to think."

"Don't try to make any of this my fault."

She only showed remorse, as she offered, "I've done some foul stuff. How many times do you want me to say it? I'm sorry. Want me to beg on my knees? Put it on my email signature, so the whole world knows? Get a tattoo?"

I sulked back to the table. In the kitchen, the French doors were wide open. My eyes were drawn to the moonlight reflecting off the pool. I needed a distraction.

Now, her voice was barely above a whisper. "I'm sorry. Even I wouldn't steal from the baby. No more lies, right? Kayla tricked off her money from the condo. I loaned money to her family and never got paid back. No idea what she did with the rest of it. Not even six months later, all the bills were overdue...told me that she was going to be evicted. Needed help. It was my money that I gave her. Not yours. Definitely not Klark's."

"You got me all the way fucked up. Are you expecting me to feel sorry for you? For her? You want pity from me?"

I answered my own questions. "Don't hold your breath. There's no way you should've been helping her sorry ass."

I sighed heavily in disbelief. My suspicions had grown into a malignant tumor. Thought that I had all the facts.

Instead, I only had fragments of incorrect assumptions. I wasn't totally right about the 529 plan. Still, she shouldn't hold her breath waiting for me to apologize.

Since we were talking about money, I had one other major card to play. "When are you paying me back for the fertility clinic?"

She pushed away from the table, folded her arms across her chest and looked at me like I had officially lost my mind. "You're on one today, huh? Why do you want that money back?"

"Because I know the truth," I hissed.

Hurriedly, I logged onto my email. Pushed the laptop in front of her. Saved her the trouble of trying to think of a lie. Watched her eyes slowly register that I was showing her an email from the ancestry/DNA site.

I couldn't help myself and accusingly told her, "Mighty coincidental that Klark and Kayla's name both start with a K."

Distracted by the email, she whispered, "No, you're wrong. I liked his initials better as K.A.R., instead of C.A.R. It had nothing to do with her."

I watched her click on the attachment. Read the results. Blink quickly like she was trying to adjust her vision. Read them again. She pushed the laptop to the center of the table and asked, "How could you? Why'd you get him tested without telling me?"

"There are much better questions. Why do those results say there's no connection between Klark and me? Did you really think I wouldn't find out?"

She was so still, I wondered if she was breathing. She stared downward, as if the answer would magically appear from the high-grade marble flooring.

"Answer me!" I threw one of the kitchen chairs clear

across the room.

The chair breaking into pieces jarred her back to reality. She blinked rapidly. Like someone trying to summon strength or courage, she glanced over my shoulder. Didn't find the answer. Stared at the ceiling. Wherever she cast her eyes, the answer remained elusive. She looked everywhere except at me and meekly offered, "Ronnie, I... I don't know what to say. I'm sorry..."

I cut her off mid-sentence and screamed, "Save it! The only things you know how to do are lie and give empty apologies. Show me through your actions. Words don't mean shit, especially coming from you. I want all my damn money back."

With shaking hands, she showed me several months of bank statements, "I'm still rebuilding my savings from when I helped my mother and made other investments in the business. I can give you, like, 5 today. Can we do a payment plan? You can charge me interest." She blew out a long puff of air and said, "If you want it all now, I'll have to dip into my 401k or sell some stocks. My liquid money is low."

My response was instantaneous. "One. Lump. Sum."

I was intent on being a bitch. She fought back tears. Again, she opened her mouth but said nothing. She ran all her fingers through her hair. With silent satisfaction, I saw the stress on her face.

On speakerphone, she called her financial advisor. In a professional manner that belied our earlier argument, she said, "Hi, Eva. This is Jenine Rhett."

"Hi, Ms. Rhett. It's late but still a pleasure to hear from you. How are you? How's the baby?"

"Klark is fine. Thank you. I've been much better. That's why I'm calling. I need to withdraw 40 thousand from my 401k."

"Are you sure that's what you want to do? There will be major tax implications. As your..."

Even though Eva was looking out for Jenine's financial interest, she quickly interrupted.   "I know...this is important. I'll deal with the penalties. This must be done, ASAP!"

"For your protection, I need to complete the two-factor authentication. This is such an unusual request for your account. What's the code that should've just been sent to your phone?"

"061716."

"Okay.   Second question: What is your spouse's nickname?"

She looked at me and mouthed, "I love you."

In response to the question, she answered, "Ronnie."

Apparently satisfied with the answers, Eva responded, "Okay, I emailed everything and will work on this right away."

While she completed the paperwork, she sneakily looked at me. Maybe she thought I'd change my mind. I ignored her. Busied myself by swimming several furious laps in her pool. I had to burn off my anger.

Purposefully, I tracked water into the kitchen. Gave her another mess to clean up.   Well aware of my intent, she cut her eyes at me but kept quiet. Instead of responding to my childish action, she said, "They're gonna murder me in fees."

She moved to touch my hands. I recoiled like she had leprosy.

"Not my problem. I bet you wish you didn't give Kayla that money. How is she handling the breakup?"

She groaned, "Not well. She slashed my tire. I'll figure

out how to handle it. She's been making more threats."

44: STILL UNCERTAIN

Weeks #2 & #3: I spent several nights, with Jenine and Klark, at her house. She asked, "Why aren't you using the keys?"

"Not interested. This isn't a magic act where you snap your fingers and the rabbit disappears. You still have a lot of work to do."

"Fine. Have it your way. I have so much making up to do."

With fierce determination in her eyes, she looked at me and assured, "We're going to be okay."

She said it as a statement. To me it was a question. I wasn't sure what would happen with us. Even with the extra time, I still hadn't come up with a better plan to eliminate Kayla that didn't involve me going to jail.

We headed upstairs to get ready for the night. Jenine told me, "You can sleep in my bedroom. I'll sleep in Klark's room."

At least she finally understood that I didn't want her to touch me. She still didn't fully comprehend the magnitude of my feelings. "That's not gonna happen. All that fuckin' y'all did on that bed. I'll sleep in the baby's room."

The next day... I saw her bed was put to the curb and a new bed was in its place. Again, I asked, "How's Kayla handling everything?"

She didn't go into details but said, "She's been calling and coming by my job. Intent on causing a scene."

As if trying to change the subject, she questioned, "Did you see the new bed?"

"Yup. Whoop dee do. We have much bigger issues than a bed. What do you do when she comes by the job?"

"We talk. She calms down. Then I get a flurry of texts and calls. It's like she's manic. For so long, it was just her and me. She didn't have to vie for my attention. Now, I have the baby and you, my babe."

I rolled my eyes long and hard. "And you say that I'm corny?"

I shook my head at the pitiful attempt to lighten the moment and her handling of the situation. "That's not the right way to deal with it. All you're doing is pouring gas on an already out-of-control fire. You can't reason with someone like that. Aren't you supposed to know that? Don't you have four college degrees?"

"You don't know her like I do."

"I'm beginning to think you don't know shit. You're protecting a troll who's given no regard to you or Klark. Why the hell do people pay you, Ms. LCSW and LMFT?"

She opened her mouth. Maybe to defend herself. Maybe to apologize. Maybe to confirm that I was right. Undoubtedly, she saw the world of hurt in my eyes. I motioned for her to be quiet and yelled, "Maybe WE don't know each other as well as I thought!"

*****

Week #4: Jenine sent me a text message. Asked if we could get together for lunch. Once upon a time, that was code for us to meet for mind-blowing sex. However, I had put her on pussy punishment, so she obviously had something else in mind.

She picked me up. More than a little curious, I asked, "Where are we going?"

She shyly smiled and said, "You'll see."

Not long ago, that look would have dissolved all my stress. Now, I was just irritated. I put on my headphones and reclined the seat. My not-so-subtle clues that I wasn't interested in talking.

We arrived at the courthouse. My aggravation increased. The workers weren't known for quick or courteous customer service. More than two hours after we arrived, we finally made our way to the front of the line. The clerk told her, "I got your stuff right here."

Jenine pointed to me and said, "Give it to her."

Directly from the clerk, I was given a certified copy, which showed that the marriage with Kayla was officially dissolved. Because I couldn't help myself and still waited for a slip-up, I asked, "Are these papers authentic?"

Of course, the clerk thought that was a stupid question. She frowned, raised her finger and looked like she wanted to tell me about myself. Regaining her professional composure, she pointed to the raised seal and judge's signature. She then not so kindly told me, "If you don't have no more questions, move to the side. You're holding up the line, lady."

Back in the SUV, I watched Jenine pull out a phone that I hadn't seen her use. She deleted all pictures of her and Kayla on the phone, social media and in the cloud.

"You know I'm not the most tech savvy-person. I see all that you're doing but what about the pics on Kayla's phone and her accounts?"

Simply, she said, "This was Kayla's phone and those were her accounts."

"Why do you have her phone?"

"I bought it, so I took it back. Reclaiming my property."

I eyed her skeptically. She quickly added, "That's the truth."

Back at my job, she stomped on phone and threw it in the garbage. I was still focused on how Kayla was dealing with the breakup. "Has she been giving you any more pushback?"

She massaged her temples. "You have no idea. My neighbors tell me they've seen her driving up and down the street. She shows up at crazy hours and rings the bell. I tell her to go home and make threats to call the cops. That's how I got her phone. She should know better than to try and intimidate me."

As if issuing a warning, she exclaimed, "People get fooled by my femininity. They don't know that I will fuck somebody up."

45: CLAP BACK

Weeks #5 & #6: Everything started with a bang. Well, several bangs that seemed to echo unremittingly. Although no one would ever consider me to be a psychic, I had a feeling things with Kayla were going to escalate. Something worse was bound to happen.

Klark spent the night with my mom. Jenine spent the night with me, even though she was still relegated to sleeping in one of the guest bedrooms. Around one o'clock in the morning, the sounds of glass breaking and car alarms blaring roused me from a deep sleep. I put on my robe and woke Jenine. Somehow, she slept through the noise.

The unmistakable smell of gasoline saturated the air. Jenine's SUV was surrounded by flames that seemed to grow each second. I rushed back in the house. By the time I returned outside, I could do little more than let loose a guttural scream. In frustration, I threw the fire extinguisher into the expanding inferno.

My coveted convertible didn't escape unscathed. All its windows were busted. The ragtop was so shredded, it looked like Freddy Kruger's handiwork. There was spray paint from the front bumper to the back bumper.

For the outrageously high property taxes that I paid, at least the cops and fire department responded quickly. It seemed like everyone who lived on the block had a front-row seat to the show. I didn't know what upset me more; the violation of my personal property or the embarrassment of having cops at the spectacle in front of my house. I was incensed.

A couple of neighbors emailed the video from their security cameras. It didn't matter that the license plate wasn't clearly visible. All Jenine and I needed to see was the black Civic with dark tinted windows.

After viewing the footage, something had to be done. "How does Kayla know where I live? Since you're still working on things but not handling anything, I'll take care of it."

"She probably followed me. I didn't tell her anything about you."

She saw that I changed from pajamas to sweats. Had some idea this may not turn out good. "Where are you going?" She hurried down the stairs and yelled, "Ronnie, stop! You said that you'd give me more time."

I grabbed my work gun, tossed it in my backpack and said, "Yeah, well, just like you, I guess that makes me a liar, too."

I had spent enough time allowing her to distract me from my mission. I wouldn't permit myself to continue being derailed. In what felt like a race, I was the first one to reach the front door.

Kayla may have vandalized my precious Audi but I had the Civic, which was parked a few blocks from my house. I still didn't have valid license plates or other paperwork. I forgot about my pledge to be careful and avoid going to jail. She may have landed the first punch. I was preparing to launch a grenade. It was time to confront her face to face.

Caution was tossed to the wind. I drove like a maniac to her apartment building. Fueled by adrenaline and unbridled rage, I was becoming more and more dangerous. Just like Kayla. Maybe we had more in common than people thinking we looked like each other and our life-threatening fixation with Jenine.

Unlike my prior visits, the neighborhood was eerily quiet. I banged on her door and yelled, "Kayla! Open the door!" Waited. Banged again. Kicked the door. Yelled louder, "Kayla! Open the damn door!" I listened intently. Didn't hear any noise coming from her apartment. Even if someone was in there, they obviously didn't want to deal with me.

I returned to the front of her building and waited. She didn't have the nerve to show her face. Before deciding to head home, I went by her job. Maybe it was the maniacal look in my eyes. No one would give me any information about her.

In the parking lot, I called her from the burner phone. Almost like she was waiting for my call, she answered on the first ring. "You're only keeping her warm for me. Those papers are irrelevant. Same thing with deleting all my pictures. She's deep in her feelings, right now. We'll start over again. I'm going to get both of my babies back. Her and Klark."

Hearing her say Klark's name was like a punch to the gut. "You're a bitch. No need to creep and fuck up my shit. I went to your spot and your job. Now you wanna hide? You running from me? Pick the place. I'll be there. I'm gonna drag you through the street. Beat the life out of you. You're not even worth the bullet that I was going to put in you..."

She warned, "This is about my wife and me and our son. I was taking it easy on you. Don't make me come for you, too. Stay in your place, little girl." She hung up the phone. Each time I called back, she banged me to voicemail.

*****

Several days thereafter were a combination of broken windows at Jenine's house and harassing phone calls to her. My doubts about her ability to handle everything only increased. I was done exercising patience. Each day, I went to Kayla's building but couldn't find her.

The third time I went by her job, the manager told me that she didn't work there. I don't even know if that was the truth. Maybe she was just tired of seeing my face.

Any other calls that I made to her went straight to voicemail. Thought she only blocked the burner phone. The same thing happened when I called from another number.

Since she was so adept at hiding, I had a security system installed. I needed video and audio evidence. Felt like it was inevitable that she'd cause more havoc.

While I remained focused on finding Kayla, Jenine remained the focus of Kayla. We were chatting on video, while she rocked Klark to sleep. "Hold on Ronnie. I think I hear something."

BOOM! There was a thunderous noise. I watched in horror when Kayla burst into his bedroom. I listened, as Jenine yelled, "What the...? How'd you...? Get the..."

"I wanna see my son. If not, I'll fuck you up..." Kayla grabbed for Klark.

Jenine turned to shield him. "He's...I told you...I'm... cops...Kayla...crazy...."

"You wanna divorce me...won't help me no more. Keep tryin' me..."

With a swing that would have made the greatest

baseball player proud, Kayla whacked Jenine across the back with a bat.

"Ahhh, damnnn.   Ohhh.   My Goddd...," Jenine screamed.

Kayla hit her so hard that it caused Jenine to drop Klark. Time was suspended, as I watched him, thankfully, fall into the crib. Jenine crumpled to the floor. Like a lioness circling its prey, Kayla pounced. She repeatedly punched Jenine about her body. Louder and louder, Jenine yelled, "Stop! Get...off...me."

An hour away and feeling helpless, I offered what I could. "Kayla. I'm calling the cops! Hope they get to you before I do. I'm going to kill you!"

On the house phone, I called 911. Kayla stood over Jenine. I had a hard time determining who made the most noise: Was it Jenine each time Kayla kicked her? Maybe it was Klark screaming from being dropped into the crib. Sensing that his mother was in danger. Could it have been me when I repeatedly threatened to end Kayla's life?

Nope. None of the above. I decided it was Kayla, who looked frantically between Jenine and me and yelled, "This is not over!"

By the time I arrived, Kayla was nowhere to be found. Two police officers had a long list of questions. I could only tell them the horror that I witnessed.

Jenine refused medical attention but she was granted a temporary restraining order.

Mercifully, Klark was unharmed. He was wide awake. At his age, the incident was already forgotten. He just wanted me to play with him.

I tried to offer some comfort, "Listen, maybe you and the baby should stay with me. At least I have my gun...if she comes back..."

"Fine. We can all stay here tonight. It's already late. Even she's not stupid enough to come back. The cops said that they'd do spot checks to make sure everything was okay."

I shook my head and asked, "Why do you keep giving her the benefit of the doubt? Hasn't she shown that she's unpredictable? Who knows what she'll do next?"

That night, my adrenaline was off the charts. Kayla had shown herself to be unstable. Like a centurion, I wore out a path pacing from the front door to the back door. Only when the sun started to rise did I get some rest and close my eyes.

*****

Days later, Kayla was arrested and served with a temporary restraining order. She was released the same day. Per the order, she wasn't to have any contact with Jenine or Klark. The next court date would be in three weeks.

At my house, Jenine complained, "My body is still so sore! Every little movement hurts like hell."

She tended to her bruises. Klark and I played with a train. I made the obligatory "choo" sounds. He laughed non-stop.

Although I was physically present, my mind was in another dimension. I tried to recall a conversation with Jenine's mother. As a victim of domestic violence, she wanted her daughter to be able to protect herself. I looked at her with ice packs all over her body and thought to myself... For someone with a brown belt in karate, she certainly got her ass whooped.

*****

Week #7:   All things considered, this week was relatively uneventful. Day after day, Jenine carried Klark through my front door. I took him from her arms.

"This is what we should have every day. Us coming home to you. Me cooking. You cleaning. A family."

"Save that bull..." I looked at Klark and remembered my declaration not to cuss around him. "Save that stuff. I just about offered that the first day we met. You were stuck on some chick that can't take care of herself. She's on a mission to make you and everybody else as miserable as she is. You..."

"Almost every day, you find a way to not let me forget that I fuh..."

I knew the profane word that dangled from her lips and scowled at her.

"...you won't let me forget that I screwed up." Softly, she asked, "Maybe one day you won't throw it in my face? Please?"

"We're not doing this tonight. I'm going for a walk." I opened the front door. Klark wailed.

"Oh no. Take him with you. Otherwise, he'll cry until you get back."

While she went into the kitchen and started dinner, Klark and I ventured outdoors. After dinner, I cleaned the kitchen and noticed her phone on the table. She had disabled the auto-lock feature.

I heard them in the bathroom. She sang a song to him, while he splashed water. I could have easily looked through her phone. What would I find? Maybe she and Kayla were still in contact. Was she lying about trying to handle everything? In less than two weeks, things would be settled, one way or the other, even though I still tirelessly searched – in vain – for Kayla. I turned off the kitchen light and went upstairs.

Jenine stood in my doorway. "Babe, I love you."

If she expected a drawn-out conversation, I was only in the mood for rhyming monosyllabic responses. "Right. Night. Night."

When she turned to head back to Klark's room, my eyes scanned her from head to toe. After all, I was human and she was fine. Made me remember one of the reasons I hadn't severed all ties. The pajamas now fit more like spandex. She complained about her body changing after the pregnancy. I was cool with the extra weight because it all settled nicely in her derriere.

In trying to lessen the throbbing desire, I put a pillow between my legs. Even though I cut off sex with her, my hormones vehemently rejected the message. Tonight would be another long and lonely night.

46: SHOW AND PROVE

Jenine had seven days left to show and prove.

Day #1: She called me in a tizzy. "Babe. I...uh...if..."

"I don't understand your gibberish. Breathe slowly and talk to me."

"...if anything happens to me...please take care of Klark. I just sent you a bunch of screenshots."

Confidently, I stated, "Nothing will..." I stopped mid-sentence.

She sent me pictures of Kayla holding a gun and pointing it at Jenine's picture. With urgency, I screamed, "Call the cops! Now! This is...violation of order...arrest...Kayla..." My own nonsensical jumble of words poured out of my mouth.

Hours later, Jenine gave me an update. "I made the report. Detective Moore told me they're looking for her. He'll call every few hours to check on me."

I watched her pace back and forth, while running her hands through her hair. That usually meant she was nervous. Now, I wondered if she felt something else. Absolute fear.

Although there was unsettled business between us, I wanted to protect her and Klark. "We can't take any chances. She knows where we live. I'm not bringing my mom into this and I'm not going to a safe house. We can do a hotel..."

"I can't even think straight. Whatever you say. I thought everything would be handled by now. Never thought it would get to this point…"

*****

Day # 2: "I did what you said and told the security people at my job's building a little about this situation. Even gave them a pic of her. Just got a call that she was here. She was making threats and trying to get upstairs to our floor. She left before the cops arrived. It's the same stuff. I make a report. She can find me. They can't find her. This is stressful."

"Don't act like you're in this alone. I've been looking for her, too. Even called in some favors…"

"Ronnie. Let the cops do their job. If something happened to you…because of me…I couldn't live with myself. Please. Promise me you'll stop looking for her."

"No. You stop talking like someone with no sense. A promise is a comfort to a fool. That's why I don't bother to make them or ask for them. Don't ever forget…this is all your fault. When I find her…"

Before I said something regrettable. Something that could be used against me in court, I hung up the phone on her.

*****

Still intent on locating Kayla, I went back to her apartment. Maybe I could put all of us out of our misery. Just like my other visits, no one answered her door. She was a fast-moving target. Despite my best efforts, I continually missed, in trying to find her.

As I walked away from her building, I heard yelling, "Police! Freeze! Kayla Denegan. Get on the ground!

Now!"

Excitedly, I turned to look for Kayla. To my surprise, the cops were running toward me with their guns drawn. Not wanting to be the next reason for a Black Lives Matter march, I raised my hands, got on my knees and yelled, "I'm not Kayla! I'm law enforcement, too! You're looking right at my badge, asshole. My gun is on my hip. My work ID is around my neck! Call Detective Moore!"

While I tried to be as still as possible, one cop kept her gun trained on me. The other ripped the lanyard from my neck. Stared at my badge. Repeatedly looked back and forth between my ID and me. Still not satisfied, he called Detective Moore for additional confirmation.

Apparently, he received the necessary information. Helped me to my feet and said, "Damn. We're sorry, Officer Glyce. Detective Moore said y'all resembled each other. Why are you here?"

I snatched my badge and ID. Coolly, I said, "First you damn near give me a heart attack. Then you insult me. That bitch don't look nothing like me. For the record, I just happened to be in the area. Supposedly this is still a free country."

Unbelievingly, they looked at each other. The woman cop offered, "Again. Our apologies. We got this, Officer Glyce. Maybe you should leave and not come back to the area."

I thought the better of arguing. Their point was made. Hopefully, I made mine, too.

While I walked back to my car, I looked at my surroundings. Kayla was like a chameleon. For all I knew, she was probably in a bush and watched everything unfold. I scanned the area and my body shook. Uneasiness, the size of a boulder, settled in my stomach.

I took the long way back to the hotel. Had to make sure no one followed me. My emotions were a roller coaster. Staring down the barrel of a gun was no joke. There was no need for Jenine to know about this incident. It just made me more determined to handle Kayla on my own.

*****

Day #3: For hours, I had been in my office. The space was smaller than a prison cell. With outstretched arms, I could touch the opposite walls with my fingertips. Even though it was voluntary, I still felt confined. Didn't matter whether the small window was open or closed.

Today, I couldn't focus. My mind was elsewhere. So far, all I'd done was stare at the walls. The papers in my "to do" pile far outnumbered those in my empty "finished" pile.

Whenever the phone rang, my heart dropped. This time, I was expecting the worst, as I answered the call from a blocked number.

Tersely, I said, "Talk."

"Uh, hi, Ms. Glyce. This is Klark's daycare. I haven't..."

Like I had been electrocuted, I jumped out of my seat.

"What hap...? Is he...? No..."

"Please...stop yelling. I can't...reach his mom. You're...emergency contact. Someone just..."

"Tell me he's...he's oh...okay." I choked back tears and felt my entire heart constrict.

"He's...one second..."

I heard voices in the background and something about an ambulance. It felt like a year passed until she got back on the line and announced, "He's fine."

The tears of joy that longed to fall were in a holding

pattern, as she continued, "I can't get in contact with his mother. Wanted to let someone know that a woman called about him today. She knew the old secret password but not the new one. We didn't give her any info."

"Listen to me. Under no circumstance is Klark Alexander Rhett to leave that daycare with anyone other than Jenine or me. Not even my mom. Do I make myself clear? I'm on my way to get him, right now."

I bolted from work and called Jenine. She answered and sounded jubilant. "Hi babe. What's up?"

"Why didn't you answer when the daycare called? Why do you sound so happy?"

"I had a session. My phone was off. I just turned it on and you called."

"What sense does it make to turn off your phone? Especially with everything that's going on? Are you even thinking, right now?" I stopped short of cussing her out and shared the news from the daycare.

Now, I heard the stress in her voice. She stated the obvious, "This is a nightmare. He can't go back there. I'll take off...rearrange appointments...maybe go see my mother. I feel like nowhere is safe."

"I'm going to pick him up now. Going to your mother's house may not be a bad idea. We'll talk later."

*****

Day #4: "Jenine! Wake up! Get up!" This woman could sleep through anything. I had been trying to wake her for several minutes.

"Why...you...yelling? What time..." She glanced at the clock. Checked to make sure Klark was okay and was adjusting her pillow, so she could go back to sleep.

"It's Detective Moore..."

Before her head hit the pillow, her eyes brightened. Now, I had her undivided attention. I put the call on speaker. Shoved the phone towards her face.

"Hi ladies. Sorry to call at this hour. Wanted to finally give you some good news. We apprehended Kayla Denegan. I don't know how long we'll be able to hold her – bail reform and all – but she's in our custody for now."

"What do you mean? With everything that she's done, she still might get out? That sounds crazy."

While Jenine tried to make sense of the good news followed by the unfathomable, I was more level-headed and asked, "Today's the court date for the final restraining order. She'll at least be there for that, right?"

Detective Moore assuredly said, "I'll make sure of it."

Despite his guarantee, we were at a loss for words. Silence filled the air. We simply stared at each other. The worry in her eyes were reflected in mine.

*****

Later that day... There was a small sense of satisfaction seeing Kayla in jail garb. Jenine and I watched the proceedings via video. The judge didn't think it was safe for them to be in the same room, even with Kayla in handcuffs and surrounded by sheriff's officers.

Lots of legal mumbo jumbo was discussed. Pictures of Jenine's injuries were reviewed by the judge. She had dark bruises on her back and chest from being kicked. Scratches on her face. A swollen eye.

In response to the judge's question, Jenine stated her case, "Your Honor, I fear for my life, my child's life and the life of Ronnie Glyce. I implore the court to take all of Ms. Denegan's threats and actions seriously. Please issue the final restraining order. To not do so would be criminal and unduly place our safety at risk."

Just like Jenine was allowed to state her opinion, unfortunately, Kayla was permitted to do the same. "Jenine. I know you can see me. I forgive you for putting me here. Making me go through this. Take some time to get your mind right. We can go back to square one and start all over again."

Jenine held her head in her hands. She anxiously awaited the judge's decision. After a short recess, the judge spoke her peace, "The final restraining order is granted. There shall be no contact between Ms. Denegan and Ms. Rhett... As is the case in these situations, I'm ordering mandatory and immediate DNA testing, as well. The matter is adjourned until two months from today. That should give ample time to sort out everything."

I was confused about the judgment. My attention was diverted back to the monitor. The judge repeatedly banged her gavel and yelled, "Stop her! Oh nooo..."

The sheriff's officer was too slow. Handcuffs and all, Kayla took what looked like a penknife from under her shirt. She stabbed herself on the chest and neck. It looked like a slasher scene from a B-rated movie. EMS responded. It was eventually determined that she needed a psychiatric evaluation. She would be involuntarily committed for a minimum of 72 hours.

"Babe. We'll get Klark. Come back. Do the swabs. Settle everything at the hotel and finally have some peace." She smiled. Genuinely. For the first time in almost a week.

*****

Day #5: For the third time, I listened to my mom's voicemail, "Hey Ronnie. Checking on you. Jenine and I are meeting for lunch and some shopping. Then we're going to get manicures and pedicures. I'll call you a little later."

I sat in stunned silence. My mom struggled to be cordial to Jenine. Her ice-cold feelings had barely thawed. As I listened to the message, again, it felt like a peace agreement had been brokered between two countries that were once on the precipice of war.

Why were they suddenly going to hang out? I didn't give it much more thought. That just meant I had my house all to myself for a little while longer. I binged on chocolate covered coffee ice cream with marshmallows and episodes of HGTV.

For a moment, I was almost giddy. It didn't last long. My home phone rang with a call from a blocked number. There was heavy breathing. I knew the culprit. In case she escaped from the psychiatric ward, I grabbed my gun and went to my front porch. Maybe we could finally face each other. Exasperated, I said, "You know where to find me. I'm not running from you. Come see me, so I can kill you."

She laughed and warned, "Be careful what you ask for Ronnie."

The line disconnected before I could respond. In frustration, I slammed the phone on the ground and didn't bother to pick up the shattered pieces.

47: OTHER PLANS

Day #6: After a long day at work, all I wanted to do was unwind. I turned the corner onto my block. Saw cars parked up and down the street. Jenine's SUV was in my driveway. So much for my night of relaxation. Trying to find the positive, at least I would get a delightful home-cooked meal.

I flicked on the light switch and damn near reached for my gun. A chorus of voices yelled, "Surprise."

My eyes darted around the house full of people that I didn't invite. Some of them I didn't even know. Because I am who I am, I looked at everyone's feet. Whoever planned this get-together made sure my unexpected guests took off their shoes and gave them socks, so they didn't track dirt onto my pristine bamboo floors.

Jenine's mother held Klark. As soon as he laid eyes on me, he fussed and extended his chubby arms. I scooped him into my arms and made my way around the house.

Abashedly, I went to Gisele. Surprisingly, her wheelchair had been replaced by a cane. My eyes apologized for being such a horrible friend. Her infectious smile and warm embrace told me that no apology was needed.

Marisa stood next to Gisele and folded her arms across her chest. She was one of the few women I knew whose breasts were smaller than mine. Simultaneously, we looked at each other and asked, "Why the hell were you ignoring me?"

I responded first. "Bitch. Don't be cute. You ignored the bat signal but show for this?" I motioned my hand around the room. "I don't even know what this is..."

She interrupted, "Don't even try it. First, I lost my phone but I called you, too. You've never set up your voicemail. You know we emailed for the first few weeks but you just suddenly stopped. Thought you were mad all over again about what I said in Phuket..."

We were intent on proving the other was wrong and reached for our cell phones. She showed me several emails that were sent to me. I admitted, "Marisa, I didn't get any of them."

Impatiently, she grabbed my phone, tapped on the screen and scrolled for several seconds. After taking a deep breath, she shoved the phone in my face. Incredulously, she stared at me and slowly shook her head. "You still don't remember to check your junk folder?"

I couldn't do anything but laugh and shrug my shoulders. "Guess I owe you an apology."

"You're ridiculous. We have a lot of catching up to do." She smiled at Gisele but whispered to me, "Think I may start spending more time in Jersey. Go and be sociable."

Just like that, I was summarily dismissed. Surprisingly, Klark reached for her. Awkwardly, she held him, while I greeted the rest of my visitors. His baby senses knew she was a good woman.

My eyes landed on my mom and bugged out of my head. Was I was hallucinating? It looked like Aunt D was cordially standing next to her. They weren't trying to scratch out each other's eyes. Hell must have officially frozen over. Not all politicians were liars. UFOs existed. The impossible was now reality.

Aunt D wrapped me in a suffocating hug. "Ronnie, I owe you so much. I know you saved me from going to jail. Your mom was out for blood, rightfully so. Thank you."

She didn't know the half. No need to share how hard I worked on convincing my mom to tell the prosecutor that she didn't want to press charges. After a lot of hesitation, especially considering the amount of money, the prosecutor agreed.

"You and my mom have a lot of making up to do. At least y'all have taken the first step. Nana's dancing in heaven."

Now, I had some words for her twin. "Hey traitor. You rocking with Team Jenine, now? Which one of you is responsible for this shindig?"

She removed my arm from her shoulder and said, "I plead the Fifth." I watched her hurry to the kitchen. My guess was that she wanted to get as far away from me as possible.

Since my mom wouldn't confirm her involvement, Jenine was the next best choice for the organizer of this event. There was no sign of her. I worked the room. Chatted with her coworkers. Sorors. Sistah friends. Did the same with a few of my coworkers. Several of my sorors and even Miss B.

It wasn't my birthday. I hadn't gotten a promotion. Everyone seemed to be in a good mood, so I felt pretty sure nothing bad happened. Why were they here?

Someone whistled loudly and got everyone's attention. All chatter instantly ceased. I watched the guests move in concert to different sides of the room. The lights were dimmed. I was left standing in the middle of my living room. A spotlight shone on me. Felt like I was on stage and getting ready to perform from a script that I hadn't been allowed to read.

From one of the back rooms, Jenine emerged. Her hair was perfectly styled. The sweater dress that she wore clung to her body and showed just enough cleavage to remind me of all that I'd been missing. I saw the engagement band that I'd given her – many months ago – was now on her left ring finger.

She made her way straight to me. Got on both knees. Took my hand. It felt like a jolt of electricity coursed its way through my body. We hadn't touched in almost two months.

The look in her eyes apologized, for almost mortally wounding my heart. At the same time, they begged me for forgiveness. She cleared her throat, took a deep breath and asked, "Babe, for so long, I've thought about the possibility of this...with you. Will you spend all of eternity, in this life and the next, as my wife? Will you marry me, please?"

In her hand, she held a symbol of unlimited potential. There was a pleading on her face that made her look so vulnerable. Sincere. No matter how much I tried, I couldn't look away from her spellbinding eyes that eagerly awaited my response.

Only she and I knew that everything hadn't been handled. There were too many people in my house. I didn't like to be embarrassed. Saying no would bring about too many questions. Ones that I wasn't ready to answer. She had me trapped. I got on both knees and said, "Yes."

*****

Everyone wished Jenine and me nothing but the best.

There was music, a little dancing and plenty of food. We partied until the cops literally came knocking. One of the neighbors called in a noise complaint. As the clock struck midnight, people cleared out of my house en masse.

My mom and Jenine's mother seemed to hit it off. They and Aunt D took Klark back to my mom's condo, where everyone was going to spend the night. Kind of like a senior citizen slumber party. Klark would make sure they didn't get too wild and crazy.

After walking them to the car, I looked towards the sky. Noticed the full moon. Heard several dogs barking furiously. Couldn't help but think they were warning about something ominous that was forthcoming.

Only Gisele and Marisa stayed behind to help clean up. During the party, they rarely left each other's side. Seemed like they had a lot to discuss. Maybe a spark was lit for them tonight. While they were busy, I caught Jenine's attention and we went upstairs to my bedroom. She closed the door, sat on the chaise lounge chair and waited.

I pointed my fingers at her. Walked back and forth. Raised my voice and asked, "How could you?"

She knew better than most how much I hated to be embarrassed. "You couldn't resist painting me into a corner...knew that I wouldn't say no with everybody in my house. You keep finding ways to outdo yourself. Have you forgotten about everything that's going on? The misery that's been our life for the last eight weeks?"

I looked at the flawless 4-carat diamond eternity ring in a platinum setting. The one I designed when we first met and I jokingly told her, "When we get married, this is my dream ring."

She saw through my façade and remembered. Gave me

exactly what I wanted.

Now, I removed the ring. Years ago, the immature me would have thrown it at her or done something worse. Now, the more mature me tried to hand it back to her.

I watched her defiantly shake her head and declare, "I know there's still work to do. How could I forget?"

She took a deep breath and offered her counterattack. "You didn't just say yes to avoid being embarrassed. You don't say it but I know that you still love me. I know there's a chance for us."

Eyes overcome with tears, she quietly asked, "Am I wrong?"

I fought the urge to kiss away her tears. Absorb them as my own. Instead, I looked everywhere except at her. I was pissed at myself for not being able to come up with a lie. My silence betrayed me. Told her all that she needed to know.

"Keep the ring. I'm committed. There's time for this... for us to work."

She watched me place the stunning ring on my dresser. I watched her walk out of my bedroom. Heard her leave my house. Wondered how things would end. There were less than 24 hours to handle everything.

48: LOTS OF QUESTIONS

Day #7 (Last Day): I left the gym. Instead of going back home, I went in the opposite direction, on my way to pick up the world's best blueberry pie. After today's excruciating workout, I deserved a tasty treat.

Called my mom for a quick check-in. "Klark and I just got back from taking Denise and Jenine's mother to the airport. Now it's time for us to eat."

"Mom, I'll make it quick. When did you and Aunt D start talking, again? Annnnnd. When did you become the president of Jenine's fan club? How did y'all get everything arranged for last night? You could've told me."

"Jenine came to me for a long-overdue talk. You know I can be dangerous, especially when it comes to you. I set her straight about several things. Your nose has been wide open over her. My eyes have stayed wide open. She understands where I'm coming from and vice versa. The air is totally cleared. I don't expect any issues."

My mom sounded like a gangsta. I wasn't sure whether to laugh or be nervous. Jenine would be wise to stay on her good side.

She wasn't quite done and continued, "As far as last night, I only had to show up and help find Marisa. Jenine took care of everything else. I had no idea that Denise would be there. I'll be honest...it feels good to start our healing process. It's been entirely..."

There was a loud crashing noise followed by Klark's

cries. "It's okay honey. It's okay." The more my mom tried to make him feel better the louder he yelled. "Everything's alright over here. I'll call you back."

The farmer's market hadn't yet opened, so I stopped to get breakfast. Jenine's picture flashed on my phone. Her ringtone interrupted my much-needed moments of solitude. I was still upset with her for putting me on the spot last night, so I silenced the phone. Took two more bites of my sandwich and my work phone rang repeatedly.

Finally, I relented. "What do you want?"

"What took you so long to answer? Where are you?"

The words poured out of her. I had to wait until she took a breath before I could respond. "I was enjoying some peace and quiet..."

"Didn't you get the messages? Released...Kayla...no jail...free."

I heard bits and pieces. Tried to make square pieces fit neatly into round holes. The food lodged in my throat. Through repeated coughs, I asked, "Did you just say that Kayla isn't in jail or the psych ward? Does Detective Moore know?"

"It's about time you're paying attention..."

In stunned silence, I listened to Jenine explain that Kayla's involuntary psychiatric hold expired today. Somehow the mental health "professionals" didn't consider her to be a threat to herself or anyone else. There was no legal ground to keep her at the hospital. Any hope of her being jailed for violating the restraining order and assaulting Jenine was short-lived. She was charged but released on her own recognizance. Didn't have to post one dollar towards bail.

"Where are you?"

"Your house. Detective Moore's the one who called me. There's supposed to be an automated notification system. I never received anything."

I grumbled, "This can't be happening. Just wait for me."

"I'm not going anywhere. Need to make some calls for work. Reschedule appointments for telehealth. See about going to my mother..."

In the background, I heard my doorbell ring.

"That's probably my package. You can sign for it."

She was quiet for several seconds and finally said, "Babe. Please remember...if anything happens...take care of Klark. Know that I loved you from the first day. I'll always love you."

"Stop talking like that. Nothing's going to happen. I'm on my way."

*****

As I got closer to the exit for my house, I noticed a helicopter that flew overhead. Felt like it was following me or vice versa. There was so much police activity that I couldn't turn onto my street. I parked around a couple of corners. Started the walk back to my house. The noise from the helicopter was deafening. I took out my badge to show the cop. She said, "I remember you from the party earlier this morning." Sure enough, she responded to the noise complaint.

Another cop overheard our conversation. In a very official sounding voice, he ordered, "Wait here." He turned his back and spoke into the walkie-talkie.

Seconds later, Detective Moore came running towards me in what felt like slow motion. A sickening feeling was rooted in the depths of my stomach and growing uncontrollably. Something was wrong.

I didn't see fire trucks or smell smoke. Jenine's car was in my driveway. Across the street, I noticed a black Civic with dark tinted windows. The license plate was all too familiar. My attempt to push past Detective Moore was futile. He held my arms in a vice grip and said, "You don't wanna...you can't..." He held his breath. Finally, he looked back at me. "I'm so sorry..."

My body went numb. Knees began to buckle. I put both of my hands on him and pleaded, "Tell me what happened!"

Dear Diary:

Once Detective Moore told me that Kayla was free, I left my job and made a beeline for Ronnie's house. How any competent mental health professional thought she didn't pose a threat was ridiculous. She was the literal blueprint for danger.

Knowing that she wouldn't rest until she found me, I waited with an oxymoronic calm sense of foreboding. Already knew that Ronnie would take care of Klark. Wanted to make sure she knew that I would always love her. I have since the first day we met, even if I had some questionable ways of showing it.

I heard the doorbell ring. It was followed by a knock on the door. No need to look or ask. We were once moths drawn to each other's flame. I had found a new light source. She was still grounded in a place where she couldn't pull herself away from me.

"You shouldn't be here Kayla. Just leave." After everything, I still tried...

"I got this for you." She held a teddy bear. Extended it to me. "Remember? Just like on our first date."

She held onto those good times, like they were nuggets of gold. Convinced herself they'd be able to revitalize our once happy marriage.

Those days were stuffed deep in the pockets of my memory. They were no longer important. I'd make new and better times with Ronnie. "That doesn't matter. You can't be here. We don't want you here."

She talked so softly, I barely heard her ask, "Is it okay if we talk?"

Her usual use of profane language was shelved. She was being too nice. My senses were even more heightened, when she requested, "May I come in?" She took a step towards me.

I stood my ground. "NO! You definitely can't come in." She looked surprised. "What don't you understand about the restraining order? It's inappropriate to invite you into my fiancée's house?"

She heard fiancée. Her body stiffened. She stared at the ring on my left hand. Felt that it truly could signify the end of us. Looked at me. Noticed the renewed determination in my eyes. Like a light switch, she flipped from caring and considerate to aggrieved and threatening. I saw her flame of anger spread in words and deeds.

"Stop! You can't come in!" I tried to block the doorway. I'm not a small woman. Could stand to lose 15, okay, 20 pounds. Like I was a ragdoll, she pushed me to the floor and barged into the house. What started as a trickle quickly turned into a tidal wave of destruction. She tore through the first floor like a Tasmanian devil. Glasses thrown. Dishes smashed. Books tossed. TV pulled from the wall. It was a mess.

I hurried to my feet and yelled, "You're destroying everything. I'm calling the cops."

Nothing seemed to register, yet I still pleaded, "Kayla. We're OVER! Get it through your head. I'm NEVER going back to you!"

As quickly as it started, her wrath came to an abrupt pause when she saw pictures of Ronnie and me. Oahu.

Costa Rica. Chicago. At the park. In one picture, I sat on her lap, with one of her damn baseball caps on my head. Our affection was evident, in the way our eyes danced, while we lovingly looked at each other. In another, our bond was sealed with a kiss.

Kayla tore the pictures off the wall. Ran her fingers along the frames. Maybe she had recollections of when that was her and me – in much happier times. She looked in my direction. The hatred in her eyes returned. Like they were Frisbees, she hurled the frames. I ducked. They whizzed past my head. Smashed against the wall. Shards of glass landed on my skin.

Change does come for everyone. She was once the love of my life. We had exchanged vows. Sickness. Health. Better. Worse. Richer. Poorer. There was just one more that we hadn't faced: till death do us part. The disgust in her eyes was another clue that she was intent on making that my reality.

I tried to call 911. She sneered. Charged at me like a bull. The phone flew out of my hand. I crashed against the wall. The wind was knocked out of me. I slid to the floor. Her hands around my throat, I was barely able to say, "Get...off...me!" Felt her squeeze even tighter. She was trying to crush my windpipe. Saw a satisfyingly wicked smile spread across her face. Wanted to talk some sense into her but lack of oxygen halted all my words. Visions of Klark, Ronnie and my mother passed before me. Didn't people have remembrances of their loved ones before they were going to die? My eyes began to roll back in my head.

No. It couldn't end this way. I gathered strength. Kneed her in the groin. Oh yeah. It hurts women down there, too. Watched her buckle in pain. I coughed uncontrollably. Gasped for the breath she choked out of me. This only incensed her more. She tried to grab me by the hair. When I scrambled away from her, she yelled louder, "This'll be way worse than the last time I kicked your ass. I'm going to kill you!"

Like an unpliable steel bar, I thought of my toughness being forged through the fire of my childhood years. The schoolyard bullies often mistook me for the poster child of weakness. At times, my razor-sharp tongue was enough to stop them in their tracks. More often than I wanted to recall, they were left with busted lips when the tall, skinny girl with the "funny sounding" accent walloped their faces. I paid attention in those karate and self-defense classes. Stupidly, they didn't think pretty girls could fight. I would need to draw on all my resources. Kayla and I were fighting like caged animals.

Unsteadily, I rose to my feet. She made more threats. Threw a wild punch. Barely missed my chin but made solid contact with my shoulder. It hurt like hell.

She was naturally strong as a bull. Anger made her even stronger. Each follow-up punch landed on my temple. I staggered back to the wall. Needed it for support. Quickly, she followed with repeated elbows to my jaw. My mouth filled with the metallic taste of blood. My knees were unsteady. Like a trained boxer, I shook it off. Through swollen eyes, I tried to track her movements.

With the speed of a cat, I attacked. Felt a surge of adrenaline. Unlike our first fight, I was on a different mission. Like vintage Mike Tyson, before Buster Douglas showed him to be a mere mortal, I punched her squarely on the nose. Once. Twice. Three times. Heard a cracking noise. Watched blood spew onto the immaculate bamboo floors that Ronnie loved so much. Heard her cry in agony. She grabbed my shirt for support. I held onto her head. Kicked her in the stomach. Snatched clumps of hair from her scalp. She wrapped both arms around my legs. We tussled. Neither able to gain an advantage, we fell onto the floor. She climbed atop me. Banged my head on the floor. I was woozy.

She felt a little too cocky. In the time she relaxed to take a breath, I gave an uppercut to her chin. Before she could respond, I punched her on the windpipe. There was a loud gasp for air, as she fell backward. I used that opportunity to get on top of her. Firmly placed my knee on her chest. Now it was my turn to bang her head on the floor. Once. Twice for good measure. She reached for my throat. Like a boxer working the speedbag, I landed a flurry of punches and elbows to her face. Little by little, I could see the wind being sucked from her sail.

But... An equalizer? A gun pulled from the waistband. Two pairs of widened eyes. Realization that it's really over. No more hope for our future? BANG! Finally. Hope for our future?

Years ago, one of my brothers found out that his wife cheated on him. He was hysterical and wanted a divorce.

I asked, "Bro, are you serious? She cheated once, right? Aren't you a habitual cheater?"

He looked at me and yelled, "That don't matter! I caught her! She never caught me!"

It wasn't an apples-to-apples comparison. I applied a similarly twisted logic to my situation. Even though my beautiful wife had been damn near perfect, I foolishly searched for something better. It hurt like hell when I learned that my efforts to repair our marriage were a colossal waste of time.

She used to be the one who rocked with me, whether we were scraping peanut butter and jelly out of jars or fine dining with Beluga caviar served on blini. Things had changed, though. Now, she was an expert in the game of "you hurt me but I'll hurt you more."

Everything I suspected was confirmed. I saw the woman my wife greeted with a huge smile at six o'clock at night. That was the same woman who bounced out of her house twelve hours later. She kind of looked like the taller, thinner, more polished version of me and drove a convertible Audi. No coincidence that was the same car I saw leaving my wife's house a few weeks ago. I did a little research. Couldn't find her on social media but still learned that she had a secure job for the government, beautiful house and didn't need Jenine for financial support.

Mentally, I was unraveling. A hurt spread through my bones like a malignant tumor. Simply waking up each day was an overwhelming task and accomplishment.

It wasn't my plan to immediately tell my wife what I knew about her secrets. I was more disappointed that she didn't have the heart to tell me. My days and nights were filled with thoughts on how to retaliate. I was determined to dish out my own measure of pain. I started with slashing her tires. After she wouldn't let me see our son, I progressed to harassing phone calls. Smashed windows. Made a lot of threats.

My wife may have been beautiful but she wasn't a punk. Even after my infantile antics, I opened the door one night and found her sitting on my couch.

"Kayla, I'm warning you to stop all of this or it won't end well for you."

"Are you trying to intimidate me?"

"Tell me what you want that doesn't include us getting back together. We can be grown-ups about this."

"It's only you and Klark that I want. I'm still not signing the divorce papers."

She grabbed her purse. Her heels clicked rhythmically, on the wooden floor, as she walked that traffic-stopping walk. At the door, she smoothed barely visible wrinkles on her skirt. Tucked loose strands of hair behind her ears. She opened the door and looked back at me. Smiled. Almost as an afterthought, she said, "Oh, I forgot...the one thing you don't know is that we've now been living apart long enough. I can divorce you, whether you agree or not."

Even in those high heels, she was quick. I picked up a vase and threw it at the door, just as she slammed it shut.

I watched it shatter in pieces and thought that was just how my heart felt.

*****

All calls to my soon-to-be-ex-wife went unanswered. She wouldn't let me see our son. I resorted to breaking into her house. Knowing that I would eventually be arrested was still worth the few minutes that I spent with him. When I tried to splinter that bat on her back, it was years of frustration and inadequacy bubbling to the surface.

My reign of terror was aggravated by the restraining order that didn't allow me to be within 1,000 feet of my soon-to-be-ex-wife or our son. Now, I had half the police force looking for me. It wasn't in my best interest to go back to my apartment. I was hesitant to contact my family. They probably couldn't help or would turn me in, for any possible reward money. My options were limited, so I chilled with a woman who had long been wanting to spend time with me. Quickly, she got tired of my tired act, so I was forced to head back to my place.

My timing was perfect. I heard the cops calling my name. With guns drawn, they were chasing after Ronnie. The look of fear on her face was hilarious. I couldn't watch everything unfold, though. I had just enough time to slip – undetected – into my building. Too bad they didn't kill her. Knowing how much that would have hurt my soon-to-be-ex-wife made me smile.

After a few days, I could no longer stand being stuck in my apartment. Not being able to see my soon-to-be-ex-wife or our son was painful. Cops were posted in front, so I took a chance and tried to head out the back door. Just my luck I tripped an alarm.

In jail for violating the restraining order, I was served with divorce papers. Part of me didn't believe that she'd do it. Seeing those papers and knowing that she was now my ex-wife caused one of the few remaining strings holding together my sanity to unravel. I wanted her to know just how much I loved her, so I grabbed the penknife before I was shuttled to our court hearing.

Court was a waste of time. We weren't allowed to be in the same room. There was some crazy talk about Klark and DNA testing being mandatory for certain cases. If they wanted blood, I'd give them more than enough to use for testing. Life had become too much to handle. Each time I stabbed myself with the penknife, things felt a little better.

*****

During our marriage, I had enough conversations with my now ex-wife to learn about different things that she considered when diagnosing people. Those talks certainly helped me get released from the psychiatric ward. I needed to thank her. It was time to finally put an end to our pain.

I didn't find her at her house or at work. I finally found her at Ronnie's house. For a moment, I had second thoughts about my vindictive plan. She opened the door and smiled at me, like she did during our happier days. My heart still skipped beats for her.

"I got this for you." I tried to give her a teddy bear. "Remember? Just like on our first date." That day was filled with so much happiness. Surely, she hadn't forgotten.

"That doesn't matter. You can't be here. We don't want you here."

This wasn't going the way I planned. Did she think I was angry with her? I came here in peace. Softly, I asked, "Is it okay if we talk? May I come in?"

Her eyes registered surprise, as she shouted, "NO! You definitely can't come in."

I heard something about a fiancée and stared at the ring on her left ring finger. Saw that it was the same one that she had been wearing on her right hand. Not only had she divorced me, she had already moved onto creating lifelong plans with someone else. I tallied up all this information and the rickety dam holding back my anger burst.

We went from the porch to the living room that I proceeded to destroy. She threatened to call the cops. Kept telling me that we were done. Each word twisted the knife deeper in my back. We traded punches, elbows, kicks and chops like fighters competing in an unsanctioned backyard brawl.

I always said she wasn't a punk. It was ugly. Painful. She was getting the better of me. This wasn't how it was supposed to happen. I needed help. An equalizer? A gun pulled from the waistband. Both of our eyes widened in surprise. She whispered four words and I had no regrets when the trigger was pulled.

51: SOME ANSWERS?

Detective Moore held my arm and walked me towards my house. He explained, "Officer Glyce. Ms. Glyce. Some of your neighbors called 911. Officers responded to the scene and found..." He gulped hard and looked at the ground. Searched for the right words. "...the victim of a single gunshot wound. I need to ask you some questions..."

I processed the news in slow motion. There was yellow police tape everywhere. People with Coroner's Office emblazoned on their jackets were huddled outside my house. From the curb, I saw her covered body in my living room. My head was spinning. Detective Moore loosened his grip. It felt like I was going to vomit.

A million thoughts crisscrossed my mind. Meeting her at the diner. Our official first date. Her enchanting green eyes. The rapturous smile that made me weak in the knees. Both pairs of her pretty ass lips. Klark. Our last conversation. The wedding, honeymoon and everything else – good and bad – that hadn't happened.

I tried to scream but no sound came forth. My mouth felt like it was stuffed with cotton balls. I was dizzy. Felt myself falling to the ground. I couldn't tell Detective Moore to catch me. Suddenly, everything went black.

*****

In the ambulance, the EMT smiled at me. "Hi. You had

a panic attack and fainted." He said it so casually. For him, it must have been ho-hum. He read the questions in my eyes and answered, "All of these machines are monitoring your vitals."

Despite his attempts to soothe me, I was agitated and tried to sit up quickly. "I know the shooting was a tragedy. We should be able to get everything under control. I'll adjust the gurney, so you can be more comfy."

How long had I been out of it? The reality of what happened was beginning to crystalize in my mind. I heard my mom's voice. Ignoring what the EMT just told me, I tried to get off the gurney. The wires and straps restrained me.

The EMT saw my distress and calmly reminded me, "Try to relax."

My mom yanked open the door and shrieked, "Oh, my baby. Thank God you're alive."

The EMT helped her into the ambulance. "I'll check on you in a few minutes." He stepped away to give us some privacy.

In all my years, today was the first time I'd ever seen my mom cry. Her tears cascaded down her cheeks and onto mine. I offered no resistance. She planted kisses all over my face, just like when I was a little girl.

With a confidence that I didn't share, she said, "Ronnie, somehow everything will be okay."

I couldn't remember the last time she told me such a blatant lie. Jenine was gone. How would everything be okay? She completed me. Without her, I'd be on life support, until God called me home. "Where's Klark? I need him with me." He was my remaining piece of her.

"He's with Gisele and Marisa. Jenine's mother and I didn't want to bring him here."

I had forgotten about Jenine's mother. She must be inconsolable. Her only child. Gone. I flashed back to the gruesome scene on my living room floor. "Mom. Get the detective and EMT. I have to see Jenine!"

With some hesitation, she cautioned, "I don't think..."

I stopped her mid-sentence and yelled, "Just do what I said!"

The machines beeped frantically. Sent my vitals back out of whack.

On any other day, my mom would have set me straight for raising my voice at her. Today, she showed me mercy. I didn't even get the grown-woman-or-not-I'll-still-whoop-your-ass-look. Dutifully, she did as I demanded.

The EMT was still talking about my vitals, so I ignored him. Focused my attention on Detective Moore. Like I was his boss, I barked, "I need to see Jenine!"

He nodded, wiped the sweat from his forehead and said, "It's not going to be pretty...give me a minute to talk to the M.E. or uh, medical examiner. I'll be back."

While waiting for him to return, my mother told me, "Close your eyes and try to relax."

If one more person told me to relax, I was going to lose it. What I wanted to do was punch something. I glanced at the EMT leaving the ambulance. Thought the better of having an outburst. Damn vitals. It was more important that I got to Jenine.

I closed my eyes and breathed in for four beats. Held it. Exhaled for four beats. I couldn't think straight. Being confined to the ambulance only made me more upset. The walls were closing in on me. I felt hopeless. Helpless. Lost.

A knock on the ambulance door broke my concentration. Now I needed to start my count again. My mom said, "Let me see what's going on."

I had no strength to argue. Slowly, I began a silent countdown from 50. Tears flowed from my closed eyes. Somewhere between counting from 45 to 44, I felt the softness of those swollen but still beautiful lips. Her eyes were so puffy, I wondered how she could see anything. Looked like she had been in a battle. She climbed atop me. Kissed away my tears. Whispered in my ear, "Babe. I told you that I'd handle everything."

Taking my hand in hers, she placed the gorgeous engagement ring back on my finger and flashed a satisfied smile.

52: MORE THAN THE OTHER KNOWS

There was no way that I would spend another night at my house. Immediately, I moved into Jenine's place. The police spent several days processing the scene. Asked a boatload of questions. They even took the clothes that Jenine wore when she killed Kayla.

Once the police gave the okay, I had my house professionally cleaned. Got ready to put it on the market. People were turned on by the strangest things. I questioned whether Kayla being killed in my house would decrease its value. Instead, it had the opposite effect. My realtor already had a slew of confirmed appointments, plus a few offers from prospective buyers who had only seen the listing on the internet.

"J, I need to go back and pack some more stuff."

"Babe, I'm going with you."

"Are you sure that you want to go back? It won't be too, I don't know, emotional?"

"You'll be with me. I'll be okay."

At my house, she was like my shadow and followed me into each room. Just about everything had been packed and moved to her house, including my secret and therapeutic journals. There was still one specific thing to organize. I preferred to do it privately.

When she said that she had to use the bathroom, I ran to the basement. Before I could get my hands on the cookie tin, I heard her coming down the stairs. There was no way she could have gone to the bathroom and washed her hands so quickly.

In the basement, she sat atop the washing machine. She looked through my high school yearbook and photo albums. She doubled over laughing at one particular picture. "It's not that funny." In trying to save face, I also told her, "That hairstyle and my clothes were very much in fashion. You're not the only one who knows how to dress nice."

With a vigorous shake of the head, she disagreed. "That shirt has NEVER been stylish nor will it ever be. My goodness. That hairstyle was made for maybe the Victorian era but not the 1990s." She laughed so hard, she was gasping for breath.

A comedienne she wasn't but that didn't stop the downpour of jokes about my poor fashion sense. "Ha. Ha. You're so funny. Make yourself useful. Give me a box. I just have a little more stuff to take with me."

The laughs got progressively louder, as she looked at baby pictures. Some of the other photo albums were placed in the box. I reached up to the top of the storage shelf. Grabbed the cookie tin. To my astonishment, it felt awfully light. Without breaking stride, I put the cookie tin into the box and opened it. I tried to hide the surprise but felt the color drain from my face. It was empty. Something was very wrong.

The wannabe jokester was no longer laughing. Instead, her eyes bored through me. The only noise in the basement was the sound of my heart, which felt like it was bursting out of my chest. I knew the gun that I swiped from the probationer was a 9mm. Was it a coincidence that was the same caliber that she used to shoot Kayla?

An uncomfortable silence hung in the air. Our eyes

locked. Suddenly, it clicked. Who would be the first to blink? At that moment, another layer of the masks that we'd been wearing was slowly removed.

A shadow crossed her face. She was the first to break eye contact. Here we go again. I watched, as she reached into her purse and pulled out index cards. I knew the routine. She said, "I'll start."

Jenine's 1st Question: My mother may be visiting next week. Can she use your black Civic, so she doesn't need to rent a car? That should give you plenty of time to get the paperwork handled at the motor vehicle office.

Ronnie's Answer: Sure.

Jenine's 2nd Question: Would you have done it?

Ronnie's Answer: You know that answer. I just couldn't figure how not to get caught. Then when I didn't care about getting caught, I couldn't find her.

Jenine's 3rd Question: Do you know that you still don't know the whole truth?

Ronnie's Answer: We have the rest of our lives for me to find out.

Now it was my turn. There were so many questions. I went for the most obvious ones.

Ronnie's 1st Question: When did you first have suspicions?

Jenine's Answer: I met some friends for drinks near your house. Saw your car in the driveway. All the lights were turned off. Let myself in. Didn't find you. I called, while I was lying in your bed. You had the nerve to tell me that you were already sleeping. I made it my mission to find out what you were up to. Once I found the gun, my plan was set in motion to finish what you couldn't and finally free myself. Kayla was never going to let me go.

Ronnie's 2nd Question: You have a brown belt in

karate. How couldn't you better defend yourself when Kayla assaulted you the first time?

Jenine's Answer: Needed it on the record that I was a battered woman. I chose not to defend myself that first time. You see that I handled myself just fine this last time.

Ronnie's 3rd Question: Why so many lies, especially about Klark?

Jenine's Answer: My relationship with Kayla blossomed and wilted on dysfunction. For too long, I played both sides, partly because I couldn't break away from her. I fucked up with you but not always in the ways that you thought.

Even now, you don't know as much as you think you know. Sometimes Kayla went to medical appointments with me because you or Diego were busy with work. She always held out hope that we'd get back together. I didn't always tell her or show her that we were done.

I kept finding ways to compound my mistakes. The trip to Jamaica was at the start of you and me. I still shouldn't have gone. In Oahu, felt like I had to give you something, so I showed you the fake papers because I didn't want to lose you. Some but not all of my dirt was done because I knew that she wouldn't let me go. I had to keep her close. In my heart, I knew that was only going to last for so long.

Thank you for forgiving me. My actions will continue to show that you won't have any reason to doubt my loyalty and love for you.

Hand in hand, we walked up the stairs. I put all of the index cards into the fireplace. She lit the match. I tossed it onto the cards. We watched them disintegrate into ashes. Again. There'd be no written evidence of our confessions.

Going through the house one last time, the few remaining boxes were by the front door. I searched for my keys.

"Ronnie, there's more..."

As we prepared to leave my house, I interrupted, "Did I forget something?"

"...I need to tell you. Remember. This is about honesty between us."

There was that word again. Honesty. Now she had my complete attention. For support, I leaned against a wall. Allowed myself to be distracted by my keys, which had been in my pocket. Clueless about what else required honesty, I asked, "What are you talking about?"

She searched my eyes but only saw confusion. Hurriedly, she declared, "I found your journals...read some entries...couldn't understand everything...your handwriting is horrible...I know...Monica...Tabitha...the real reason you don't drink alcohol. I'm proud of you for keeping your sobriety through all of this..."

"Believe me. It wasn't easy."

I shook my head to clear the cobwebs. I thought back to sitting in my shower. Finding the strength to pour the tequila down the drain.

"How long have you known about everything?"

"Only a couple of weeks..."

I swallowed my nausea. Silently, I replayed her words in my head. I blinked rapidly. After several minutes, I still hadn't said anything.

As if moving in slow motion, she stepped towards me and cautiously asked, "Are you mad at me?"

I put up my hands. She stopped on a dime. Unlike my journals, she respected this boundary.

Mutely, I continued to think about her revelations

and question. She knew my secrets. The alcohol. My shameful actions against Monica and Tabitha. The vice that has been around my neck. Maybe now I could truly be free.

Honestly, I shared, "I'm not mad. I'm relieved. Purged. Glad that you don't think less of me. Those chapters are finally closed. I'm ready to keep moving forward."

53: REVELATIONS

From the listing to the closing, my house sold in thirty days for significantly more than the asking price. To help me feel more at home, Jenine used some of the money and transformed the basement into my oasis. Paraphernalia from the Chicago Bears and my beloved sorority decorated the walls. Two nice touches were the glass-encased jerseys and volleyballs, which commemorated my number being retired at Whitney M. Young High School and The University of Alabama. For extra amenities, she added a huge flat-screen TV and surround sound speakers. I even had a massage chair/recliner that would help me to relax, after a long day.

Since I moved in, things had been going well. She cooked. I cleaned. Klark thrived. I was looking through the mini fridge, in my private piece of paradise and listening to "Kind of Blue," Miles Davis' iconic jazz album.

My phone rang. "Hey Marisa. What's good love?"

"So much is good. Almost so good that I'm nervous. It feels unreal. Gisele is amazing... We're taking our time in getting to know each other, though..."

"Sounds like you have a song in your voice. Are you still taking me to lunch today, so we can properly talk about your sabbatical and you diggin' Gisele?"

"No doubt. It'll be a marathon session, so be ready. I'm gonna grill you about Jenine, too. I got lots of questions."

Jenine opened the basement door and yelled, "Babe, come here!"

"You have no idea. I could seriously write a trilogy of books about J and me. Text me the info for the restaurant. My better half wants me. Peace out."

I hung up the phone. Usually, Marisa didn't pry. She knew that I valued privacy. I'd give her a little more than the usual. Just to keep her off my back.

I made my way up the stairs and asked, "What's up?"

"There's something you need to see." She pointed to an email from the ancestry/DNA company that processed the swabs for Klark and said, "Read this."

The email started with an apology and mentioned the error being against their high-quality standards. It ended with the recommendation that I resubmit swabs. There was an unexpected error in the processing of Klark's sample, which invalidated the results. As if it would make things right, the company offered to reimburse the cost of the original tests. They'd send replacements, which would be submitted for rapid processing, all at no extra charge.

While I reread the email, Jenine came back with two unopened Manila envelopes from The Family Division of the county courthouse. One addressed to her. The other to me. "You told me to show you and not tell you. Remember?"

I nodded my head unsure where this was headed.

"Read these, too," she demanded and tossed them to me.

As instructed, I opened her envelope, which showed the biological relationship between her and Klark. That was a given. I looked at her and shrugged my shoulders.

The other paper showed that there was no genetic relationship between Kayla and Klark. Oh. What a surprise.

Slowly, I opened my envelope. Pulled out the paper. No more doubts about why he looks like me. The paper verified the genetic relationship between my son and me. Sent my heart soaring to unimaginable heights.

Arms folded across her chest, she stood near the island in the kitchen. Through narrowed eyes, she said, "If you want more proof, I'm cool with you resending the swab for OUR son back to the company."

Excitedly, I shook my head. "That won't be necessary. We're all good. I'll make sure you get all the money back for the fertility clinic."

She waved her hand nonchalantly. "No worries. Use that money for our honeymoon."

I looked back and forth between the papers and the email. Even with the incredibly good news, my smile slowly faded. I confessed, "You know...this may sound petty but Kayla won't know about the test results."

She extended her arms, drew me into the warmth of her body and whispered in my ear, "Since we're about honesty..."

That word. Honesty. Again.

My entire body stiffened. I tried to pull away. She clung to me like a drowning person holding onto a flotation device and whispered, "Before I shot Kayla, the last four words I said to her were, 'He's not your son.'"

Case File #1913

Death of Kayla A. Denegan

The investigation considered that Jenine wasn't notified when Kayla was released from the psychiatric ward. According to the video footage, Kayla went directly from the psychiatric ward to Jenine's job and house. When she couldn't find her at either place, she went to Ronnie's house where everything unfolded.

During the follow-up interviews, Jenine stated that Kayla attempted to rekindle their romantic relationship. Once she learned of Jenine's engagement, she forced her way into Ronnie's house. All of this information was supported by footage from the security system.

Based on the forensic evidence and Jenine's version of events, once inside the home, Kayla made multiple threats to kill her and damaged property on the entry level. Undeterred at being rebuffed, Kayla continued asking for another opportunity to work out their issues. Jenine reminded her that she was in violation of the restraining order and tried to call 911.

Kayla became more enraged and commenced a physical attack, wherein Kayla brandished a gun. Feeling that her life was in danger, Jenine continued to defend herself and tried to disarm Kayla. A scuffle ensued. Kayla suffered a fatal gunshot wound to the chest.

Beyond Jenine's official statement and interviews of neighbors, the forensic evidence, threats, documented history of domestic violence and emotional instability all supported Jenine's killing of Kayla.

Decision: Justifiable Homicide – Case Closed

I guess Jenine did handle everything.

Nadi Hemden

As a child, the author wanted to be a pilot or a minister or a sportscaster. Now an adult, she works with children but still dreams of doing something else. Often, she thinks about pursuing a doctorate to bookend her other degrees. This book represents her initial journey into being a published author. Writing it was therapeutic and helped her work through one of life's more challenging chapters.

For business and pleasure, she enjoys traipsing around the world. She has visited 6 of the 7 continents and more than 60 countries. Ultimate bucket list: visit every country in the world. More realistic bucket list: Bhutan. Maldives. Antarctica. No matter where she travels, her heart longs for the West Indies.

When not accumulating passport stamps, she is usually spending time with her mother and godson, taking long bike rides, exploring nature, serving the public through Delta Sigma Theta Sorority, Inc., agonizing over Les Bleus and trying to find unforgettably good pizza.
Twitter: @nadi_hemden   Facebook: Nadi Hemden

www.ingramcontent.com/pod-product-compliance
Lightning Source LLC
Chambersburg PA
CBHW022027240626

47154CB00007B/2295